WINGSPAN

WINGBOUND SERIES: BOOK THREE

HEATHER TRIM

This is a work of fiction. All characters, places, and events portrayed in this novel are either products of the author's i magination or are used fictitiously.

WINGSPAN

Published by TrimVentures
www.trimventures.com

Hardcover ISBN: 978-1-7329090-5-2

ALSO BY HEATHER TRIM

THE WINGBOUND SERIES
Wingbound
Wingless
Wingspan

Supernatural Superheroes

Join the email list for new releases and more. Go to www.heatheraine.com

PRAISE FOR WINGBOUND

"Unexpected, funny, serious, wonderful,
and above all; magical."
-Fantasic Books & Why to Read Them

"Spellbound by Wingbound... I was swept away
by visions of the castle in the sky."
-Author A.C. Gaither

"Sprawling castles and desolate oceans
in a soft, simplistic fairy-tale writing style."
-Bookish Creature

"A new world, new cultures, adventure, danger, triumph,
true-to-life characters, humor, romance, and dragons."
-Author Melissa Keaster

DEDICATION

To my Big Fam:
You're my favorite band of misfits.

Prologue

ALOUETTE

It doesn't much matter anymore. I am the enemy. As I wait to die, the guardians bring irons. Metal scrapes on stone, echoing through the prison. I sit in the corner alone. My cell mates are gone—tried for their crimes, killed, or released back to their loved ones. I have no loved ones left. My parents are dead, and Dayson, my betrothed, hasn't come to see me since we were ripped apart. He is done with me, no doubt. I think of his crystal blue eyes, and my soul aches.

"Alouette." A voice rattles me as a key unlocks the gate. "It's time."

My limbs hang hopelessly with no fight left as the guardian places an iron on each wrist and ankle. He pulls me to my feet, and my legs barely hold my weight. I haven't eaten in days. When I waver, he catches me. The sadness, the fear of what comes next, and the despair chokes the life from me.

I close my eyes, avoiding his face because it will be filled with disdain for me and for who my father was: Roi du Ciel, the murderer king of Ellery. He killed the rightful king's family and helped us all escape this prison of an island. To rebuild and expand. But he was unkind to our people, taking them by force and killing all who stood against him. Because of him, I am ashamed of who I am.

The guardian pushes me toward the door. Step by labored step, I leave my cell. My heart breaks at the thought of how many people died at my father's hand. I should die too because I didn't stop him. I am his only kin left, and I let our people down by not reasoning with him or standing up to him. I stood by. I watched, passive and powerless. Their blood is on my hands.

Raging voices fill the prison hall. My name echoes with curses, wishes for my death, and my father's name. I'm pushed down the hall and something hits the side of my leg. Feces. More hits me on the chest from the same direction, wet and dripping. The smell makes the back of my throat constrict. It matches the stench of my sins. The yelling assaults my ears. With each step, another person throws excrement from the buckets in the corner of their cells. I accept their hatred with every putrid hit.

"Enough!" the guardian bellows at the other prisoners. "You're getting it on me. I will not stand before the advisors smelling like your shame. Next one will get the whip!"

Topside, the light of day stings my eyes, and I accept it as another deserved punishment. Standing before the advisors, my mind is incapable of focusing on their words. Their mouths move, their voices reverberate, but I don't know what they are saying until Advisor Caedus, with nostrils flared in disgust, says the one word I do understand.

"Death."

Tears spill from my eyes. My insides are hollow and dead anyway; it's time my body caught up. As I am escorted to the door, someone shouts, and a fight breaks out. Dayson lunges toward the guards, hair mussed and blood at the corner of his mouth. A flash of emotion wraps itself around my neck. I can't breathe. Two powerful guardians drag him away. *What is he doing?*

The memory of the day my father and Dayson made the marriage agreement invades my mind. "She will be your wife. She will be queen. You will honor her position above all," my father said. He laid Dayson's hand on mine and walked away. The courtyard was silent as I gazed up into his eyes. His dark hair was neatly slicked away from his face. His jaw tightened, and I didn't feel worthy of his beautiful face. Dayson smiled sweetly and kissed my hand. I've always questioned whether he was marrying the crown or marrying me.

Outside, at the edge of Ellery, I am mesmerized by the orange sun on the horizon. It burns my eyes as my irons are exchanged for ropes. The guardians are careful not to touch me and the excrement splattered on my body as they tie ropes around my wrists, wings, and legs.

"Glad we're not over water," one guardian says as if I'm not here. "I hate carrying the weights all the way out here to make them sink."

They wrap the rope around my chest and wings until I am completely restrained. One of them curses and wipes his hand on my thigh. I wish they would put something over my head so I don't have to see.

Both guardians spin my immobilized body toward the

castle looming over me. It stands for everything I failed to do.

"One, two, three," they say together, and with hands on my shoulders, they both push me off the side of Ellery.

I cry out. I hate myself for making a sound. My insides wrench as I fall. My wings instinctively try to spread and catch me, but they are useless. All I can think as I fall from my home is *I deserve this*. A criminal's punishment. For not helping my people when they needed me the most.

The underside of the island is dark and grows farther away. I close my eyes against the inevitable, but all too soon I hit something in midair. I am jolted from my descent as arms wrap around me. *Is this what it feels like to die?*

Opening my eyes, I find Dayson cradling me. His eyes are bloodshot, and a fresh trickle of blood seeps from his lip. His gray wings are pumping and carrying me away from my death sentence.

My head swims with emotions, and I can't sort one from the other. Tears stream down my face. I hear myself wail, terrified and relieved at the same time.

We soar into the shadow of the trees below and the island above. Close to the ground, he darts between the trees toward the north. I weep and close my eyes against the reality that I am still alive.

We burst from the woods over a small pond. He slows and lowers us into the frigid water. The air is knocked from me as the chilling temperature touches my toes, knees, then torso. He submerges me before I can brace myself. One hand embraces me, and the other washes the filth from my body, rubbing each spot regardless of how disgusting it is.

He brings water to my cheek and gently washes the stench from my skin. I tremble. More tears blur my view. His blue eyes brim with tears. I reach his face with my shaky hands bound together and wipe the blood from his mouth.

Leaning in, he touches his warm lips to mine. He plunges his hand under the water, scoops up my body, and walks to the edge of the pond. Trudging through the weeds, he sets me down in a grassy area. It is brown and bristly, but solid and safe.

He unties the ropes. When I am free, I reach for him and wrap my cold arms around him. I hug him, crying into his warm neck.

When I pull away, he asks, "Are you okay?"

No. I'm not. But I don't know how to tell him that.

1 Changes Afoot

LEDGER

The smell of burned bark and thatch stings my nose and my heart. Kicking up ashes in my path, I make my way between charred log walls, determined to do my part to redeem our devastated village.

Weeks before I arrived home, a vicious army of savages attacked and killed many of our men and took others prisoner, including my father. They burned our sacred grounds and several cottages throughout Balfour. The sadness drifts from person to person as I pass them on the path, with their downcast eyes and quiet pondering. Still, I'm so relieved to be home and at peace while we rebuild and expand, the calm drowns out my own sense of loss.

A scraping sound makes me cringe as I come around the back of the cottage. Several winged men are taking off a layer of blackened bark. Luckily, this cottage only needs a good scraping and a new roof. Three other cottages did not fare so well. I load a handful of tools and nails in a bucket and pull the rope through the pulley, sending it flailing through the air.

"Thanks, Ledger," Elder Jubal calls from the rooftop, pulling the bucket over the thatched roof line.

Finally, he appreciates what I do around here. I puff up my chest and stride through the village square, heading back to the workshop to begin the next project of forging five hammers.

The island of Ellery is a grand stalactite hanging high in the sky with a tan stone castle atop, gliding across our southern border. When I was a little boy, it used to seem enormous and ominous. But today, even with the gray clouds overshadowing it, I am unafraid.

It feels strange that I'm getting my wish. The Ellerian people are leaving the island in the sky to live in our village. They've had the worst year in their long history. They lost their rightful king, were enslaved on the ground, and even when they made it back to the island, they didn't have enough supplies to survive. Their one glimmer of fortune was finding the last living member of their royal family living in this little village: my grandmother, Huyana.

She did what I only dreamed of. She opened our village to the winged people, who we've been at war with since before I was born. But we are at peace, and now we know we are one people. Balfourians and Ellerians are kin.

With many hands, we can not only rebuild but expand our village to accommodate the many Ellerian people. Everyone is pitching in. The Ellerians are learning new skills. Some are learning how to fell pine and spruce trees, some stack the log walls, and others are building the thatched roofs. There are already three homes in various stages of construction. It is beautiful to see the winged and the wingless working side by side.

A shadow darts over me, and I jolt. Belamy, an Ellerian with black inky wings, bronze skin, and a brilliant white smile lands beside me with an armload of sheets, blankets, and clothing. “Watch out, little buddy,” he says.

I frown and resist the frustration clenching my stomach. Another Ellerian lands nearby with several stools, and another with a small table. They are unloading as much furniture and supplies as they can carry off the island of Ellery before it drifts too far away.

Even if we don’t get everything, it circles our world every year, and we can finish emptying it next harvest. When the Ellerians lived on the island, they used to fight us for huge supplies of grain, corn, and other crops. Our wingless warriors were no match for their nimble, winged guardians. I am so relieved the war is over. Especially because Alouette can live here now, my dear friend with beautiful white wings, dark flowing hair, and a heart shaped face that always looks like she’s smiling, even when she’s sad.

“Hey, Ledger?” Belamy calls as I reach the other side of the village square. “Deveraux is looking for you.”

“Who?” I don’t yet know all the Ellerians.

“Our blacksmith,” he shouts back and leaps into the air. His jet-black wings carry him toward the island in the sky.

His answer worries me. Another blacksmith will get in my way. I pick up the pace, walking the western path beyond three rows of log cottages before reaching my father’s blacksmithing workshop. The original building burned down when I was about two years old, back when it was made of logs. Now his shop is the only structure made of stone in the entire village, and rightly so.

The sky is gray and overcast. A drop hits my arm. Rain must be coming. I round the corner of the stone building and feel another drop and another. Before entering, I glance up at the grayness. Without warning, a deluge of water hits me in the face and splashes down my throat. Someone on the rooftop giggles. I heave and cough, clearing the water from my lungs. Hollis leans over the flat roofline, holding an empty bucket.

Her laughter fades while she climbs down the ladder inside the workshop and races out to me. "Sorry, sorry, sorry." She slaps me on the back, as if it will help me stop choking.

I put one hand up and lean over for one last, good cough. "Hollis!"

"You weren't supposed to look up," she says, holding back a smile. "I'm sorry, Ledger. I didn't mean to drown you." She pushes her eyebrows together and smiles apologetically.

I shake my head. "Why would you throw a bucket of water on me?"

"I don't know. I just wanted to get a laugh out of you. Lately, you've been so…" She sticks out her bottom lip. "Glum."

"What the skies is *glum*?" I squeeze the water from the front of my shirt.

"Sad, mopey, boring?"

I chuckle and step into the dark shop, brushing the wet hair off my forehead.

"Yay, you laughed." She claps her dainty hands together. I light the wall lanterns, illuminating the room and her golden hair. Her cheeks are flushed, and her blue eyes are wide with joy. I love when she smiles like that. She's wearing a pale blue dress that hugs her tightly and drapes to her calves.

I resist giving her another chuckle. "We are engaged now, which means you need to start acting like an adult."

"What? There's no rule about that." She puts one hand on her hip and stomps her foot.

"If there was, would you follow it?" I put away a few tools and pull out the ones needed for the next project. I lay them neatly in a row, in the order they will be needed.

"Probably not," she says through a bubbly laugh.

I actually love that she doesn't follow rules. She inspires me to take risks and come out of my fearful cave. So I pause my work and risk saying, "What if I asked you not to pester me like that anymore?"

"You think I'm a pest?"

Holding my hands out and indicating my dripping wet clothes, I carefully consider how to best answer. *Yes, you're a pest* could be followed by Level One Anger. *No, you're not a pest* could be followed by her pestering me to tell the truth. I sit on the small stool at the bellows and pump it to get the furnace burning hot. "You know I love you. I just need you to love me back differently. Nicer. Fewer shenanigans. More… gentleness."

She bursts out laughing.

Is she not taking me seriously? Her blonde hair swishes about her shoulders, and her slender body bounces. Once she regains her composure, she places a hand on my cheek. "I can't promise no shenanigans. But maybe I won't throw water on you again."

"No more tripping, either." I grunt, pressing the handles of the bellows together, over and over.

"Fine."

I stop and hold up a finger. "And no more tickling."

Her eyes widen and the corners of her mouth droop. "You don't like tickling?"

"Not really." I prepare to explain how it makes me panic. Instead I say, "But I am willing to tickle you. You seem to like it." I smile in hopes I haven't hurt her feelings with my requests. I love her attention and her lightheartedness, but her pranks sometimes feel like attacks.

I swallow my fear that she will reject me as a smile spreads across her face. Her blue eyes sparkle as she puts out her hand to shake. "You've got yourself a deal." I take it in my hand and kiss her soft knuckles.

"Mister Blacksmith?" A hefty Ellerian with thick shoulders and gray wings nearly touching the ceiling crashes into the room. He is carrying two heavy leather bags, with a third strapped to his chest. He pants heavily as he sets them on the floor with a thud. "You would not believe how fast you plummet with all these tools." He chortles, and his belly bounces up and down. It hangs over his belt a little, and I wonder how he keeps himself aloft at all.

Hollis snickers at his comment. It takes me a moment to realize he must have flown down from Ellery with all of it. I fake a laugh in response.

"This is Ledger," Hollis introduces me.

"Oh, yes. I'm Deveraux," he says. "Is your village smithy around?" He glances out the door.

His question irritates me, but he doesn't know he is being

rude. I clear my throat and make my voice lower than usual. "I *am* the blacksmith." I put out a hand.

He grabs my forearm, and we shake. "Right. Okay. You're a bit flimsy for a blacksmith." He grips my bicep with his other arm, then pats me on the shoulder.

Hollis stifles a laugh as the man lets me go.

I rub my arm where he squeezed me too hard. "I've been apprenticing for six harvests, but my father was taken prisoner, and I've had to take on all the responsibilities myself."

The man nods as if that validates my position. I wish my father were here. He used to speak well of me to the Balfourian elders when they preferred my father make them a sword. *You won't be disappointed in his craftsmanship,* I remember him saying once.

My heart aches for him. *Is he still alive? Have the savages killed him?* Shame grips my head. We should be tracking him down.

Deveraux pushes my neat line of tools to the side and slams a heavy bag on the workbench. I press my lips together in an angry line and stare at Hollis. With her eyes wide, she shrugs.

2

Plea to Stay

TOLLIVER

With a bowl of my mother's steamy morning stew and a hunk of bread wrapped in cloth, I step through the front door of Kava's father's cottage.

"Where's my darling wife this morning?"

Healer Clovis is hunched over a book with a spread of herbs while flames lick a pot of boiling water, sending a strange odor into the air.

He points a finger at the back door. "Kava's out back." He is always mixing new healing tinctures to help the sick and wounded. He must be making something important with how little he says, so I leave him to his work.

I push through the back door to the makeshift tent set up as a medical ward. There are three cots on both sides of the small room. Old Man Dudley is asleep on the far right. He came in with a fever yesterday. There's a winged man asleep across from him. His tan wings hang off the side of the narrow cot and touch the floor. Neelie, the Ellerian nurse, said he is chronically ill and didn't want him to be far from the medical ward. I search for her, but she isn't in yet.

Kava is dressed and wrapped in an apron. Her long brown hair frames her warm red cheeks and hangs past her elbows. She usually pulls it back before attending to a patient. She is busy already tending to an Ellerian man who is moaning in bloody agony. He must have come in this morning.

Kava sets a few supplies on a table next to the writhing man and pushes her hair behind her ears. She notices me, and her eyes brighten. "Can you hold him down while I stitch his cut?"

I set the bowl on the shelf by the door and join her. The man's white wings are splayed out beneath him awkwardly. I push the wing nearest to me inward. It's strange how warm it is. Pulling his arms across his chest, I lean over and hold him down so he doesn't thrash in pain, hurting himself or my pregnant wife.

At first glance it isn't noticeable, but I can tell her belly is slightly swollen. Our child is growing.

Kava grabs a needle with one hand and pinches the gash closed with the other. Her fingers move gently and aptly as she sews up the wound. She bites her lip with a pained expression on her face and lets out a breath when she finishes, clipping the thread close to the skin after each stitch. The man relaxes as Kava scoops a bit of salve and gently brushes it over the stitches.

After wiping off on a towel, she places a warm hand on my arm. "Thank you, love."

Releasing the Ellerian man, I face her. "You are amazing at what you do." She responds with a smile as I take her in my arms. "I brought your morning meal." I nod toward the shelf.

"In a minute. I need to bandage him up."

"How'd he get cut?" I ask, as someone scuffles through the tent flap.

"Tolliver." Angus's loud voice is laced with intensity.

"Keep your voice down," Kava whispers, nodding at her other sleeping patients.

Angus frowns, and a muscle in his jaw tightens. He points at me, then out the door with a wild look in his eyes.

Kava folds a clean bandage and lays it on the wounded Ellerian's gut.

I follow Angus into the morning sun outside the tent. His voice is still curt and loud when he says, "We need to leave. Today. We need to get our fathers back, Tolliver. They could be torturing them, or…"

"Angus, yes, yes, I know."

"No, you don't. They slaughtered almost all of our men. You didn't see it, Tolliver. I had to bury their broken bodies. Days and days of digging." He inspects the callouses on his palms, then balls them into fists. "We need to go after them."

"We will—"

"Then why are you standing around here playing nursemaid?" Angus shouts, face flushing with rage.

I stand up straight. "Get off your high horse, Angus. There's a lot to do around here. I've been building all week. Fran and Shurl's cottage is nearly ready—"

"I don't care about any of that!" He throws both hands in the air. "It's all meaningless unless we can bring our men back. The Ellerians will take over our entire village if we don't do this."

"Who? Take over? You're not thinking, Angus."

"I'm the only one who's thinking. The longer we wait to save them, the higher the chance the savages will murder them all. So let's go! Let's get an army and track them down. I can't wait any longer. We must leave!" His voice shrieks and I shush him as Kava appears in the doorway. I hook my arm behind his neck and drag him farther from the tent. Its thin walls, made of mismatched sheets and quilts, can't block his panicked voice.

"Okay, Angus. Pack what you need. We will leave in the morning."

"I'm packed. We should leave now."

"No, I need to talk to Kava so she doesn't hate me when we return." I run a hand through my hair and sigh.

"We need an army, Toll," he says, grinding his teeth.

I shake my head. "We don't have an army. At best we have a ragtag militia. And that will have to do."

"No—"

"Yes! We will take whoever we can get, and they will have to suffice. If you can't stand that, I will tie you to a tree and leave you here. You are useless when you aren't thinking!" I stand nose to nose with Angus as his eyes bulge and his breath wafts in my face. I don't blink, and he backs down. "Go tell Ledger we're leaving in the morning. I will get whoever I can to join us."

He turns away.

"Angus," I call before he gets too far down the path. "Get your head right."

He squints with the sun in his eyes, gives me a curt nod, and disappears around the corner.

"You can't be serious." Kava is several feet from me

with her hands on her hips. Her nostrils flare, but before she can say anything else out of anger, I reach for her.

"Someone has to rescue them, Kava. Whatever it takes."

"It doesn't have to take you." She purses her lips.

"Who else can lead a battalion of men to rescue them? No one. There's no one."

"Angus can."

"He's in no condition…"

"What about Ledger?"

I laugh and squint against the brilliant sun as a bead of sweat trickles down my forehead. "Ledger? There's no way."

"He's different, you know." She drops her hands and wipes them down the front of her blood-stained apron. "He can go. He brought me home safe. Even saved me from a pack of wolves. He can take Angus, Bernhard, Hollis, her dragon..."

"Yeah, but who else? Ledger is no kind of warrior. But I am."

"You're needed here. To rebuild." She places her hand over her pregnant belly. "And I need you." My eyes drift to her abdomen. "Our baby needs you—alive."

My fingers press hard against my temple. Everything inside me grinds against itself. Instead of saying anything else, I grab her and hug her to me. Her hair smells of sweat and lavender.

I can't agree to this. I must go. I must find my father, my Balfourian father. The longer they're missing, the higher chance they're all dead. I will find a way to tell her how it is going to be. We will be back in two moons at most.

I release her and stare at the ground as she walks off.

My shadow is so small beneath me. I feel it shrinking and boxing me in. I consider convincing Angus not to go at all and imagine his reaction. With his state of mind, even implying it could get my face bashed in.

Could Ledger lead them? He led them home from Ellery, but he didn't lead them in battle against fierce barbarians. He's not a warrior. I am. Without me, they will all be slaughtered.

I glance up at the haphazard tent of made of old, frayed fabrics attached to the backside of Healer Clovis's house: Kava's childhood home. The opening in the side of the tent frames a woman. She watches me with sad eyes and crossed arms. When our eyes meet, Kava frowns: a plea to stay.

***

Instead of strolling to the meeting of the elders and advisors, I jog. As the air fills my lungs and my heart rate picks up, I make longer and longer strides until I am sprinting. I'm irked she would dare ask me to stay as arguments gallop through my mind. *She knows I've been planning this. She knows they need me. My father needs me.*

I race around the inner circle of cottages. The people come and go from their homes, obstructing my path. They frustrate me as I slow to avoid a collision. *I know in my heart I'm the leader of the front-line battalion, and the front line is heading east. I must go.*

When I make it to Elder Tillman's home, I slow to a walk. The front door is wide open, welcoming each elder and advisor to the morning meeting. I climb the stairs and step through the door. I shake off my irritation and put on a good face—relaxing my brow and feigning a smile.

"There aren't enough," Advisor Cabot says. "If we are going to make more, we must dismantle the looms and bring them as well."

Three of the five Ellerian advisors are present. Advisor Gabriel is seated at the meeting table across from my mother, Adaya. Advisors Cabot and Merle stand beside the hearth discussing looms. Cabot is short, round, and elderly but quick-witted.

"They are enormous," Advisor Merle says. Though he is younger and taller, he is quite passive. He turns slightly, and his white wings knock something from the mantel. It crashes to the ground. "Oh dear. My apologies."

Elder Tillman grabs a small towel. "It's no problem. Let me get that." He uses the towel to scoop up the remnants of a shattered clay jar and swipes the small shards toward the hearth and into the fire. "Join us at the table," Tillman says.

Merle folds his wings tight to his back and sits on the bench beside Advisor Gabriel. They both have a serious look on their faces. Advisor Cabot sits beside Merle and continues their conversation.

I join my mother on the other side of the table. She pulls her blue skirts close to make room for me. I slip between her and Elder Chasen on the bench. He smells of sweat and cabbage. I hold my breath until the gagging sensation fades.

Elder Jubal clamors through the room, tossing a tool belt near the door. "Who's missing?" he asks, as if he's in charge. He strokes his graying beard and takes in the room. I dismiss several hateful thoughts in an attempt to appear impartial to his presence.

"We're here." Advisor Tiberius, my Ellerian father, climbs the porch steps. He enters with my grandmother on his arm. His white wings brush either side of the doorway on the way in. Behind them an older Ellerian man with dark brown skin, hazy black eyes, and gray wings enters: Advisor Samhul.

At the entrance of my grandmother, something in the room shifts. I stand and show her the reverence she deserves. Grandmother smiles as each elder and advisor stands. She strides to the head of the table, pushes the chair aside, and waits until we are all seated.

All four of the official elders are present. I am still an apprenticing elder. My mother should have stepped down so I could step in when I arrived home. Angus is also apprenticing. With his father missing, he should officially be an elder but hasn't been instated yet. He should get sworn in today. *Angus should be here.* I consider looking for him but decide against it as Grandmother, Queen Huyana, begins to speak. "How is the first stage of transition going?"

"Well," Jubal says in a commanding voice.

"Not you," she interrupts. "I want to hear from the Ellerians first."

I raise my eyebrows as Jubal's shoulders slump ever so slightly. I take a bit of pleasure that she put him in his place so early in the meeting.

It's obvious we are still two separate people groups pretending to be one. The winged and wingless. Anyone with wings is on that side of the table, and those without are on this side.

“As I was saying while we were walking over here, Your Majesty,” Advisor Tiberius says. “Everyone has a place to sleep. Most of them are in temporary tents in the Hundred Harvest… area, clearing, whatever it is called.” Huyana smiles as Tiberius continues. “The group meals we started offering yesterday work perfectly for everyone. That was a good decision. As people get more permanent homes, they can begin to make their own meals, which will lighten the load of the cooks over time.”

“Superb,” Grandmother Huyana says. “Let’s address the fact that we need more people to help cut down trees for the new cottages. Who can coordinate the effort?”

No one says anything. She purses her lips and makes eye contact with each person around the large wooden table. She isn’t quite intimidating as an old, petite lady. Her hair is a dull white and her wrinkled skin has seen many years in the sun. But her determined nature and fierce gaze have made grown men cower. She is the granddaughter of the original royal family of Ellery, even though she is wingless. She was lost from Ellery as a small child—*because* she was wingless.

Merle moves first. “I can take care of it.”

“Thank you. I know we all have plenty to do. It’s going to take continued effort to get this village running smoothly again. Are there any other pressing issues?” Her voice carries the air of confidence it always has.

I gaze at her in respect. Surely this village is in good hands so I can do what I need to do—find the men of Balfour.

I rise from the bench. “I’m putting together a group to rescue the men who were taken by the savage tribe.” Someone to my left gasps, but I don’t care who.

"There's no time for that," Jubal says.

"There is always time to save our loved ones." I frown at him.

"They could already be dead. It's not worth the effort. I vote no." He folds his arms across his chest.

"I wasn't asking for permission. Especially not yours." I hold myself back from shouting at him.

At the other end of the table, Grandmother's eyes hold my gaze. Stern and thoughtful.

"Pass the word." She glances from person to person around the room. "Anyone who is willing to go. We will send you with anything you need."

"We will meet at my mother's home after midday meal." Around the room, the only one who meets my eyes is Tiberius. I try not to seethe with hatred at the rest of them because I know they won't pass the word.

"Will do," Tiberius says.

At least I have him.

As Grandmother moves on to the next subject, I consider the first people to ask to join us: Belamy, Estefano, and a few more.

"I would like to address the issue of Caedus," Grandmother says as she slowly takes her seat. "It's been four days since his mutiny. Ellery will be out of range by tomorrow, and we must take him and his cohorts out of the prison cells by this evening. Any suggestions?"

I barely pay attention, listing all the things we will need: food, water, weapons, medicines.

Kava's request flashes through my mind. I scowl and chew the inside of my cheek. I understand why she's asking me to stay, but *she* doesn't quite understand what's at stake. I love her fiercely and will miss her over the next few months while she's safe at home.

3

Cared Enough

LEDGER

"Only Balfourian *men*!" Angus shouts from the platform in the middle of the village square. "You may join us to get our fathers back." His face is fiercely red, merging all his freckles into one.

The people of Balfour stop their work and listen to him, but there's something strange happening. They are silent.

"Join me," Angus demands. His eyes squint against the harsh light of the afternoon and his forehead glistens with sweat.

Someone mutters nearby, then Ryllis and her younger brother walk away, followed by another and another wingless Balfourian. The few Ellerians around the square simply stare. My sister, Mila, and her friend, Myst, whisper to each other and snicker in Angus's direction.

I clomp to the platform as the village square clears out and everyone rejects my cousin's cry for help. I agree we must go find our fathers, and I know Angus means well. But his plea comes across as judgmental and demanding. No one will answer an invitation like that.

His shoulders droop and eyes close as I climb up the three steps toward him.

"You okay?" My voice comes out in a whisper.

He answers with an angry sneer, grinding his teeth together. Angus tips his face to the sky, his red curls fall back from his face, and a tear trickles from his eye. I understand why he's so angry. His father and brother are missing, possibly dead. He walks away, more sad than anything.

I want to tell him what his message sounded like, but I don't want to tell him he's wrong. The one thing I know about Angus is he believes he's never wrong.

There is no one left in the square, neither Balfourians nor Ellerians. Rhythmic hammering echoes around the wide space. To the southeast, several cottages are being rebuilt.

The Ellerian people came to live among us in peace. I never thought I'd see this day. All I ever wanted was peace between our people so I could be friends with Alouette—beautiful, white-winged, Alouette. She is the reason I was gone for the last year. She was missing, and my village was happy there were no more Ellerian people on the floating island that travels past our village every harvest. But I had to find her and make sure she was safe. Surprisingly, I did.

I aim toward my father's blacksmith workshop and descend the platform, leaving scuff marks in the cold, dry dirt. Angus is right, we need to rescue our fathers. But he's expecting the wrong thing. The only men left in Balfour right now cannot come with us. They are old, most of them grandfathers or village elders with obligations. I press my fingers to my temples, easing the pain in my head and heart. Many of us in this village are fatherless and broken.

Especially Angus.

I should ask the elders. I whirl all the way around. Tillman's home is on the corner of the square. I come around the front porch, ready to stomp up the steps and through the front door, but the elders and advisors are funneling out. I step out of their way feeling like a slow-witted dud.

Tolliver comes around the corner. "The word is out that we need volunteers."

It doesn't matter if I am too late. Tolliver, yet again, has picked up the slack. I sigh with relief and smile at him. "Thanks, brother."

"Oh, we're brothers again? That's fantastic." He raises an eyebrow at me and I freeze, my eyes wide. He lets out a laugh. "I'm just kidding."

He hooks his arm around my neck and guides me eastward. I should get back to the shop, but instead I go where he leads. I put an arm around his waist and walk with him.

He says quietly, "We won't get many volunteers. I hope Angus knows that."

"No, Angus doesn't know. He demanded only Balfourian men go with us."

He heaves a heavy breath. "Once we get on our way, he will be fine."

"Or we can direct his rage at our enemies."

He stops short and spins me toward him. "You understand these savages are nothing to mess with, right?" His face is serious with a hint of fear in his eyes. I nod as he says, "Meet at Mother's cottage after midday meal." He ruffles the hair on the top of my head like I'm eight years old again instead of eighteen.

I consider grabbing his hand and twisting a finger back, but I don't want to be wrestled to the ground.

"I have a few others to ask to join us," I lie as he walks away. There aren't any Balfourians who would want to join us. Out of the few Ellerians I've met, the only one I haven't asked yet is Alouette.

4
Save Him

ALOUETTE

Between flights to and from Ellery, I stop in my parents' quarters on the thirteenth floor. I was barely conscious the first time back in these rooms after my father died. I was incoherent. My chest aches remembering when they attempted to execute me. I nearly drop the items hidden in several grain sacks slung over my shoulder. I set them down gently on the stone floor right inside the front room.

The room is washed with white light from outside the door. The padded bench with pilling, gray wool fabric sits along the right side, and I touch the darkened stain on the nearest corner. I push away the memory of skinning my knee as a young girl and having to tend to myself without my parents' help. My family's table and chairs still sit beyond the fireplace on the left side of the room.

I catch my reflection in the tray propped on the mantel. My dark hair is jagged and unruly, contrasting starkly against my white, buttoned shirt beneath my tan, fur-lined coat. My black leather skirt hangs nearly to the floor over calf-high boots. I lost all my beautiful dresses at my father's castle on the ground. I swallow hard at the memory of dressing fancifully while half our people were slaving away building his wretched castle. Ledger's mother gave me these clothes, even cut a space for my wings.

Smoothing my unkempt hair, I take deep breaths to slow my panicked heart. I need to stay focused on secretly stocking the closet with everything I will need when I leave Balfour. All of Ellery is being unloaded for them to live in Balfour. They plan to never return to the island, so they are scavenging everything not fixed to the floor.

I've gone back and forth a hundred times about leaving. If I'm going to go through with it, I'm going to need things. They must be hidden away before the other guardians haul them to the ground. Linens, stocks of grain, dried herbs, medicines I might need, and cookware. My mother's pots and pans will work, as long as no one makes off with them.

"Alouette?"

A distant voice startles me, and I yank my wings in tightly to my back. I drag the first grain sack into the closet and quickly pull the door shut. As I shuffle back to the front room, Ledger comes through the doorway.

"What are you doing?"

I fiddle with the furry hem of my coat. "I… I'm visiting my parents' quarters."

Ledger saunters to the hearth and runs his hand along the stone mantel. "I've been looking all over for you. Thought you might be here."

I peek out the front door, worried someone followed him. He is alone. I relax my wings and my stance.

"Is it strange to be back here?" His voice is even, free of

judgment.

I frown. "Strange. Yes."

His dark curly hair is quite long now, nearly to his shoulders. When we were children, we used to play on the mountainside, rolling down a grassy knoll. Leaves and sticks used to get stuck in his wild mop. He was much smaller then. He has changed so much: scruff on his chin, a man-sized nose, and taller than me by a whole head.

"What are you doing up this high?" I attempt to sound nonchalant, but I startle at every noise outside my door.

"I came to ask you something."

I hold my chin high and anticipate whatever is coming. My mind flips through all the possible things he could ask. I feel trapped and found out, especially with a full grain bag at my feet.

He clears his throat. "I was hoping… I mean, would you come with us to rescue my father? Tolliver, Angus, and I need anyone we can get." He looks at his feet, something he does when he's nervous. I find it endearing that he's still the same boy inside. He waits patiently for my answer.

"I can't, Ledger."

His brown eyes meet mine, pleading and sad. "But why? I know you don't want to be in Balfour."

"You're right. I don't." My voice comes out flat.

"Then come with us." He starts talking faster. "It's not exactly safe, but at least you can get out of Balfour for a while."

I shake my head, grappling for a way to tell him why. "I can't—I'm not staying in Balfour anyway."

"What? Where—"

"Come here, Ledger." I reach toward the closet. I open the door, and he gazes upon my supplies.

"What's all this?"

"I'm stocking up. I'm staying on Ellery."

"Alone?" His chin does that sad quivering move, making my heart ache.

"Yes." I close the door and wish it had a lock. I shouldn't have shown him. "I must get out of here." With a throbbing head, I march through the front room. I flap my wings to get me out of the room quicker, hoping he will follow. Laying my hands on the stone railing, I brace myself. *I should get him as far away from my secrets as possible.*

The wind whips through the inner tower of Ellery and muffles Ledger's voice. "I wish you wouldn't leave, Alouette. You'll be all alone."

I sense the panic in his words.

But that is exactly what I want. "I need to get as far from you as possible."

"Me? What did I do?" His eyes scrunch with hurt and too many questions.

"Yes, you, Ledger." I regret saying it as I cross my arms. He waits for me to explain, and I grapple for a reason to change the subject. "How did you get up here?"

"I—oh, Belamy and Estefano." He shakes his head. "I need to know why you think you have to leave." He raises his voice at me. "Why do you have to get away from *me*?"

He waits and waits for me to respond.

The question stands between us like a rabid jaycoon threatening to eat one of us alive. Of course it's me it's after.

My thoughts pound louder and louder until I can't hold

them in, and I blurt, “Everyone I love dies!” Panting like I flew around the entire world, I press a hand to my chest. “I can’t risk losing you too. I must get as far from you as possible. Bad things happen around me. I can’t stop it. And you’re in danger for being my friend.”

“Alouette.” He steps closer.

The way he says my name reminds me of the day he dragged me from the burning cottage. He desperately screamed my name. I feel the pain of the flames and the losses of that day. It was the day my father was slaughtered at the hands of the Lianminese. The day I would’ve been burned alive, had it not been for Ledger. He saved me. And now I must save him.

“Alouette, please,” he says again. “If you leave, you’re still losing me.”

“But at least you’ll be alive.”

“I’m not in danger being around you. Remember? I saved *you* from that fire. You don’t mean this. I know you.” He reaches for my hand.

“No. The girl you knew died that day.” I step back to avoid his touch. “I’ve made up my mind. Goodbye, Ledger.” Tears fill my eyes and I let them fall as I stomp away into my old and new home. I slam the door in his face and press my wings against the cold wood, hoping he won’t push through it. He doesn’t, and it makes me cry even harder that he lets me shut him out so harshly. I deserve to be punished for treating him so badly. I bite down hard on my cheek until the pain inside me subsides, at least just a little.

5 The Horror

LEDGER

After mulling over and over our conversation, I shove Alouette from my mind. Slumped over a bowl of porridge beside Hollis, I stare into the distance at the woods surrounding the Hundred Harvest sacred grounds. The tents tied between the trees blur as I daydream about the mission before us.

Trekking again through the wilderness. Vulnerable to wild animals. Out in the elements, rainstorms, mud, and eventually snow. I don't like traveling. It's too much work. Too many surprises. I'd much rather wake up on my comfortable mat in the corner of the loft, follow the same routine of breakfast stew, firing up the forge, and making new tools and weapons every day.

I take another bite of porridge. I'm startled when a hand pounds the table next to me, jostling my bowl. Tolliver says, "Ledger, meeting time."

My heart leaps into my throat.

He continues walking and pounds on the table next to several others around the dining area.

"Well, let's go," Hollis says. She is already out of her seat, gathering up her empty bowl and spoon. I follow her, gobbling the rest of my porridge in three big spoonfuls. We drop them in the basins of water at the edge of the dining area, and she slips her hand in mine as we head toward the village. My heart keeps up the unsteady rhythm, and I'm nauseous, knowing I have to leave the comfort of my home to find my father.

Hollis drops my hand and hurries ahead of me, yanking open the back door and traipsing into my parents' house. I catch the door before it slams, and I follow Hollis into the living area. Sweat beads on my forehead when we stand beside the blazing fireplace.

My mother sits with her hands folded on the table, watching everyone enter.

Angus is standing near the head of the table with his arms crossed. I avoid eye contact. Beside him is Bernhard, who is much taller with a less confident demeanor. His shoulders slump forward, and his mousy brown beard is scraggly like it actually takes effort to grow. It's hard for me to believe he is willing to face this enemy again.

A few Ellerians enter through the front door, their wings brushing the top of the doorway. Belamy, with his black wings and somber brown face, takes a position near the hearth. Beside him, Estefano pushes his long, brown hair behind his ears and exchanges a wary glance with him.

Another Ellerian enters that surprises me: Char. The man who threw Alouette against the prison wall while we were on Ellery. I scowl but clear the expression from my face before he looks in my direction. When he makes eye contact with me, I nod then feel stupid for doing it.

Four other Ellerians I haven't met yet crowd into the room. Then Hellwig, the dragon keeper, saunters in and gently pushes the door shut. His white hair is as bright as his white wings. The small man stands beside hulking Belamy as they exchange jovial words.

It's strange that there are more Ellerians available to go than Balfourians. I don't know what I was expecting. The only other Balfourian men alive are elders.

Tolliver and his Ellerian father—wings and all—enter through the back door, slamming it loudly. Tolliver addresses the group. "Thank you for coming. Each of you expressed interest in helping rescue some of our men."

He is interrupted by the front door opening. Everyone watches Ryllis step over the threshold. My eyes widen as my wingless red-headed neighbor joins the ranks of brave men willing to take on a dangerous task.

Her cheeks flush as she scuttles over beside Hollis. Hollis loops an arm through hers with a big grin.

"As I was saying," Tolliver continues. "Thank you for your willingness to join this mission. If you know of any others who might wish to join, please, bring them. We shall meet after morning meal in the square. Bring whatever supplies you need. Travel may be long. They have a twenty-four-day head start. We are unsure how far our men have been taken. Angus is a skilled tracker. Is there anyone else who knows how to track?"

"Aye." One of the new Ellerians raises a fist. His pale, sandy hair falls in his face, and he doesn't move it.

"Okay, Angus and…" Tolliver raises his eyebrows in

question.

"Zander."

"Angus and Zander can track their direction."

"They headed east for at least a day," Angus says.

"Good." Tolliver nods at our cousin, then addresses the whole group. "You'll need weapons. Ledger has a few new ones in the smithy shop you may be able to use. My mother—er—Adaya will share what she knows about the tribe."

He holds his hand out to her, seated at the table, and she clears her throat. My mother gazes into the eyes of each one around the room. When she meets my eyes, my heartbeat picks up its pace.

"They came down from the mountains in the northwest without warning." She speaks with confidence, the tone she used to take with us kids when she would give us direction. "Our perimeter battalion was dispatched already, off to the south in anticipation of Ellery's return. Their eyes were on the sky, not the mountains or the village. The intruders tore through the village, chasing our children, terrorizing our families. Sage reached the village bell first. She rang and rang and rang—"

Her throat makes a choking sound as tears well in her eyes. "When our warriors came, the savages had already breached the village. They fought in our streets, outside our front doors. Many mothers of Balfour dragged their children into basements, where we used to hide from the Ellerians. Some of them didn't make it to their own homes but hid with neighbors."

She pauses and Advisor Tiberius takes a step forward. "We've seen these sorts of roving tribes before. They don't stay in one place for very long, but travel the countryside in search of a fight, to pillage and take. We've not met with this specific group of warriors before to know who they are or what they want." He nods reverently to her and she continues.

"You will know it is them because they wore red leather armor covered with metal rivets. Their iron helmets come to a point on top with a wild animal's tail jutting out, like that of a wolf or a fox. Most wore metal masks, making them look like monsters. Bernhard can help identify them. Oh, and Ryllis as well."

"What of their weapons?" Char crosses his arms.

She glances over at Char and rises from her seat. "They carried long, curved swords in leather sheaths. Those who rode on horseback carried spears with four sharp points. Their round shields were a mosaic of metal and leather. Their leader wore a larger helmet lined with fur and bore a chain with a spiked iron ball. It was covered in blood after he—" Her voice rises in pitch and stops abruptly.

Char uncrosses his arms. His face softens and jaw drops open.

Mother swallows and stands up straighter. "As our men poured in from the south, their warriors cut them down one after the other. I've never seen such hatred and intensity in killing. They were ruthless."

Sorrow shines in her eyes with unshed tears, but I can't reach her on the other side of the table.

"They had us surrounded. It seemed like over half of our village was slaughtered. But Fergus…" She glances at me and quickly away. "He somehow disarmed their leader. He seized the vicious weapon that killed his own father moments before. He blew the shofar with a sword at the man's neck. He knew we were beaten. If they kept fighting, we might all be dead."

My insides twist at this new information. I didn't know how my grandfather died. I wish I didn't know now. I look around the room at each one present. *Are they willing to die like that?* Tolliver catches my eye and flattens his mouth in a line, giving none of his feelings away. The Ellerian guardians in the room are already armed. *Are they powerful enough to get my father back?*

My mother continues, "Fergus proposed a deal, difficult as it was because they did not understand our language. He and the rest of the men surrendered to them in exchange for leaving the rest of the village alone, even though the they had already started torching the cottages.

"Fergus didn't release their leader until all their men left the village. One of our women, Ria, reported that Fergus wounded their leader to get them to relent. The last Ria saw of Fergus was him being knocked unconscious and dragged off with the rest of our men. By her count, there were fifteen left."

I take in a panicky breath as my body shakes in fear. I knew they were vicious people, but they may kill us all for simply approaching them.

I can't slow my heart as I squeeze Hollis's hand. I can't subject her to this. I can't let my sweet Hollis see the horrors my mother described. She can't go with us into this battle. The only thing slowing the blood in my veins is the idea of Hollis staying home.

“I’m sorry. This isn’t my fight. I can’t…” an unfamiliar Ellerian man with dark gray wings says. He pulls the door open and walks out. *I don’t blame him.*

6
Sweat and Worry

TOLLIVER

By midafternoon, we are back to thatching a roof just off the village square.

"Here you go, Tolliver." Advisor Tiberius hands me a bundle of combed wheat reed, the perfect crop for thatched roofs.

Standing on a ladder beside my biological father, a pang of guilt almost tips me over as I take the reeds. It took me a year to find him. We met a mere three days ago, but I must leave again to hunt down my adoptive Balfourian father. But my curiosity about my birth family keeps me rooted on the ladder, thatching a new roof beside a man I barely know with enormous white wings. It's my last day to ask him what I need to know before I head east.

When he hands me another golden bundle, I lay it alongside the previous one and hold it in place with a long metal reeding pin. There are hundreds of questions I want to ask him.

"Advisor Tiberius, can I ask you a question?" I tap the base of the bundle with the palm of my hand so the ends of the reeds follow the pitch of the roof.

"Please." He lays a hand on my shoulder. "Call me Tiberius. Or, when you're comfortable, you can call me Father. Whichever you wish." He gives an awkward smile.

"Okay. Thank you." I return the expression with a hint of doubt, but I appreciate his effort. I feel guilty for the thought that he should earn the title of Father.

There is barely a breeze today even though we are high on a roof tying down bundles of thatch. It is the first cabin he and I are helping build. Tiberius wipes a cloth across his forehead despite the cooler temperatures of autumn. He stretches his white wings and flaps them, wafting the air across my skin. I smile at him.

"What were you going to ask?" He accepts more reeds being passed up his ladder from below.

I watch him stack them against the roof beams. "What was my mother like?"

He hands me a small metal crook with a far-off look in his eyes. "She was beautiful with a quiet ferocity."

Pulling out a small handful of reeds, I lay them horizontally across the bundle. I hammer several metal crooks into the wood beams underneath, pinning it all down permanently.

I catch a glimpse of his face. He is almost smiling as he talks about her.

"She was my guiding light. She kept me true." He smiles wide and stares into the distance.

"What was her name?"

"Oh skies, you don't even know her name. My apologies." He clears his throat. "Her name was Asha. She was a midwife. There was nothing she adored more than babies. Of course, I always hoped she loved *me* more." He winks and hands me the next bundle of reeds.

If she was a midwife, perhaps that was the reason she knew about the wingless children being smuggled off Ellery.

As I batten down the next few bundles, he tells me about their wedding day and how she fought with her father about marrying him. Her father thought she could do better. "But when her mind was made up, come dragon or gale force winds, nothing could move her."

We laugh together. I see a lot of myself in how he describes her.

The bell tolls three times in the village square, announcing the evening meal. I drive the last few crooks into the roof and slip my hammer into my belt. I only now notice the sun dipping toward the horizon and the clouds reflecting its orange light.

"Meet you down below," Tiberius says. His wings carry him downward, leaving the ladder to me.

We walk through the village between the wingless and winged people heading to the clearing around the Hundred Harvest Tree. All the high tables from Ellery's dining room are positioned around the stump of our sacred Tree. Several Balfourian women stand behind a table serving a barley and venison stew and crunchy bread. Tiberius and I take our bowls and sit together at table on the outskirts, where it's quieter.

Sweat collects at the edge of my forehead as I spoon up the steaming meal and listen to Tiberius talk about the mother I never knew.

"The advisors were terrified of her. Advisor Zeru once came to me and asked me to keep her away from him." He chuckles at the memory. "She was only as tall as my shoulder." He stands and holds his hand at shoulder height. "Zeru was the brother of the king and a head guardian. And he was afraid of my little Asha."

I laugh and gobble up every word he says about her.

"She could never stand for injustice, Tolliver." His voice changed to a somber tone. "She was devastated when she had to give you up. But she would never let them kill you. Several babies had already made their way to Balfour in years past." He leans forward and whispers, "And other cities as well."

He takes another bite and I grind on those words. *The wingless children of Ellery are spread all over the world?* My heart sinks at the sad thought.

He averts his eyes in shame. "She couldn't allow you to be killed. I didn't know about any of that until after you were gone. I only held you once. I kissed your forehead." He touches his forehead and his eyebrows pinch together in pain.

My throat constricts. Sorrow and regret are evident in the slump of his shoulders and in the overused frown lines on his face.

"It broke her spirit to lose you, our firstborn son. All she ever wanted was to have a child of her own. The fact she had to give him—you—away, tore the heart from her chest. For two years she walked around with vacant eyes. When her belly began to grow again, part of her began to blossom. She started coming back to me. But…" His voice trails off and he inhales sharply, as if describing how he lost her in childbirth is too painful.

"I am here now." I reach across the table.

After a few moments, he meets my eyes and takes my hand. "I am sorry I was not allowed to raise you, but you have grown into a strong and genuine man. It's more than I ever could have hoped and more than I deserve." His eyes pool with tears, as do mine. "Your mother would be so proud of you."

"Thank you," I choke out, trying to maintain my composure.

Turning back to the stew in front of me, I eat quietly. As I ponder what he said, I realize I should stay in Balfour. I shouldn't leave *my* child. I want to see him—or her—come into this world. I want to kiss my child on the forehead.

I push a hand through my hair, wiping away the sweat and worry. *I shouldn't go.* I shouldn't leave Kava alone in this. I would never forgive myself if something happened to her or our baby.

7 The Rage of Hollis

LEDGER

It's taken me all day to work up the nerve to approach Hollis. To tell her—no—beg her not to come with us. It shouldn't be this way. I should be able to speak my mind, regardless of the consequences. But it's Hollis. My Hollis. She is fiery and opinionated. *Skies, save me.*

I follow her around the backside of the North Mountain, overlooking the various shades of trees in yellow and red and every shade in between. The sun droops close to the horizon below a layer of blazing orange clouds, flooding the world in its glow.

I make several attempts to breathe through the sour churning in my stomach. I imagine again and again that vicious tribe coming over this very mountain pass and attacking my people. One of them tore my grandfather apart. Grandfather Galefire was an old, gentle soul. He should never have had to fight in battle. He was forced to be on the front line until the men returned from the southern border. My head aches at the thought of Hollis going with us to face the savages in battle. It's the only thing keeping me walking alongside Hollis to her favorite spot so I can say what I need to say—confidently or not.

As we come around the mountain, the cliff drops off to the left.

"Okay, this is about as far as we can go without having to climb straight up," Hollis says. Her face is upturned with a big smile. She points at a dark cave on the side of the mountain. "She's up there."

"Can you call her?" I ask, not really wanting to see that dragon again.

"Of course." She puts her hands on either side of her mouth. "Tristeh! Tristeh, come!"

A screech echoes from the cave. A shimmery red dragon darts from the opening and propels herself into the air.

"Tristeh!" Hollis waves her arms. "We're down here."

The dragon twirls in the air and pauses, aiming at us. If Hollis weren't so good at calling her, I would think she was preparing to attack. The spikes around her eyes protrude up like she's angry. The talons on all four of her feet swipe at the air as she speeds toward us. That will never cease to terrify me. My heart thumps an uneasy rhythm, barely leaving room for my twisting guts.

The dragon lands before us on the cliffside, already saddled—but not muzzled. Her scales are a brilliant red in the evening sun. They reflect the sky and make her appear like a burning bed of coals.

"There you are, my sweet." Hollis coos at the beast. She runs a hand along Tristeh's neck as far as she can reach. Tristeh has grown. Hollis can barely reach her shoulder as she taps the scaly upper leg.

Tristeh leans forward on one knee. "Come on, Ledger." Hollis crawls up Tristeh's bended knee and onto the clean white saddle. Seems Hollis has been cleaning it up, polishing it maybe?

With trepidation, I approach the beast. It could cough and burn me to a crisp in a matter of seconds. Part of me wonders why I put myself in this kind of danger. Hollis says something and Tristeh extends her wing to me. I climb the warm, leathery surface until I reach the shell-like scales of Tristeh's back. Long spikes have grown up along her spine. I'm surprised there's room for Hollis's saddle. With a gulp, I settle behind her and strap myself in.

Hollis shouts, "Tristeh, fly!" and we are off the ground between heartbeats.

Tristeh's powerful wings propel us into the fiery sky. Hollis directs her with body movements, leaning to the right. Tristeh flattens out her wings and tips to the right.

The air streams past my ears and in my mouth, drying it out. Because I'm smiling. *Am I enjoying this?* My heart rattles in my chest, but it's more excitement than terror this time.

Hollis directs the dragon to a clearing in the woods with a small pool of water. I've hiked this far only once.

Tristeh lands beside the pond. Hollis and I fall forward when Tristeh sticks her whole head into the water. Hollis chuckles as she throws off the saddle belt and scrambles down an outstretched wing.

"Thirsty girl," she says and walks under the dragon's extended neck. I follow her to the ground.

Tristeh steps back from the water, exhaling through her

nose. The surface of the water splashes and swirls violently. Hollis calls to me from the other side of the dragon. "Look at the sky, Ledger. Isn't it beautiful?"

I consider walking around the backside of Tristeh, but her tail is swishing back and forth. I learned at an early age never to walk behind a horse. My cousin Berthold got kicked in the side of the head and was unconscious for a full day. So I follow Hollis under Tristeh's neck. Once I'm clear of the dragon, I find Hollis sprawled out on a patch of grass beside the pond, staring up at the sky. As she leans back on her elbows, the warm evening light reflects beautifully on her face and in her blue eyes. Her blonde hair and blue skirt pool in the grass around her. I very much want to kiss her.

Instead, I sit beside her cross-legged and gaze up at the peachy, swirling clouds over the top of the fading blue sky. We sit in the quiet until Hollis says, "I gathered a lot of food for tomorrow. Mother let me take almost all the ripe berries we found."

I sigh, remembering what I came here to tell her.

"Thanks." The blood in my veins race throughout my body. It pounds in my head as I rearrange the words I need to say. "I need to tell you something, Hollis." I keep straight faced and watch the clouds move ever so slightly.

"Oh?" She gives me her full attention.

Watching her out of the corner of my eye, I say, "I need you to stay here."

"Out here?"

"No, in Balfour." My chest constricts as the words come out.

"What are you talking about?"

"Tomorrow. I need you to stay home. After hearing about—"

"No way," she interrupts.

I face her. "Listen, after hearing how my grandfather died—"

"I'm going, Ledger."

"Please, Hollis. I'm not asking. I'm telling you. You need to stay home. They are bloodthirsty barbarians. They are horrific fighters who will slaughter you, no matter who you are. Girl or not."

"What?" She sits up and crosses her arms. "Are you kidding me?" Her voice reaches a high pitch and Tristeh whimpers behind me.

"I'm serious. Please. I need you to stay here. I can't lose you too—"

"No. I'm not a child. You can't command me to hide in the cellar."

"I know that."

"Then don't!" she shouts. "Don't tell me to stay."

"Just—"

"No!" She leaps to her feet. "I can't believe you. After this year together on Ellery. We faced a lot of dangers together."

"I know but—"

"Together, Ledger. We are stronger *together*!" She screams the last word and heads toward Tristeh.

I snag her arm. "I can't lose you too. I lost my grandfather to them. My cousin, my uncle… maybe even my father." Tears blur my vision. I don't mean to, but I can't hold in the fear that is clawing its way out. "I can't lose you to them. They are more vicious than anyone we encountered on Ellery this whole past year, even Wolfman's tribe who kidnapped you. I need you to stay here. If you go, I'm not going." I let her go and cross my arms. I need to stand up to her. Make her see the reality before us.

"I can't believe you," she growls and stomps to Tristeh's side. "I'm not someone you can command! I'm your wife—I mean, betrothed." She mounts the dragon and shouts, "You have a lot to learn about me, Ledger. I know you're the grandson of the queen and all that, but I'm not your subject!"

With that, she latches herself in and Tristeh takes to the sky. "Wait!" I call. "Don't leave me here," I mutter. She is too far away to hear my protests. I swallow the bitter truth of her words. This is a first and hopefully a last. But part of me is settled. I wanted her to stay home. I've never commanded her to do anything. But I just did.

The setting sun is halfway hidden on the horizon. It's going to take me half the night to get back to Balfour. My shoulders slump as I walk south, keeping the blazing orange eye to my right.

8 Acidic Tears

ALOUETTE

In the early morning hours, with an armload of sheets and a sack full of medicines, I fly down from Ellery to deliver them to the medical ward in Balfour. It's the last load I'll deliver before I drift away from this place for good.

My fall from the island flashes through my mind as I descend, sending a shiver through my body. My wings work through the air and carry me faithfully to the ground without fail. I swallow hard as my feet touch the ground. I shake off the feeling from the ends of my toes to the tips of my wings.

Adjusting my full arms, I climb the steps of Healer Clovis's cottage. A commotion grows behind me, and I turn just in time to get out of the way of several children. They scramble up the steps, dart across the porch, scale the railing, and leap off into the alley in some sort of game of follow-the-leader. The next child's feet pound loudly on the wooden floorboards. I freeze and watch him take the dangerous leap. One after the other, they run past me. I consider stopping the last boy. He leaps off the railing. As he lands out of view, he cries out.

The door whips open. "Alouette," Kava blurts. "What happened?"

I point in the direction of the obstacle course. "Some kids were jumping off your porch."

A child's wail grows louder in the alleyway, and Kava races to the railing. "Oh my stars!"

She dashes down the stairs. I cross the porch, wondering what he did to himself. I anticipate the worst, because the worst always seems to happen when I'm around.

A child is lying on the ground with his foot facing the wrong way. I'm suddenly woozy and unable to breathe.

"Alouette!" Kava's voice cuts through my shock. "Why didn't you stop them?" She looks me full in the face with anger in her eyes. "Don't just stand there and gawk. Get down here!"

A stab of guilt cuts me. I drop the load of sheets and set the bag of bottles down alongside them. I fly down the stairs, flitting through the air around the side of the cottage, and land beside them.

The boy is screaming and writhing in pain. The other children chatter nearby. "It was an accident," one of them yells.

Between the broken boy's screams, Kava snaps at me. "Let's get him inside." Though he is probably only twelve or thirteen, he is quite hefty. She slides an arm under his right leg. I copy her, sliding an arm behind him and under his left leg—the broken one.

"One, two, three, lift," she says as we stand. He barks a panicked cry as I lift him.

Kava nods toward the back of the house. "That way."

The sway of my steps bumps against his twisted ankle and he cries out in pain each time. Anxiety runs through my veins. It's like I can't avoid hurting people.

Once we lay him on a cot inside Kava's medical tent, I slip out the side door. *I've got to get out of here.* I press my fingers to my temples. My wing gets stuck in the opening, and I yank once, twice to get free. Panting and frustrated, I leave a few feathers behind in the rush to get away from her and the broken boy.

Someone calls my name as I turn away from the healer's house. Preparing to be reprimanded again for not stopping those kids from jumping off the porch, I glance around.

"Alouette," the elderly voice calls from several doors down. She is seated on a bench with a worn quilt laid across her lap. "Come here, dear," Queen Huyana says. Her wrinkled cheeks display a sweet smile. Her hair is neatly combed, and she's dressed in a modest white underdress with a faded red overdress tied in a zigzag pattern across her slender chest.

I pad to the front of her cottage. She taps the bench next to her. I don't want to get that close to her but climb the stairs anyway.

"That was not your fault," she says. "Kava was being very hard on you." She has a perfect view of the healer's home and the place where the boy fell.

I tuck my wings tightly against my back and sit on the bench beside her. I turn toward her slightly so my wings can hang off the bench. I don't know what to say.

"She can be pretty harsh." She sighs and places her hand on mine. "I've been meaning to talk to you. How are you doing?"

I don't want to tell her how I'm doing. I want to dart into the sky and fly away. I want to leave this place and all these people behind. "I'm well," I lie.

"From what I can see, you're not well. You lost your father this year. And no one is well for a long time when that happens."

Her words douse me with the frigid truth, and I shiver. Meeting her gaze, I can't stop the tears from pooling in my eyes.

"Then, you lost your betrothed. You won't be well for a *very* long time."

I hang my head as my mind drifts to Dayson. He died doing the right thing, but he did so many unforgivable things. For skies' sake, he tried to assassinate this woman sitting next to me. I swallow back the sadness and banish thoughts of him from my mind. His blue eyes, his dark wings, his protective arms, his intense care.

"Sadness is not a rabid beast we must chase away. It is a justified reaction to losing someone you love. In your case, losing *two* people."

My breath catches in my chest and I hold it, waiting for the feelings of complete brokenness to pass. But my head is light and my body is in pain, pleading for air.

Queen Huyana continues with no outward reaction from me. "I lost my husband when the savages attacked our village. Every day, I take time to cry and let out how I feel robbed and wounded. Because the more you hold it in, the more it will kill you from the inside."

With that, I let the cool air fill my lungs.

"And forgive yourself, Alouette. You couldn't have done

anything to save either of them."

Her words break open something inside of me like a dam that's been breached. It bursts out in a mournful wail. It starts low and guttural, growing into the most painful cry, pushing the pain throughout my body. Acidic tears burn my cheeks. I can't stop for a long time. The old woman slides an arm behind my back and pulls me close.

Though everything in me tells me to run away, get on that island, outrun the sun, get as far away from people as possible, something else tells me I should go with Ledger. But I'm so toxic; I fear what it will do to him if I'm nearby during the most dangerous thing he's ever done. I can't let the last person I love die. Dread overwhelms the sadness pouring from my eyes. Eventually, the tears dry up, and I glance at Ledger's grandmother.

"Thank you." I feel vulnerable and uncomfortable. I straighten my buttoned shirt and my wings ache to stretch out.

"You're welcome, dear," she says.

I realize what I must do.

9
Uneasy Rhythm

LEDGER

After I gobble down my morning stew and kiss my mother goodbye, I sneak out the door before any of my siblings wake up. Surely, they would make it difficult to leave. I rush to our meeting place, hoping Hollis will be there, waiting with the others to say goodbye. Bernhard is there with his mother and younger brothers. His mother is fussing over him. She seems sad and worried. Several Ellerians wait with bags thrown over their shoulders and anticipation in their stance. There are old and young winged people grouped around each one. I can only assume they are families.

Hollis is nowhere to be seen.

I need to see my grandmother before I go. I take the northeastern path so I can walk past Hollis's cottage. Maybe I can run into her in a coordinated accident. Shuffling along at a quick pace down the second row of houses, I slow to a walk, listening and peeking around. There is no one, no noise, as if everyone is still asleep. The sun isn't even cresting over the horizon yet. But it will be soon. I stroll by Hollis's place and continue to Grandmother's cottage a few rows back.

I quietly climb the stairs and hold a hand up to knock.

"Come in, dear," Grandmother's calm voice calls.

I push the door open and find her sitting with Neelie and Sybella, two Ellerian women, around the table near the hearth. I'm surprised she is up and around so early. I guess she isn't as frail as I thought when I arrived home several days ago.

"Have you come to say goodbye? I was going to see you off." Quiet strength emanates from her entire being.

"Yes. Well, sort of." I lean down and hug her small frame. "Last night, I told Hollis she can't come. She left me in the woods. I had to walk back—that's not the point. I made her really mad. I knew she would be upset but—"

"She will be fine, dear." Grandmother smiles with a slow blink.

I suddenly feel bad for chattering on and on at this early hour but can't stop myself. "She isn't in the square waiting to say goodbye like everyone else. I just need you to keep an eye on her." I wring my hands. I love her, and if something bad happens, I don't want that fight to be our last conversation.

"I will," she says. "Have you eaten?"

"Mother had food ready before I got up." I smile at the thought. At least my mother and grandmother are supportive.

Footsteps pound up the front stairs, and the door flings open. Neelie and Sybella turn with a start. I'm startled by Tolliver fumbling into the room. His lip is bleeding. His right eye is purple and beginning to swell.

"What happened to you?" I ask.

"I just—" Tolliver pants. "I've been looking for you

everywhere."

I gape at him, unsure what to say.

He dabs a finger on the cut on his lip as he approaches the table. Grandmother hands him one of Grandfather's old kerchiefs. Pressing it on the side of his mouth, he says, "I just talked with Angus. He's not too happy with me right now."

I frown and refrain from asking the obvious question.

He scowls. "Angus did this to me because I'm not going."

My whole body shudders. "What? Why?" I sound angrier than I meant to.

Sybella stands, kisses her mother on the cheek, and heads for the door in a flurry of feathers and worry. She and Angus have been growing closer since they've been in Balfour.

Tolliver's sandy blond hair falls in his eyes. "Kava asked me to stay. I wasn't going to. I was fully ready to ride into battle and bring home a victory." He removes the kerchief from his lip and runs his bulky hand through his hair. "I can't leave her. She needs me. My child needs me. You understand, don't you, Ledger?"

I've never heard him plead with me. The tone of his voice is foreign. Vulnerable. Almost sad.

"You'll be back before the baby comes, Toll."

"You don't know that. What if you wander season after season and never find them?"

"You think we won't find them? Angus is the best tracker—"

"No, I know he'll find them. He's like a tracking dog, but he's a bit rabid right now. He'll bite them. Which is why he can't lead." Tolliver shakes his head. "And I can't leave

Kava again." His eyes scrunch.

I understand why he needs to stay. The worries about this journey scream through my mind. Nothing is going the way I thought. "What are we going to do without you? You're the battalion leader. We can't—"

"Yes. You can." He points a finger to my chest, sending my heart into an uneasy rhythm. "*You* must lead them, Ledger."

I shake my head over and over and over.

"You always act so incapable. Do you have any idea who you are?"

I frown.

He says, "You cared enough to go find the Ellerians when no one else in this village would."

"So did you," I argue.

He shakes his head. "No, I went for my own selfish reasons. You even dared to rescue Alouette from that burning cottage."

"Yeah, but—"

"No! Don't discount yourself anymore. You even had the gall to get in the middle of a battle to stop everyone from killing each other. You can lead them, you can find our men, and you can bring them all home."

I stagger back, like he's put a heavy weight into my hands. *Me? Lead them?* My thoughts skitter like roaches in the dark as he continues talking.

My grandmother smiles mischievously. I lower my eyebrows at her and almost ask, *Can I really do this?*

She nods as though she heard my thoughts.

"It's your time," she says. Neelie nods as well.

Slamming from one emotion to the next, I've been on fire with fear and worry for hours, but my older brother's words have thrown a bucket of water on it all. I stand and smolder in the moment, thinking of the possibilities. If he believes I can… maybe I can.

I need my father back.

Kava needs Tolliver.

It's now or never.

Tolliver is right. I *have* to do this, regardless of who is going.

***

"Thank you for your willingness to go on this journey to rescue the men of Balfour," Tolliver announces from the platform in the village square. His black eye is still swollen and purple where Angus punched him earlier this morning. "There is great honor in being willing to sacrifice your life for another. The men who were taken prisoner will be truly grateful when you bring them home. Thank you, brave crew." He claps for us. No one claps along. Our guts are full of gurgling worry. Many who are joining the mission have a wide-eyed, panicked expression on their faces.

The end of his disheartening speech tells us to strap on our bags. We've loaded down Old Man Dudley's mule with weeks' worth of supplies, sleeping mats, and extra food.

Bernhard's mother is on the tips of her toes kissing his cheek. Ryllis whispers to her brother and pats him on the shoulder, probably saying something reassuring about her return. Angus stands on the path ready to go. That's all. Four of us Balfourians are going. I heave a heavy sigh. Considerably more Ellerians have volunteered to go: Bellamy, Sybella, Char, Estefano, Hellwig, and three others I haven't officially met yet.

Tolliver makes his way over. "You ready, Ledger?"

He meets my eyes and I realize I am taller than him now. Not by much, but I'm definitely looking down at him. "I don't know anymore." My voice cracks. He blinks and pretends he doesn't hear it, when normally he would take a jab at my pubescent voice.

"You'll have plenty of time to prepare to encounter the savages," he says. "It will probably be days until you catch up with them."

"Maybe," he says. "I thought Hollis would at least be here to say goodbye." I glance back and forth around the square, too tired to start another journey. "Tell her I love her, would you? I can't stand it that she left it like this. Do you know she ditched me in the middle of the northern woods on the far side of the North Mountain? It took me half the night to get back."

"No, I didn't know." He puts an arm around my shoulders. "She will get over it. Just focus on your quest. I'll watch over her while you're away. Then when you get back, you can marry that wildcat."

I give a half-hearted smile and shrug.

A shofar blasts to the east, and everyone milling about the square glances into the sky. The island of Ellery is fading into the distance, barely visible because of the clouds. A group of guardians descends slowly toward us. More and more people flood into the square, mostly Ellerians. Many of them have angry expressions on their faces.

The shofar trumpets again, louder this time. One of the guardians in the sky lowers the twisted ram's horn from his lips. Several others are carrying a man—Caedus, a murderer and traitor king of Ellery. My mouth hangs open at the sight.

As the group of guardians drop from the sky into the square, a group of Ellerians rush forward with loud shouts and swords drawn. Someone yells, "You killed my wife!"

"Ledger, you need to go!" Tolliver releases my shoulder. I stand frozen, and Tolliver yells again. "Get your people and go!"

I meet Tolliver's eyes. "But—"

"I'll take care of this. You don't have to worry about it. Just go."

***

As we leave the village, the clang of swords makes my stomach do somersaults. I resist the urge to turn back. That's what Tolliver deserves. If he's going to stay, hopefully he will have enough trouble to make it worth staying behind. The more I think about him, the harder my teeth press together until they grind with a harsh scraping sound.

The thirteen of us walk in silence. Angus heads up the pack. I'm on one side and Sybella, who he calls his *winged savior*, is on the other. Belamy and Estefano are close behind, then Ryllis and Bernhard leading the overloaded mule. The rest of the Ellerians follow us silently.

Feels like a death march. As soon as I think the words, tears of terror sting my eyes. I turn my head away from

Angus and open my eyes wide, hoping the morning air will dry them out. *I don't want to die. I want to grow old with Hollis, have hordes of kids, and smith things till I'm too old to hold a hammer.*

I hate the way we left. It felt flat and sad. No one was there to say goodbye. No one was excited for what we are about to do.

By the time we reach the river, the chaos of the village fades into the distance. The flow of water is the only thing I hear. I pull out my water pouch and fill it before crossing.

"What do you think you're doing?" Angus asks with a condescending tone. "The cattle are upriver. Do you want diarrhea?"

I feel like a fool when Belamy laughs and leaps into the air. He flits over the water, keeping perfectly dry, while Bernhard and Ryllis traipse through the stream in their boots. The mule keeps a steady rhythm as it follows them across. The water is only ankle deep at this point, but it is wide.

Looking Angus directly in the eye, I empty my pouch and flick the last drops at him. He doesn't flinch, but follows Sybella across, along with the rest of the Ellerians who've joined our group. I guess I should find out their names, aside from Hellwig and Char.

Splashing my way across, I slip a few times on the pebbly riverbed. I catch myself and keep walking, pretending like I don't feel like a complete idiot.

"What are your names?" I ask when I catch up with two of the unfamiliar Ellerians.

"I am Swarley," the biggest one says. He is a burly guy with a thick beard and long dark hair falling nearly to his elbows and messily around his feathery gray wings. Dayson and his father were the only gray-winged Ellerians I've known. I wonder if they are related. I feel tiny next to his hulking size.

"You're a warrior—I mean, a guardian?" I ask, remembering their word for it.

"Yes, and a hunter," he says. Then he points at the man next to him. "This is Zander. He is a tracker and dragon rider… when Hellwig lets him." Swarley chuckles.

Zander's mouth twitches, but a smile never forms. He has shoulder-length sandy blond hair, and the top half is tied back. His white wings are folded tightly against his back as we ascend the grassy hill. Zander's eyes never change expression, and he says nothing. The wordless ones always worry me; I never know what they are thinking.

"Glad to meet you," I say to them both, then point to the Ellerians ahead. "Who are those other two?"

"The smaller one is Terrowin," Swarley says.

"The one with white wings?"

He glances up at Terrowin to confirm, as if it's something he doesn't notice. I guess he wouldn't. He grew up with winged people his whole life. Terrowin is the one who stomped out of the meeting yesterday. I wonder what made him change his mind.

"Uh, yeah. We call him Cookie because he was one of Ellery's finest cooks. I hope he brought that herb mix he uses on roasted boar." Swarley elbows Zander, who gives an almost imperceptible nod.

Swarley takes enormous strides up the knoll, probably one for every two of mine. At least he is friendly.

"The other is Eljah," Swarley continues. "His father was one of the best swordsmen on the island. King Halcyon's head guardian, until Ciel killed him. It's a shame."

"What does Eljah do?"

"Oh, he's just a washman," Swarley says. "But his father taught him the sword. I haven't seen him participate in any swordplay since he lost his father, but I'm pretty sure he could best at least half of us." Swarley glances from person to person as we reach the top of the hill as if making a tally in his head.

"Why didn't he become a guardian, if he's so skilled?" I frown.

"Hates it, I guess." Swarley shrugs his massive shoulders. "And those two up there are Hellwig and Char."

"Oh, I've met them before," I say as muttering erupts up ahead.

I catch sight of Alouette at the top of the hill, with billowing white wings. Relief fills my lungs. I exhale my frustrations, feeling a little more confident.

Alouette's dark, wavy hair cascades down her shoulders as she stands with her arms crossed. She wears a thick, fur-lined brown coat. One side of her black skirts is tucked into one of her tall black leather boots. Her dark demeanor contrasts starkly against her feathery white wings. They stand at attention behind her, as if ready to take flight.

I invited her and she said no. But now she is here. Maybe she needs to tell me something? I scurry to the top of the hill.

Panting, I ask, "What are you doing here?"

She takes a moment to notice each of the people who tagged along. She frowns at one of them and answers, "I thought I would take you up on your offer."

Several bags lie beside her and I realize she is serious. I stand upright. "I'm so grateful." I can barely contain my relief and excitement that she is here.

Char mutters, "Like we need another *girl* on this mission." I'm irritated that he is so rude. His black hair hangs in his eyes and the dark stubble on his chin makes him seem unkempt and dangerous. He scowls as he shoulders past her and walks down the back of the hill, followed by the rest of our troop and the mule.

"Where's Hollis?" She lifts her bags and secures them over her shoulder.

"I don't know exactly." I shrug at the true statement. "She's mad at me." I can't admit where Hollis is. Alouette might change her mind and leave.

Alouette joins me in step. Before we descend the other side of the hill, I take in the sight of my little village. The concentric circles of homes are being filled in with new cottages. One roof is being completed. Another has only walls. *Goodbye, Balfour.*

With a sigh, I search the skies for a red dragon. I don't know where in the wild world Hollis could be. Probably in Tristeh's cave on the back side of the North Mountain. I pinch my lips together and kick myself for not running back there to check before I left, even though there's no time for that. It's so hard to leave her like this.

Goodbye, Hollis. Sadness fills to my eyes and nearly spills out.

I head down the other side of the east hill. The Ellerians mutter amongst themselves. Several of them leap into the sky: Swarley, Zander, Char, and the other two—the cook and washman. I scowl, wondering what they're doing.

Hellwig announces to the group, "Wilhelm is aboard Ellery. I will fetch him, and we will catch up with you." Hellwig's brilliant white hair stands high on his head, and the excitement in his eyes make him seem years younger than he actually is.

"Who is Wilhelm?" I ask.

"The green dragon," Hellwig says as his wings unfurl to twice his height. "He's the last one left."

The five Ellerians dart through the sky without him. I can't see Ellery from here, but they head in its general direction, I guess.

I'm irritated by our lack of organization. I didn't know the green dragon was coming along. "What about Tristeh?"

"Tristeh is not a battle dragon. She was the most unreliable dragon I ever trained. She refused to learn the most basic things."

My heart rate picks up as I think about Hollis riding that untamed beast. *I rode on that thing.*

Hellwig continues, "I didn't bother preparing her. She can stay here with your Hollis. She has captured Tristeh's heart."

Unsure if that's a good thing, I nod. Hellwig's white wings flap and lift him into the sky. He salutes, touching two fingers over his eyebrow, then points at me.

Angus grunts beside me as we descend the hill toward the lake. "They could have taken us with them."

"It would take two of them to carry one of you," Alouette says.

Angus counts on his fingers and says, "There's enough of you to carry us four."

"Not everyone likes doing that. It's very awkward to carry someone while flying. Besides, no one would want to carry that stinky, old mule up there." Alouette continues to walk alongside us which makes me wonder something.

"Why aren't you going with them? I thought you hated walking."

A brief smile appears, then falls quickly from her face. "I chose to come along, knowing there would be a lot of traveling the Balfourian way."

Asking Alouette was the best risk I ever took. A silly grin spreads across my face. I'm relieved she is here. It makes me wish I didn't tell Hollis to stay behind. I don't want to do this alone—without her.

10
Dark Secrets

ALOUETTE

It takes half the day to pass the lake beside Ledger's village. My feet already ache from every step on the hard ground, not to mention the traipsing up and down the hills heading east. I'd much prefer being on Ellery, gliding steadily along, gazing down at the rugged landscape. Now I'm committed to touching every bit of the scraggy terrain.

Beneath the canopy of evergreens, we walk on soggy pine needles. At least the ground is padded through this part. As we crest the top of the hill, the trees thin out into a wide meadow. It takes my breath away—the beauty of the wildflowers, purple and white dispersed among wispy yellowing grasses. Ledger comes to a halt beside me.

"I know where we are," he says reverently. His eyes are serious, and his chin quivers. "It's the baby graveyard."

"What does that mean?" Ryllis, the redheaded girl asks. She takes the first step between the waist-high flowers and grasses, brushing them with her hands.

"When they smuggled babies off Ellery, this is where my mother—and my grandmother before her—used to meet them." The volume of his voice lowers. "She said, most often they'd be dead. With and without wings. Many of them were second-born children…" His voice drifts off.

"Which isn't permitted on Ellery," I finish his thought.

"This is where she would bury them," he says with sadness in his voice.

He gazes over the field as Ryllis, Angus, and the other Balfourian make their way across, pulling the mule along by its rope. Its lips grasp at the tall grasses and chomp a few stalks as it walks.

Ledger's shoulders droop, and I'm impressed by his compassion for people he doesn't know. Babies he doesn't know.

"Come on," Ledger says, and I follow his first step into the meadow. Angus and Sybella follow in quiet respect, along with Belamy and Estefano.

The sun is directly overhead, warming me from the top down. The wispy flowers tickle the tips of my fingers as we weave our way across.

"There's one." Ledger stops and points to a mound of dirt with short grass sprouting around it.

"How do you know?" Belamy asks. "It just looks like a random lump in the ground."

"Look closer." Ledger crouches down and pushes the grass aside. There is a pile of three flat rocks, stacked perfectly. "My mother would mark the spot with three rocks, as a memorial."

"Here's another," Estefano says from a few paces away. "And another." He points between the flowers.

"There are even more over here," Ryllis calls, nearly

halfway across.

The air gets stuck in my throat as they each find more and more burial sites for the lost children of Ellery. I choke as I back away. I hold my head in my hands as an intense sorrow bubbles up from deep in my belly. *There are so many.*

Surprised by the weight of grief, I can't shake the heaviness on my chest. I'm so overwhelmed with the horrors of this beautiful field that I barely notice the footsteps coming from behind us. Ledger leaps up, draws his sword, and pushes me behind him. Angus tromps ahead of him and shouts, "Who's there?"

Birds sing. Crickets chirp. No one responds.

Ledger steps up beside Angus. "We know you're there." Ledger takes a slow, careful step toward the shadows of the evergreen forest. It feels ominous, holding dark secrets, until a child's giggle trills through the air.

"Hollis?" Ledger calls, relaxing his stance.

After a few moments, a small voice trickles over the wind and birds. "It's me." Out of the shadows of the wood steps Mila, Ledger's eleven-year-old sister. "It's me, Mila."

"And me, Myst." A smaller girl steps into the light. Ledger stomps toward them.

"What are you doing out here?" he yells.

Angus throws up his hands. He walks away from them, refusing to be slowed down.

Mila is taken aback with a frown. "I was trying to catch up with you. I know you needed more volunteers. Since Tolliver isn't coming, I thought—" The words spill out at an alarming rate until Ledger cuts her off.

"No! You can't come."

She puts both hands on her hips and stomps toward him. "And why not? Ryllis is here." She points at the red head. "And Alouette? You're here?" She gives me a big smile and runs to me. I open my arms in time to be engulfed in a tight hug. She barely comes up to my shoulder as she presses her head against my chest. I glance at Ledger.

"Stop hugging her," he says to me, then turns to her. "You're not coming." He sticks out his chin in anger.

When Mila pulls away, she twirls around to address Ledger, and her long brown hair flicks into my face. "You need all the help you can get." She waves her arms wildly. "Clearly you're down to the bare minimum here. Where in the name of sanity are the rest of the Ellerians? Did they ditch you too? Where's the dragon? Great skies, you need me more than I thought you did."

"No, I don't. They are off—no—I don't need to explain anything to you. Go home!" He points emphatically to the woods, then steps toward her pointing again. Every muscle in his body is taut and his lips purse tightly as he stares at Mila.

The other little girl groans. "I told you we should have asked first."

"Myst, you're not helping. We don't need to ask. We are here, and that's that."

Myst nods warily at Ledger.

"No," Ledger says. "You're going home." He looks at the sun above us. "You have plenty of time to make it back before sunset." He grabs Mila's shoulders, spins her around, and pushes her towards the woods.

"You don't get to boss me around, Ledger." She pushes

back against his hands.

"Yes, I do. Tolliver put me in charge. I get to choose who goes. And you can't go." He pushes her once more, and she stumbles away from him.

Myst sighs, throws up her little arms, and walks toward the trees. Mila shouts after her. "Myst, get back here!"

"I'm hungry. Let's go home," the little girl says. She stops and smells a flower.

Mila growls and yells at Ledger, "Fine! I'll go. You're a crazy person not wanting my help!" She stomps off.

Myst reaches into the tall grass and plucks a flower out. When Mila reaches her, she too pulls a handful from the ground.

"Stop it!" Ledger blurts. "Don't pick those!" He scrambles toward them. "Leave them be." He falls at their feet, hold his hands out for the flowers in their hands. "Don't you know where we are?"

He sputters. I walk over and explain, "This is where the lost children of Ellery are buried." I reach for Mila's hand. She lets me take it. "Your mother cared for many of the babies that the women of Ellery weren't allowed to keep. Most places around this wide world didn't have someone like your mother, so our children were tossed out like garbage. Mila, we need you to stay in Balfour and care for your mother. She needs you. She works hard to keep things running in Balfour. With as much death as she's seen in all these years,"—I wave a hand over the meadow of purple and white flowers—"she needs someone to support her. Can you be that someone?"

I watch her expression melt from tense anger to droopy

sadness then intense determination.

“Yes,” she whispers. “I can do that.”

“Thank you.” I reach out another hand, and she lays the flowers in my palm. She hugs me again and walks slowly away. Myst follows along.

Ledger and I watch them disappear into the woods.

I hold the flowers out to him. He takes them, wiping a tear from his cheek. He tucks their ends into the dirt with a sigh.

On the Anvil 11

TOLLIVER

"We made an agreement," Jubal complains. "We have equal say, and it is not equal. There are more Ellerian advisors than Balfourian elders. I make a motion to remove two Ellerians and—"

The room erupts in shouts. Ellerian men stand with their fists in the air, shaking them at wingless Jubal. He stands tall, with hands on hips, arrogantly pushing out his chest.

"As far as I can see, we are quite even." Tiberius speaks over the loud voices. They quiet down to listen as he puts out both hands. "Five advisors. Five elders. And our mutual queen."

Jubal shouts back, "There are two Balfourians who do not belong in this room. Adaya is merely the wife of a deceased elder and—"

Mother gasps and stands with the rest of the angry men. "How dare you!" she says in a tightly controlled voice. "My husband is *not* dead."

Jubal clears his throat. "He is not present, then. She is the wife of an *absent* elder. And Tolliver is simply an apprentice.

Why are there two representatives from the same family? It's preposterous." Spittle flings from his mouth.

"Now, now," Grandmother says in her queenly voice. "Jubal, sit down. I've heard enough of your grumblings. I understand your frustrations; Fergus's family outweighs your own. Adaya is a perfectly suitable alternate for Fergus until he returns. So, Tolliver." She turns her eyes toward me. "I'd like you to step down as apprenticing elder until we can better organize."

"But Grandmother—Your Majesty—"

"Tolliver, you have plenty of other duties besides participating in the drudgery of these arguments. Besides, we didn't gather to discuss positions." She glares at Jubal. Then her gaze softens as she meets my eyes. "Take a break. Put your focus on rebuilding."

Clamping my mouth shut, I refuse to say anything that will get me into more trouble. I shoot a hateful glance at Jubal and catch the smile playing at the edge of his upturned mustache. He should be the one walking out the door right now. As I get up from my seat beside my mother, the conversation continues.

"Advisors, your apprentice must step out as well," she says, glancing at a young man standing behind Advisor Cabot. His son. He hunches slightly and heads slowly to the door.

"I know it doesn't make us even, but my vote counts as two," the queen smiles and chuckles to herself. I slip around the table behind her and head for the door. "Is there anyone who would like to step down? No? Then let's discuss the real subject at hand: what do to with Caedus and Talon."

I step out the door after the other apprentice with his large gray wings. Pulling the door shut behind me, I hold fast to the handle. I don't want to go far from the door. I want to hear what they are discussing. *Why would Grandmother remove me at such a crucial time?*

Cabot's son addresses me. "That didn't seem necessary."

"I agree." But I don't want to talk to him. I want to eavesdrop on the conversation in that room.

"I'm Zane, by the way." He holds out a hand and I quickly shake it.

"Tolliver."

"I know who you are," he says as he takes a step down the stairs, acting like I should follow him.

I refuse to move my feet.

"You're the grandson of the queen."

The tone of Grandmother Huyana's voice drifts through the door, but I can't make out the words until I realize what Zane just said. "I was adopted by her daughter. Actually, Tiberius is my birth father."

"You're Ellerian?" he asks, with round-eyed confusion.

"You realize we're all Ellerian, right? We all came from that island at one time or another. The wingless were banished to the ground at first, then eventually… never mind."

He tips his head to the side.

Frustration grows in my belly. I want to yell at him to move along and stop being ignorant. Instead, I say, "If you don't mind, I'd really like to hear what they're saying."

"I don't think that's allowed." He makes it off the porch, and I worry he will come back to listen as well.

"Then I'll get thrown in lock-up alongside Caedus." I

shrug.

He shakes his head and walks off. Finally.

I lean against the door with my ear and listen to their voices.

"Then Caedus and Talon will be executed at nightfall tonight," Grandmother says, followed by a long stretch of silence. "If there was a chance he could be redeemed, you would tell me, wouldn't you?"

A man's voice begins, "I wish it were so. I tried to get Caedus to see the truth for years." As he continues, I realize it's Tiberius. "He made those plans in secret to kill anyone in his way to become king. He sent an assassin to murder you without the consent of the advisors. He wouldn't listen to the consensus of our council and staged a take-over, locking up those who opposed him, myself included. He has chosen to be a lost cause."

Sweat beads on my forehead as I listen. It is a complete injustice, being turned out into the street. As irritation piles on my shoulders, I step away from the door and head down the stairs into the afternoon sunlight. I close my eyes and tip my face to the sun, searing my eyes with streaks of fire and frustration.

My hands feel jittery. I need to do something. I need to hit something. I take long strides toward the blacksmith shop until I arrive at its stacked stone walls. Smoke wafts from the chimney and the clang of metal against metal reaches my ears. I step inside the door to find a hefty man sweating over the anvil with a hammer in one hand and tongs pinching hot iron in the other. He glances up and smiles beneath a silvery beard that is clipped closely to his chin.

“Good-ay,” he says. “What can I make ya?” His gray wings hang loosely from his back and drag slightly on the ground.

I stop short and realize this is the Ellerian blacksmith. Ledger too has been replaced. I resist the pain shooting through the depths of me. “I want to hit something,” I blurt.

He belly laughs.

“I mean. I am the blacksmith’s son. Well, I was…” My words come out in stupid spurts as my anger rises.

“I thought his son was that other little guy,” the Ellerian says, eyebrows knitting together.

“Oh, that is my younger brother,” I say.

“Well, I’m Deveraux.”

“Can I help with that? Looks like you’re starting a sword?”

“Aye,” he says. “That I am. If you’d like to have a go at it, I’ll prepare my next project. Show me what you can do.” He smiles wide and hands me the hammer and tongs.

Now I have to prove myself as a blacksmith? The pain in my gut reaches my heart and I clamp my teeth together as I swing the hammer onto the iron over and over and over again. I flatten one side and flip it over to smooth out the other. Sweat bursts from my skin in this blazing hot room.

Deveraux chatters about making tools and the difference between Ellerian weapons and Balfourian weapons. I barely listen as I work out my frustrations on the anvil. It takes me back to my early apprenticing years with my father. He was patient, but firm. He wanted perfection, not sloppiness.

As I swing the hammer, I remember how much I hate this trade. Hate the sweat. The clang of metal smashing against metal. The smell of burning coal.

I'm not a warrior anymore. Our enemies are now friends, and Ledger has stepped up to be the warrior to save our men. Abruptly, I stop swinging. I'm sinking into the hole Ledger left behind.

The hot iron slips out of the tongs and hits the stone floor with a loud clang. *If I'm not an elder and not a blacksmith, then who the blazes am I?*

***

Caedus and Talon were hanged from a tree in the eastern woods beyond the cattle yard. The sun is setting somewhere beyond the grumbling clouds, making it seem as though night is upon us. I wait to speak to my mother as the humidity rises and the wind picks up. She stayed long enough for their bodies to be lowered into the ground. The somber event is sobering for all Balfourians and Ellerians alike. Treason will not be treated lightly.

"Mother, may I speak with you?" I ask from the edge of the woods.

Lanterns hang all around the gallows and sway in the wind. My mother's face shows a bit of shock. I didn't mean to sneak up on her.

"Sure, Tolliver," Mother says, continuing along the path toward Balfour. "Walk with me to check on the children."

I join her in step. "Why you didn't stand up for me today?" It comes out more demanding than I intend.

The path between the trees grows darker as we walk beneath the canopy. Storm clouds crowd the sky and the air grows thick, threatening to rain at any moment. Anger rumbles in my chest and I have a hard time holding it back.

"Tolliver, your father was working closely with the council to keep things running efficiently. Fergus was a great leader. I know what he would want for our village, and I want to make sure he is proud of how things play out." She pauses and looks up at me. "I know you'll make a great elder someday, but Fergus would want his ideals upheld, and I'm fully ready to fight for them." She frowns and continues walking. The sky groans in the distance and a light flashes.

"I would too, but you let me get kicked out of that room. It was quite unfair." My voice is strained and I clear my throat. "Why would Grandmother do that?"

"You don't know how much is at stake right now." Her voice is tense and quick. "Do you think your feelings matter more than our village's survival?"

Her question hits me in the chest, and I stand up straighter. Keeping a close rein on my feelings, I justify my frustrations. "I am an asset to the council."

The air whips around us as we stop before the stream between us and Balfour. She puts a hand on my forearm. "These are tenuous times. If we must ask you to step out to gain a stronger foothold of peace between Balfourians and Ellerians, then we must."

"I can help with that. You *know* I can." I grind a fist into the palm of my hand. My skin prickles with a cold mist as the sky churns above us.

She drops her hands to her hips. "You realize there were three of our family in that room, not just two? *They* didn't even realize it. You, me, and Huyana. We used it as an opportunity to level the table."

I am the lowest on the list. Anger clashes with embarrassment and explodes in my mind. *Shame on her for using me like that!* I search for the appropriate thing to say as thunder crashes through the air with an immediate flash, and we both startle. I press my lips together tightly and refuse to yell at her.

Even though the people have left us behind, headed toward the village, she steps closer to me and lowers her voice. "We all have our uses, Tolliver. I am being used in your father's stead. Am I supposed to be ashamed of that? You provided a perfect opportunity for the queen to gain favor with the advisors and elders alike."

My heart races at the pace of her frustrating words and the whipping wind. I want to argue or say something to make her feel guilty. But the way she drops her head and her hands, releasing the tension between us, gives me pause.

She purses her lips and whispers, "Do not tell anyone, but Huyana will soon dissolve this monarchy into a republic. She wants the elders and advisors to merge into one group. She even wants the people to vote each council member into their position. That way, one family does not have higher say than another. You were a demonstration of good faith that she will reveal later."

I raise my eyebrows and suck in the cool air, blowing away the barrage of negative emotions. The mist turns into a sprinkle and cools my flushed cheeks.

Before I can apologize, she sighs and says, "Like I said, there is more at play than you know. And I'm going to help her get us to that point. Before he was taken, Fergus was working us toward a new system where everyone has a voice." She slides her hands in mine. "Help me, Tolliver. Help me by not making a big fuss about being asked to step down. Be the man I know you are, loyal regardless of the circumstances. Please?"

Her kind words brighten the path.

I realize I'm being selfish and short-tempered. "I'm sorry, Mother."

"I will always be your mother, and Fergus will always be your father. We raised you and *know* you." She presses her hand to my heart as the rain pours heavily on us. "But we are peers now. You have earned the right to call him Fergus, and you may call me Adaya," she says with a sad smile.

I'm old enough to call her by name, but everything inside me doesn't want to let go of calling her Mother—it feels like it will change everything.

She kisses me on the cheek and leaves me on the path at a fork in the road. Do I let myself get swept downstream or barrel forward? I'm halfway between who I thought I was and someone else entirely. I'm not exactly sure who that is or how to find him. I wade across the rushing river as the rain starts pounding down.

12

Fear of Falling

LEDGER

"Ledger, there they are!" Bernhard shouts. He stands up a little straighter with his scraggly bearded face toward the sky and pointer finger outstretched.

We all gaze up in the direction he's pointing. A green dragon descends toward us. Winged Ellerians follow right behind. It's been an entire day since they took off for the island. It's difficult to tell how near to sunset we are because of the cloud cover.

We walk out from among the trees into a small clearing no bigger than a Balfourian cottage. The giant dragon drops into the small space. Hellwig unlatches his belt and darts down from the dragon's back. Beside me, the mule's eyes widen, and it snorts and bucks to move away from the scaly beast. I know exactly how it feels.

"I can't believe this is as far as you've gotten. Did you stop?" Char's dark eyes scowl.

"What do you mean? We've not stopped walking all day," I say, offended by his offhanded comment. "We didn't even stop for midday meal. We ate while we walked."

Char laughs mockingly. "Ellery is quite a distance that way." He points east. "With the rate you're going, we'd be better off boarding Ellery and riding it until we find them."

"No," I say. "What if they suddenly head north? And we're up there, wandering off in the wrong direction."

Belamy lands beside me. "Didn't make it very far today, huh?"

My skin crawls with irritation, and I want to shout at him for saying it.

"We made excellent time without you here," Angus says. He steps aggressively in Belamy's direction, and I put a hand on Angus's swelled chest.

"We did just fine. How are things in the sky?" I ask Hellwig. He's about the only one I can trust at this point.

Waving his hands in the air, he says, "It's a beautiful day for a quest!" He looks like a wild man with his windblown white hair and red cheeks.

Angus steps up to take charge. "Okay, let's get moving. We will continue east as far as their tracks take us. If we keep up a good pace, we can catch up with them in a couple of weeks." He shoulders between Belamy and Estefano's black and white wings. "Hellwig, you can keep to the skies if you'd like. Watch for any surprises. I'll track them down here. Let's go."

He heads into the woods. We follow him up the sloping hill in silence for quite some time.

Of course, Belamy is the first to break the quiet. "I hate walking," he says. "It's so… primal."

Estefano chuckles. "And unbefitting."

"And tiring," Eljah says.

"Haven't we been here before?" asks Estefano. They laugh with him.

Belamy points at the nearest tree. "Yes, I've seen that tree before, but from a lot higher up."

"Shut up, Belamy!" Angus shouts without turning around. He tromps ahead to the top of the hill. On the other side, it drops off into a deep ravine.

"I remember that too," Belamy says with a smile.

Angus turns to the right, following the trail of dusty footprints. He glances over the drop off.

"Would you mind giving each of us a lift across this thing?" Ryllis points at herself and Bernhard.

"Sure, I'll carry you," Belamy says, taking Ryllis's hand in his.

"We don't need them to carry us," Angus says. "We just need to find where the barbarians crossed." He scowls and walks along the edge overlooking the gorge.

"What about the mule?" Ryllis strokes its short mane.

Belamy pulls several ropes out of the saddle bag and nods to Estefano. He loops one rope under the front legs and hands either end to Char and Swarley. Then he tosses the other in front of mule's hind legs, to Estefano.

"This is definitely something I've never carried before," Swarley says with a grin.

"Look!" Angus calls from down the path. "They dropped a tree for a bridge."

Belamy steps to the edge. There is a giant tree at the bottom of the gorge. "But they also broke the bridge," he says.

I step beside him and notice it has drooping and drying

leaves on its branches. It hasn't been there long.

Angus's voice emanates from the woods. "We can simply fell another tree."

Belamy calls into the woods, "You sure we can't simply scoop you up and deliver you to the other side, Angus?"

Angus steps out from the tree line and waves a hand. "I'll take care of this." He drops his packs, rummages around, and pulls out an ax. My father would have called it a hatchet because it's quite small. He disappears into the woods once more.

Belamy nods to Estefano, Char, and Swarley. They each wrap the rope around their arm, or over their shoulder, and heave the mule into the air. Swarley laughs with a grunt as the mule's *heehaw* echoes through the ravine below. They fly the flailing beast of burden over to the other side in a matter of minutes. By the time they land and release the thing, they are all laughing and joking about the worst that could have happened.

The Ellerians sit down in the dirt, sprawl out on boulders, and lean against trees while the mule munches on some wilting grass.

I realize my mouth is a gape when Angus lets out a groan. I step between the trees as he hacks at the towering pine. "Can I help, Angus?"

He doesn't say anything for a long while, as he mutilates the tree. "Naw," he finally says.

"Seems we should have taken them up on their offer," I whisper.

Alouette stands nearby, as well as Sybella. I am embarrassed for Angus as he tries to act like he is fully capable of making this trip with no help. I *know* I can't make it without help. I need Angus, I need Alouette, I need Belamy. And right now, we could already be over there. But I feel like I'm supposed to support my crazy, red-faced, ax-wielding cousin. Maybe this will work off some of his intensity.

Ryllis and Bernhard sit in the dirt. He lets me drink from his water pouch because I forgot to refill mine. Peeking over the edge, my stomach twinges. I hate heights. But I notice a stream below.

"Alouette," I say in a hushed voice. "Could you fill my water pouch down there?"

She glances at Angus, who has gouged the tree about a quarter of the way through.

"Sure." She takes the pouch in her hands and walks slowly to the edge of the ravine. Her wings flap several times as she walks right off the edge. I am envious that Ellerians have no fear of falling. *Must be nice.*

Angus chops vigorously until he's halfway through. Then he steps to the backside of the trunk to cut out a wedge. Hopefully it goes the direction he wants. He didn't attach ropes for us to pull it toward the ravine, and before I can ask, a loud crack echoes through the woods. Followed by another and another, until the large pine tree slowly bends and falls across the crevasse.

"Yeah!" Angus pumps a fist in the air and yanks his packs onto his back. "You coming?" He smiles victoriously.

The rest of us get up and meander to the branch-covered log.

Sybella's tan wings flap, and she is in the sky before Angus climbs onto the log bridge. Traveling with Angus is always interesting. Nonetheless, his leadership creates too much conflict. I shake my head at the idiocy that it is taking this long to get across.

"Where's the mule?" Angus puts his hands on his hips.

I nod across the ravine and Angus's eyes darken as he sees it standing among the Ellerians. He stomps halfway across the fallen tree and disappears into the branches jutting out in all directions.

I swallow hard through panicked breaths, and then climb up and balance on the tree trunk. I inch across the log to the branches and feel a lot better with something to hold onto. I hold each I can reach as I follow the center of the tree across the ravine.

I'm nearly there. The tree bounces beneath me with each step as the trunk narrows at the top, and I fear we will break it and go tumbling downward. My whole body pulsates with the fear of falling. Alouette stands below with my full water pouch… just waiting.

Angus leaps off ahead of me, and I hurry to the end. I dive out of the tree and lay in a heap on the solid ground.

Ryllis and Bernhard follow quickly across and step over me to join the others.

When Alouette darts up from the gorge, I drag myself out of the dirt. We continue our walk into the darkening woods in silence, mule in tow. What Angus did was unnecessarily dangerous; I inwardly bristle.

The cloudy sky grows grayer until I can barely see my own feet with each step. "I think it's time to make camp," I say.

Angus doesn't say a word but continues as if I said

nothing.

"Angus, let's camp for the night."

"I really think we should sleep on Ellery tonight," Belamy says.

Angus spins around. "How would we stay on their track by doing that?"

I don't understand why he isn't calmed down now that we are on our way to find his father and brother. He should be happy that we are doing this.

"He's just making a suggestion, Angus."

Belamy nods at me, and a weird feeling chokes me, like I'm siding with Belamy over my cousin.

"Camping here will be fine," Sybella says. She drops her satchel and weapons belt near a tree, and then follows Angus over the crest of the hill. The quiet mutter of their voices drifts over the ridge, but I can't understand what they are saying. Hopefully she can talk him off the insane cliff he's hanging from.

Zander blows a brown, swirly ram's horn shofar, calling in Hellwig and the dragon. I don't know where they're going to land without a decent clearing for that enormous dragon, but I tie the mule to a sapling near a mass of bushes.

Each of us finds our own place to sleep on the ground. I sidle up to a tree that has turned almost entirely yellow and kick up a pile of leaves for a makeshift mattress. I scrape a spot at the center of all our beds to build a fire. Belamy walks out from among the trees with an armload of wood and plops it into position. Estefano kneels and strikes his flint over and over, trying to light the fire.

After relieving myself in the woods, I come back to find

him still striking that stupid stone. Then Hellwig and the dragon walk through the trees from the north.

"Maybe you should let the dragon light that," I say.

Belamy bursts out laughing like it's a joke. Estefano scowls at me. Hellwig brings the dragon to the edge of the camp and pulls the saddle from its back.

"Hellwig," I call, unsure if I should ask. "Can the dragon light the campfire for us?"

The old man wobbles on his feet and gasps so loud, I worry he will fall and hurt himself. "Never do we allow a dragon to breathe fire!" he says curtly.

"I—umm—oh." I choke on my words.

"They should never understand that their fire should be used. It is very dangerous." He shakes his head. "Very dangerous."

"Okay." I relent and walk away with my hands up.

I think of Tristeh and the time Hollis had her light a campfire for us. It seemed quite simple and controlled. But another time she nearly burned us all to death when she defended us against a pack of wolves.

***

I awake to the creaking and popping of a stretching dragon. I peek in its direction, and Hellwig is already by its side, pulling the muzzle from its enormous jaw. My heart leaps in my chest, and I worry it may scorch us all. But I remember that Hellwig said Wilhelm is well-trained.

Hellwig walks him out from beneath the trees, climbs aboard, and the green dragon leaps into the sky.

The sky is slightly gray-blue as the dark of night fades. Belamy and Estefano eat beside the dead fire pit with one tendril of smoke snaking skyward.

"Where's he going?" I ask.

"To feed the dragon," Belamy says. "Don't want him getting hungry."

I shiver and sit up in my bed of leaves. Belamy laughs at me and points at my head. My cheeks warm as I pull several leaves from my wild morning hair.

I stretch and start packing my things. "Where's Char and… what's his name?" My mind is groggy, and I can't think of his name. Swarley's friend. Swarley, the biggest of us, is sprawled out behind Belamy, bearded chin hanging wide open, and a loud snore startles me.

"Zander? He's scouting out the direction the tribe went next."

"Oh, yes, he's a tracker," I mutter. I need to remember these guys and keep them straight in my head. *Zander the tracker, Zander the expressionless tracker.*

I glance around in the morning haze for Angus. He's beginning to stir beneath a tall oak. He appears so peaceful and calm. A sensation of dread wells up from my gut. *I wonder how rotten he will be today.* I wish he would stay asleep a little while longer.

As the sky spreads with orange light, I take a silent moment to myself in the woods. When I return, Angus and Sybella are eating together. The other Ellerians are packing their things. The swishing of beating wings fills the air as Hellwig shouts from overhead. "Zander says the path heads directly east for quite some distance. Maybe a day's walk."

"Thanks," Belamy shouts and waves to him between the branches of the trees. "Just what I thought." He turns to me. "Shall we take to Ellery? We can send Zander out to follow their path for long distances. He's like a keen owl on the hunt. You should see him. He surprises even me."

"No," Angus disagrees loudly. "We stick to the ground."

"Angus—" Bile rises in my throat. "I don't know. Seems smart to me." I turn to Alouette. "What do you think?"

She shrugs. "You know I'd rather fly than walk. Whatever you decide."

Bernhard stretches his lanky arms with an awkward wide-mouthed yawn.

"Bern, what do you think?"

His voice comes out with a groan. "That's got to be better than this. No offense, Angus." He holds up his hands and takes a step back.

"I like the idea. Let's do it," Ryllis says.

Angus's eyes grow dark and his cheeks redden. Sybella touches his arm. "It may get us there faster, Angus."

It's as though the lot of us are trying to convince Angus. Technically, he's not in charge. I am. I swallow the fear of making a decision that trumps him. "Then it's decided. We will board Ellery," I say quietly.

Before Angus can respond, the branches above our heads part and two Ellerians drop into our midst: Zander and Char.

"Ledger," Zander addresses me, and I'm surprised by his eye contact. "There's something you've got to see." The way he says it, sounds bad. Really bad. His expression doesn't change as he walks away.

Char breezes past me and the intense look in his eyes

unnerves me.

Zander says, “Follow me.”

Everyone is strapping sleeping mats to the mule, grabbing their things, and heading in his direction. I freeze, terrified about where Zander is leading us. As a breath finally reaches my lungs, I strap my bags to my back and hurry to catch up.

I glance back to make sure we didn’t leave anything behind. The mule is munching on a tuft of grass. I scramble over, untie it, and pull it up the hill when I notice Angus. He stands with his bags in hand, muscles taut. His jaw pushes out angrily, and I wave for him to follow. “Whatever it is, I can’t do this without you, Angus.”

We walk silently over the next hill and through a trickling stream. The crowd of winged and wingless in front of me stop. Releasing the mule, I shoulder between their rigid bodies until I see it.

There is a partially rotting corpse face down in the drying leaves. I recognize the style of clothing. A woven cotton tunic. Black wool long pants. *This is one of our own.*

I muster the strength to step out from among them. Angus follows me, and I swallow hard. I don’t really want to know who this is.

Angus kneels on the other side of the body and rolls it toward me, revealing the lifeless face of Cullen, Hollis’s older brother. His gut is sliced through and it’s as though every drop of blood has drained from him.

I turn my face away as my stomach heaves. I can’t look at him. I walk away in shock.

Angus mutters behind me, “He needs burial.”

I can’t think. Alouette says something to me, but I can’t

make it out. A hand is on my arm, taking me away from the stench of death.

I sit on the hillside, watching Zander, Belamy, and Angus dig a hole nearby using all the wrong tools. One has an ax, another has a machete, and another has a short sword.

Once the hole is dug, I join them. Six of us push our hands under Cullen's broken body, lift him, and gently lay him in the pit. I take the machete from Zander and help push the dirt over Hollis's brother. When he disappears beneath the soil, I fall to my knees and cry. *How will I ever be able to tell Hollis about this? This will crush her.*

Angus puts a warm hand on my shoulder and whispers, "Let's go, Ledger." Tears gather in his eyes. "You're right. We must get there faster. Ellery is the only way."

I look into his brown eyes. *This is what it took to sober you up?* But I keep the angry thought to myself.

He helps me up, and we divide the Ellerians two by two to carry us to Ellery.

They argue for several minutes who should carry the mule, when Hellwig suggests we feed it to the dragon. Ryllis gasps, and I blink at them. *It doesn't matter. A man is dead.*

"Let's release it into the wild," someone says.

I shake my head. "Can the dragon carry the mule to the island?"

"I can't guarantee a smooth ride," Hellwig says as he prepares the dragon. We each take an extra item off the mule, and Char moves it into a grassy open space. We all watch Hellwig take the dragon in the air and direct it toward the open grassy spot where the lone mule stands.

In a flurry of wings and a loud *hee-haw*, the dragon grabs

the mule around the belly with its enormous claws. I worry it will puncture the mule, but its legs gallop in midair for quite some time.

Trio after trio takes off and follows the dragon and the mule toward the morning sun.

There's nothing like the disconcerting feeling of drifting over the treetops in the arms of Belamy and Estefano. My blood races through my veins for a good portion of the morning. Eventually, I trust their grip and regain my nerve to look down. When I do, I remember the years of Alouette taking me into the sky as a boy. She was easier to trust.

I'm surprised that it takes most of the day to reach the island drifting east. It would have taken much longer to reach this point on foot. I hope we haven't lost the savages' trail. Zander seems confident that he can monitor their path from here on out.

13
Glowing Red Eye

ALOUETTE

When we touch down on the surface of Ellery, Sybella and I release Ryllis—the only wingless girl among us. It's a shame four people in our group don't have wings. My arms hurt from carrying her over acres and acres to reach our island—home.

Angus is dropped off by Swarley and Char. They each stretch their achy arms. Belamy and Estefano set Ledger down. Hellwig sails by and sets the mule on the surface without coming to a stop. The little beast squeals at the dragon as Ryllis rushes over to grab the rope around its neck.

I coax my feet to carry me toward the castle as the sun drops below the horizon. I could drop into bed at this moment and sleep for days. Another group lands behind me, but I know it's the other Balfourian man with Cookie and Eljah.

I meander through the grand entrance, down the hall, and into the courtyard in the center tower of the castle. I close my eyes because my wings know exactly where to go as they lift me into the air. My body dangles from them. A muscle in my arm spasms from holding Ryllis.

Before I get far, Ledger calls from below, "Alouette, where are you going?"

"To bed," I mutter.

"Did you see this?"

Down below in the waning light, he is approaching the fountain in the center of the courtyard. King Rayven's statue is still standing atop, wings outstretched, strong, and bold. Ledger kneels, and I stop my ascent. There is a crater beside the fountain pool.

"I don't remember seeing this the last time I was up here." His voice is thick with concern. Against my tired body's wishes, I flit downward and land beside him. He runs a hand through the jagged bowl-shape, about the size of a picnic basket.

"It looks like someone dropped a boulder from thirteen stories up, making this large indentation." He picks at the edges. Dark gray stone crumbles in his hand.

I crouch next to him and touch it. It feels like lava rock.

Several people enter the courtyard through the grand entrance behind us and Ledger calls them over. "Belamy, what do you suppose this is?"

The black-winged guardian gazes over our shoulders. "What in blazes?"

Char shoves me aside, and I hit my knee on the cold stone floor. He blocks my view of the strange formation with his intrusive white wings. Every time he is near, an uncontrollable fear grips me around the throat. *He was one of my executioners.* My hands shake as I face him.

"Looks like the remnants of a dragon's egg," Swarley says as he saunters by.

Ledger jolts. "Dragon's egg? What?"

Swarley heads down the royal hall, and right before turning the corner, he says with a goofy grin amid his burly beard. "Someone laid an egg. Right there." He yawns loudly and disappears around the corner.

I face Ledger. "The only female dragon I know of is…"

Ledger's eyes grow wider than a full moon. After a second of shock, he stands and races down the Grand Hall. I must fly to keep up as he heads down the dungeon stairs, past the prison cells.

His shadow disappears around the swirling stairs, plunging into the depths of Ellery. I am out of breath by the time I reach the bottom and catch sight of him darting into the dragon's cave. Surprisingly, there are torches lit nearly halfway around. I exit the stairwell onto the platform overlooking the cave. Bars extend from the platform to the ceiling, creating a massive enclosure for many large beasts.

Ledger makes a sharp righthand turn down the stairs around the outside of the cage. His footsteps echo off the cold stone ahead of me, until a girl's voice reverberates around us. "Ledger?"

"Hollis?" Ledger replies.

As I take the first step down the stairs, a silhouette of a young woman emerges from the darkness inside the dragon's cage.

"What are you doing here?" they both ask at the same time.

"Oh my stars, Ledger—don't be mad!" Hollis prattles on and on, apologizing for being on Ellery. "I'm so, so sorry. Tristeh brought me here and wouldn't leave. I couldn't…"

Hollis stands inside the dragon's cage with her hands up. She is half concealed in the darkness in her black leather pants, boots, and a black fur vest over a white tunic.

"Hollis, I need you to come here!" Ledger shouts, angry and desperate. She scuffles to the bars and Ledger grabs her in an awkward hug with the wrist-thick metal bars between them. A sniffle and a quiet cry emanates from between them. It is too low to be Hollis's voice.

"Thank you—thank you—thank you, for never obeying anything I tell you," he says.

"What?" she says, pulling back to see his face. I stand on the second to last stair watching them and feeling uncomfortable when he presses his lips to hers in a needy kiss. I consider turning around and giving them privacy, but Ledger pulls away and says, "I have to tell you something."

My heart aches for what he is about to tell her.

Before he can continue, she says, "I have something to tell you too!" Her smile is bright and her blue eyes shine with tears. But they must be happy tears, because she bounces in his arms saying, "I want to go first. Please, pretty please?"

I shake my head, knowing she is missing all his signs. She must think he is so relieved to see her that he's crying, and I *know* that's not it. Remorse emerges from the depths of my heart. I've always known Ledger is a good person, but I didn't value his mild and subtle nature. I should never have chosen Dayson over him.

Ledger clears his throat and says, "Sure, you first." He squeezes her to him for a moment more, then releases her.

She notices me and smiles. "Alouette! Hello. You can come too. Bring a torch." Hollis heads to the gate.

Ledger has a sad expression in his eyes. I give him a reassuring smile and pat his shoulder. He walks away with shoulders slumped, and I follow him along the outside of the cage. He pulls a torch from the wall as we approach the gate.

Her energy is tangible as she dances on the tips of her toes while pulling the gate open slightly. Out of the darkness of the backside of the cage emerges a loud hiss.

"Oh, hush, Tristeh!" Hollis shouts. The door squeaks shut behind us as she takes the torch from Ledger. "Oh Ledger, I'm so glad you're here. I can't believe you're okay with the fact that I'm here. Wait till you see this. You're going to flip." She titters on and on as we walk along the water trough in the far-right corner, into the deepest darkness of the cave.

She holds the torch up as we reach the back wall. In a pile of rocks, perched right on top, is a perfectly smooth egg-shaped stone the size of a large watermelon—even bigger than that, actually.

"Tristeh's going to have a baby!" she says, beaming. "I didn't know she was old enough. But when Hellwig helped me pry it off the courtyard floor—"

"Hellwig knew you were here?" Ledger interrupts.

"Well, yes. But I was supposed to leave by—"

"He didn't even tell me." Ledger's face is covered in flickering light. He turns back to her. "Why wouldn't he tell me you were here?" He frowns and crosses his arms.

"No, you see. I was supposed to be gone by now. But Tristeh…" Hollis sputters over her words as they spill out too fast for my tired mind to keep up. "Tristeh would *not* leave Ellery. I had the egg in a satchel that I made from a grain sack. It was as heavy as an anvil. But at least it worked.

It was secure—"

"Get to the point," Ledger says, lowering his eyebrows at her.

"Anyway, when I mounted Tristeh, with the egg and everything, out there…" She points out the back exit of Ellery. Her arms start flailing as she talks louder and louder. "Tristeh would not budge. I gave her all the signals and commands. She would not fly. I'm sorry, Ledger. I even got down and tried to push her off. Of course, I couldn't move a dragon that is so much bigger than me. I'm so sorry, Ledger. I should have been gone by now. I've been trying to figure out what to do."

"Hollis," Ledger says. "It's okay." He pulls her into another embrace. "Do you understand what I'm saying? I'm glad you're here. I needed you, and I couldn't go back to get you." He breaks down crying again.

His emotions pick at the scab over mine. I didn't realize my feelings were so close to the surface. I bite the inside of my cheek to ward off the tears.

Hollis breaks in, "Oh good, I thought you were teasing me. You would tell me if he's teasing me, right Alouette?"

I nod as she hands me the torch. She hugs him back. I back away, feeling a squeeze of jealousy over their closeness. To distract myself, I step closer to the egg. It is a solid dark gray. It's more like a smooth, oblong boulder than an egg. It stands out against the jagged rocks that are stacked all around it, protecting it. I reach out a hand, and before I touch it, a streak of red slides around it. Tristeh hisses over my head.

I meet the dragon's glowing red eye. My heart thrashes in my chest as she wraps her tail around her offspring. "Sorry, girl," I whisper.

"Oh yeah, she doesn't like anyone touching it," Hollis says. "You should have seen what she did to Hellwig. Whew! That man won't be able to sleep on his back for weeks!"

"What?" Ledger's voice cracks. "He's wounded and didn't even tell me?"

"Sorry, Ledger. I made him promise not to." Hollis touches his face and his lips loosen. He hugs her again. "What did you need to tell me?"

The breath goes out from my lungs. *I can't be here for this. I need to leave.*

"Oh, umm, can we get out of here?" Ledger asks. "I found out something about Tristeh that doesn't exactly make me feel safe with her anymore. And now that she is a mother—if she is anything like a bear with cubs…"

"Oh, she is, Ledger." Hollis chuckles. "She is."

I follow them back to the door of the cage. They walk hand in hand. He is a whole head taller than she is. She doesn't stop looking up at him lovingly as she unlocks the gate and lets us out.

"Come on, Hollis," he says when she shuts herself in.

"Oh, yes, of course." With an embarrassed giggle, she squeaks the gate open and slips out, latching it behind her. "I feel like I'm a mother too. I haven't left her side. Since Tristeh is like my baby, does that make me a grandmother?" She laughs at her own strange joke as we make our way around the outside of the cage.

I walk faster than they, hoping I'll hit the stairs and be gone before he tells her. I can't handle another person's emotions, let alone the ones ripping their way out of me. My head buzzes with exhaustion, and it's as though I'm sleeping on my feet.

"Alouette, would you stay?" Ledger asks. His face is desperate and pleading.

I nod and rub my sleepy eyes.

He takes Hollis's hand and guides her to sit on the stairs. I sit down next to her, shoulder to shoulder, tucking my wings to one side.

"Hollis." His eyes glisten in the torchlight. "We found your brother."

She smiles and nearly jumps up.

Ledger kneels before her and reaches out for her hands, holding them firmly in his. He shakes his head, and she straightens.

"Listen," he says with a gulp. He lets out a long sigh.

Hollis looks at me inquisitively and back at Ledger as the smile falls from her face.

"Cullen is dead."

She sucks in a sharp breath as her mouth drops. She is stunned for a bleak moment. "Oh no! Oh no!" she sputters. "Cullen?"

"We found him this morning and buried him," Ledger says.

"How?" She struggles to get the word out.

Ledger shakes his head.

"How, Ledger, how?" Hollis cries.

Still shaking his head, he says, "No. You don't need to know that. All you need to know is that he was killed by the savages. We found him and gave him a proper burial. Okay?"

Tears stream down her pale cheeks. She leans against me and cries on my shoulder. "Oh, Cullen."

I slide an arm around her as Ledger slips onto the step on her other side. I'm too tired to fight the sadness. I remember what Queen Huyana said about crying each day. I let the tears fill my eyes and drip into my lap.

Peering over Hollis's head at the young man holding her, I wish I had run away from Ellery with him. I knew he wanted to ask me but was always so afraid. If I had, maybe my father would still be alive. The thought makes my stomach jerk as a cry tries to escape my lips. But I keep my mouth sealed shut and refuse to cry out loud.

We hold Hollis in a quiet embrace until her weeping subsides. It is a strange several minutes, participating in their closeness. It makes my throat dry up as a callus forms over my heart. I shouldn't let anyone get so close to me ever again. Everyone I love dies. They are cursed by having me around. I release Hollis and slowly stand.

I carefully tiptoe up the stairs as they remain locked in a sad embrace. I consider packing a few things and taking off before we get too far. Then when they find the rest of their men, they won't all be dead.

14
An Encampment

LEDGER

When we arrived several days ago, we found a few beds left on the island for each of us to sleep in. Swarley claimed the royal chambers. We actually couldn't find him that first day because he was passed out on the fluffy, room-sized mattress. I wonder why they didn't offload that mattress. Maybe it was too big? I was perturbed that he got there first. That's where I slept most of last year on the island. But he is the biggest guy among us, and his forearms are as thick as my head.

Belamy and Estefano brought a mattress down from the higher floors for me so I didn't have to climb the stairs in my annoyingly wingless state. They tossed it from the fifteenth floor. It cheered up Hollis a little bit, watching it plummet wildly past each level of the tower, slapping onto the third-floor railing. Estefano had to push it over, and it landed in the middle of the courtyard below, right in front of the Ellerian fountain statue.

This morning, we are sitting together around several makeshift tables, each made of a door on stacks of stones pulled from the crumbling wall outside. All fifteen of us sit on piled stones because there are no stools left on the island either.

Terrowin, the cook, made grain-meal flavored with cinnamon. Apparently, he carries a roll of seasonings in his pack to make any food into a delight to eat. I'm glad he is here.

I take small bites of my cinnamony grain-meal to savor it and scan for Alouette. She's not here for the second morning in a row. "Where's Alouette?"

Hollis answers, "She's hiding out."

"Why would she need to hide out from *us*?" I scowl. Alouette's desperate and broken words come flooding back, the reason she wasn't going in the first place. Something about needing to stay away from me. I wonder if I hurt her feelings or something. "Is she upset with me?"

"I pretty much think she's mad at the world," Hollis says. "And rightly so. She's had a rough go of it lately with losing Dayson and her father."

Sometimes Hollis makes so much sense. I'm embarrassed that I didn't think of it first. But I *shouldn't* have to think of everything.

Zander the tracker finishes his meal and pulls a satchel over his head and shoulder, leaving his wings free to move. He's been spending the daylight hours tracking their path so that through the night he can sleep and know we are still on the right trail.

"I'm going with you today," Angus declares.

Zander doesn't say anything. His dirty blond hair falls around his face, half-concealing a frown.

Swarley interjects, "Seems he'd be faster without a

wingless one in tow. No offense intended."

"I don't want to fly with the guy the whole time," Angus says with a sharp tone. "I'll go my own pace after he drops me on the ground. Zooming along the ground like he does, what if he misses an important sign? We can't afford to lose the trail now."

Zander stands up straighter and one eyebrow raises slightly. It's a small movement, but it worries me. Not many can make that man's face move. I anticipate a fist fight due to Angus's tactlessness.

Angus continues, "I'd like any clue as to how they are living. See if we can figure out how they are holding our men before we catch up with them." He shovels grain-meal into his mouth and waits for Zander's reply.

With a sigh, Zander finishes his meal. Before walking away, he says, "I'm leaving in a few minutes."

"I'll be ready." Angus gulps down the rest of his breakfast.

They both walk off separately, and I doubt this will go well.

***

By late afternoon, a shofar blares from above. I barely hear it from the dragon's cave. Hollis and I look toward the stairs. By the time we get to our feet, it sounds again, louder this time. We walk side-by-side, and when it alarms a third time, we run up the steps, out of the cave, and up the winding dungeon's staircase to the main floor of Ellery. I make it to the top before Hollis. Out of breath, I stop and suck air into my lungs as she darts past me toward the inner courtyard.

A fourth blast of the shofar from behind me stops me in my tracks.

"Where is it coming from?" Hollis yells. She whirls around, and we follow the alarm through the Grand Hall to the surface of Ellery. Voices come from outside as we exit the wide-open doors of the castle. My heart jolts. *Are we under attack? No, the savages don't have wings.*

Outside, Zander hovers over Belamy, Estefano, Char, and Swarley, speaking loudly and out of breath. "…an abandoned encampment. It's worth taking a closer look, so I came back to get you." He makes eye contact with me as Hollis and I step into their circle. His feet touch down and his wings tuck behind him. "Would you like to check it out, Ledger?"

"Yes," I say, surprised he would go through the trouble of coming back for any of us. Terrowin joins the circle followed by Eljah.

"Angus is already there," Zander says. "Who else is in?"

They each agree, even Hollis. She puts a hand in mine. "What about everyone else? Ryllis, Bernhard, Alouette?"

"Let's wait for them," I suggest.

Zander puts the shofar to his lips, and I plug my ears in time for the ear-splitting call to cut through the air. In the distance, the mule tied to the fountain makes an ugly honk in response.

"I'll wait a few more minutes, but—" He stops as Ryllis and Bernhard hurry of out the grand entrance toward us.

"What happened?" Ryllis shouts from across the wide rocky space.

"They found something we need to see," Hollis replies.

I turn to Zander. "Hellwig won't care to go. We left him in the dragon's cave. Where's Sybella?"

"Oh, she's on the ground with Angus," Zander says. "Pair up."

"What about Alouette? Should I fetch her?" Belamy asks.

"Let's leave her be. I haven't seen her in a couple of days," I say.

Belamy gives his attention to Hollis. "It'll only take one to carry this one. I'll take her."

Hollis giggles like it's some sort of joke, and my head throbs. I want to punch Belamy. Instead, I consider how to keep him from touching any part of her. "I thought you were *my* flying buddy," I say.

He turns to me with raised eyebrows and a goofy grin. "Oh, Ledger, you love me."

I scowl at him and ball my hands into fists. "Skies, Belamy, why do you have to be so strange?"

His loud laugh echoes off the castle and slaps me in the head. My cheeks warm.

"You have the best reactions, Ledger. I'm just twirling your brains. Come on, let's get down there." He scoops an arm under mine, and Estefano grabs the other. They yank me haphazardly into the sky, making me really yearn to ride the dragon instead. Big old Swarley scoops Hollis up into his muscular arms and darts into the sky.

Belamy nods to Estefano. They lean forward and beat their wings faster. My eyes water from the sheer speed of our flight. Someone shouts from behind us. Belamy glances back, then redirects us slightly north. It takes quite a few minutes of my hair flapping in the wind to reach the clearing northeast of Ellery.

As Belamy and Estefano drop me on the ground, my feet tingle as they hit the hard dirt. I clear my dry throat and wince. "Thanks, a lot."

Three by three, they all land in the clearing. Then Swarley touches down with Hollis lying in his arms. I saunter over to her and pretend it doesn't bother me. He sets her on her feet as she pulls her wildcat vest tightly around her.

"That was a cold ride." She shivers and walks with me through the drying grass.

It's obvious people were here for an extended time, like nothing we've seen up to this point. There are worn paths between matted areas. As I inspect a round indent in the grass, Angus emerges from across the small clearing.

"There you are," he says with a smile. He is miles different from how he was this morning. "They camped here for quite some time. There was an enormous bonfire in the middle of it all. They had three tents set up here in the clearing and six others in the woods. Adaya was right. There are a lot of people in this tribe." He points back to where he came from.

Worry seeps in the backdoor of my mind. *Were there any dead bodies?* With Angus's bright-eyed reporting, it seems unlikely, but I'm afraid to ask.

"I can't tell where they kept our men, but they had a grouping of horses over here." He directed me to the far side of the field. There is a fat stake protruding from the ground with a circle of chewed grass all the way around it, along with many hoof-prints. "They moved them at least twice, because there are two other circles of eaten grass over there and one on the opposite side of the camp."

He gazes around. "Well, let's keep searching."

"I'll let you guys figure out what they did here, and I'll keep tracking them until dark." Zander glances at the sky. "I've got a little less than half the day left."

I nod at Angus. He says to Zander, "Go on ahead. We've got this covered."

Without another word, Zander takes to the sky. His white wings quickly disappear into the blue.

"Angus," someone calls from the woods. I follow him toward their call. "Over here." Belamy waves us over as he inspects a tree. "It looks like there was something wedged in these branches. Between here… and here." He points at another tree several paces away. He rubs his forefinger on a spot where the bark was worn away in the crotch of the branch, then walks to the other tree and does the same. "Yep, definitely."

"What does that mean? It isn't like any tent I know of," I say.

"No, I've seen tribes tie their prisoners' hands together, thread a pole through their arms, and hang it between two trees. See, it's low enough for them to sit on the ground with their hands tied over their heads." Belamy sits in the dirt and raises his hands over his head with his wrists together.

Angus puts his hands on his hips. "You might be right." He walks along the area and taps each swirl of dirt. "Looks like there were… six tied here. They left impressions in the dirt."

Belamy scrambles up from the ground. "How many are

we searching for?"

"By my count, fifteen. Well, now that we found Cullen—" Angus searches the area, probably for Hollis, and lowers his voice. "Now it's down to fourteen." It was kind of him to consider her feelings.

"Then there should be another spot like this around here somewhere. Or two. Unless they murdered the rest." Belamy rubs his head, gazing around the wooded area.

We spread out and search the woods around the clearing. Finally, on the other side is another grouping of six impressions in the dirt.

"That only makes twelve." Estefano shakes his head.

"That's not a good sign," Angus says. "They must have killed a few more on the way."

I put both hands on my head and grab handfuls of hair. The pain I inflict distracts me from the pain in my heart. *Please, let my father be alive.*

"You can't be sure how many were taken, Angus," Hollis says, scratching her chin.

Angus shrugs. "But at least now we know how many made it this far. Twelve."

"They treated them like animals. I wonder how they were able to eat or relieve themselves," Swarley says in a serious tone.

I'd rather not think about how they are being treated. It bothers me enough that they are in the custody of such brutal people. At least there are twelve poor souls we can save.

The journey back to Ellery is short, as it catches up with our position. Belamy and Estefano drop me off at the entrance of the dragon's cave along with Hollis. They fly off toward the surface.

Hollis's eyes are glassy. "I was worried we were going to find someone else down there." She swallows and fiddles with the fur on her vest. "Like my father." The corners of her mouth drop, and her chin pushes up. I reach for her and fold her small frame into my arms as she quietly cries.

"We will find them, and we will bring them home, Love." I sigh, hoping I'm not lying to her.

15

Angry Energy

TOLLIVER

After several days of completing the second cottage, I settle in for the night with Kava. She always seems to make the bed before we turn in for the night. I watch her straighten the blankets and fold it over neatly before slipping between the sheets. I crawl in and slide an arm around her.

The footsteps of our roommates up in the loft echo through the room. There aren't enough cottages for all the Ellerians who have moved to town, so some of us are stuck sharing. At least our room has a door on it. Merton and Arla are quiet and keep to themselves. Though, in addition to the dust, little bits of white down feathers clump in the corners of the main living space. His wings are white and hers are some shade of tan with darker brown dapples.

Kava leans toward the nightstand and blows out the small oil lamp. Kissing the top of her head, I consider the fact that we've only been married for half a year. Then a terrible thought hits me. I don't exactly know what day we were married. Every marriage in Balfour happens either at the Harvest Festival in the fall, or Delineation Day in the spring. I hope to the high heavens she knows what day it was. "You realize we won't have the same anniversary as everyone else in Balfour?"

She jerks, as if she had already fallen asleep. "Isn't that nice?" she mumbles.

"Do you remember what day it was?"

She chuckles softly and yawns. "It was a pink moon."

"Huh?" I grunt, confused at what she means.

"The fourth full moon of this year. When the moon rose in the sky that evening, it was pink."

I appreciate her impeccable memory. "It was a special day," I say.

"Yeah." She sighs and says, "I love you." Minutes tick by in the fading twilight until her voice drifts through the air again. "I've been meaning to ask you something." She adjusts herself to face me. I can barely see her eyes in the dark. "First, I want to say I'm sorry Angus took his frustration out on you."

I smile, even though she probably can't see it. "Better me than Ledger."

She gently touches my black eye. "I've been thinking. You might not like this, but I think it's a great idea, and I'm hoping you'll at least consider it. Even for a moment. Think about it."

"Think about what?"

"I know you're feeling a bit lost—after being asked to step down from the council and not going to rescue your father. You've sacrificed so much already—I hate to ask, but I think it's important."

"You need to let me in on what you're talking about.

You're not making any sense."

"We are both very busy, which means I don't get to see you much. I miss days like we had on Ellery throughout the last year when it was just us. Waking together. Talking over breakfast. Taking strolls around the castle. Working together. I miss it. I miss you." She sighs.

"I miss you too," I say, trying to figure out what she's getting at.

She sits up, settling her hands in her lap. "I'd love it if we could move to my father's cottage—to the medical ward."

"I know you would like that, but it wouldn't work," I say. She can't be serious.

"Then we'll be right there together instead of having to walk back here each night. We could even have morning meal together before you go… and do whatever it is you do."

I push up on my elbow to get a better view of her as my eyes adjust to the dark. She's completely serious, almost pleading. Everything inside me resists the idea. It's as though she wants to move back to her childhood home.

"Isn't this place good enough for you?" The words come out without a second thought.

"Toll, this place is fine."

I sit up to face her. "I don't want to live in the same house as your father, Kava. You know that."

She scoots closer. "We could get more time together. Maybe you could even apprentice as a healer."

"No! I'm apprenticing as an elder!" There's no way she's asking me to do this. I'm exasperated as she pleads with me. She puts a finger on my lips—making me want to swat it away.

"Please hear me out." She crawls close and touches my hands. "It's not a bad idea. You're actually perfect for this work. The sight of blood doesn't bother you. Because of your years in battle, other people's pain doesn't deter you. We can move out of this cottage, away from these people we barely know, and live at the medical ward. So we are right there and working together."

I suck in a curt breath. "No. No way. First of all, I'm *not* living under your father's roof. I'm apprenticing as an elder. I'm a warrior, training as a front-line battalion leader."

"What front line?" Kava meets my intensity. "There isn't a front line anymore, and if there was, they left *days* ago without you."

"You asked me to stay!" I can't believe her audacity.

"Yes, I *asked*. But you didn't have to stay. If you were a warrior, you would have gone. I think you know deep down that's not who you are."

I fire back, "I am the son of a blacksmith. I'm not a healer."

"*Are* you the son of a blacksmith?"

The question slams me right in the face and my swollen eye throbs. Heat rises in my chest at her appalling words. "I was *raised* by one, apprenticed as one—"

"Toll, please. I'm just saying that you can be whoever you want to be. Not who you feel *obligated* to be. I'm simply presenting you with another option."

"No, you want me to do what *you're* doing. I'm no midwife, Kava!" I leap from the bed and fumble around for my tunic. "I'm a warrior. A leader!"

Suddenly, the room is too small. The walls press in on

me and I need to get out. I need to run the stairs of Ellery, but I can't get there. I'm wingless and incapable of flying or doing what I want to do. "I can't. I can't do this." I find my shirt, throw it over my head and tighten the string on my sleep pants.

"Where are you going?"

"I need to get some air."

"It's time to sleep, Toll," she whispers.

"Don't tell me what it's time to do!" I yank the door open and stomp from the bedroom. I jam my feet into my shoes and snatch up the vest lying on the bench by the front door.

"Everything okay?" Merton calls from the loft. He and Arla peer down from their bed. I have no privacy in my own home.

"Everything's fine. I need to go for a run," I say, hoping that's what I'm doing. I slip on my shoes and dart out the front door.

***

The cool night air hits me full in the face. I jog down the stairs and around the path between the outer circle of cottages of Balfour.

I can't believe Kava's asking me to be an entirely different person, a healer, of all things. I've already given up so much for her.

I turn right after the last cottage, the one with the nearly finished roof, and run along the backside of the village. Regret grips my chest as I run too hard and too fast for my lungs to keep up. I'm not living the life I want to live. *I should have gone to rescue our men. I wanted to go but didn't. Does that really mean I'm not a warrior?*

The sky is a fading gray-blue curtain behind the black silhouette of trees. The glowing moon watches me pass each cottage until I reach the road along the river leading to the mill. I careen to the right and follow its long solitary path.

I should be an elder. With Father missing, Mother should have stepped down as soon as I arrived home. My heart sinks at the lost opportunity. *But she is one of the main people keeping this village together. And doing a good job.* Facing that fact, I shove my feelings of jealousy aside.

As the mill comes into view, I notice light and dark spots in the thatched roof. It will need to be replaced soon. It overhangs the dark logs framing the building. On the right side I can barely make out the giant wheel turning, but I hear the splash of the water.

As I run, memories of the times I've helped Kava with a wounded person flash through my mind. I helped her set Hollis's broken leg and helped attend to Angus when he nearly died of inhaling smoke and ash. This morning, I held that man's arms while she sewed him closed. She's right, blood doesn't bother me. I didn't think it was a big deal. *I don't mind helping now and then. But making it my life's work?* The idea of it puts a bad taste in my mouth, and I spit it in the dust.

The mill is tucked between tall trees and the rushing river. I jog to the closed door and stop in front of it as another thought strikes me. *She wants to live with her father again.* It feels like a punch to the face. Wincing at the pain in my black eye, I tighten my jaw and growl.

Turning from the mill, I run away. Harder this time. My feet pound the dirt. I drown out the chirping night frogs, running as fast and as hard as I can, using all the angry energy in my body.

The trees swish by in a blur, and I realize tears cloud my vision. *It's like she doesn't trust me enough to live with me and is looking for a reason to move back home. I should confront her father. Maybe he's pressuring her to move back. Maybe he put her up to asking me to apprentice.*

Glistening Blood 16

ALOUETTE

Making my way down from my quarters to fetch more water, I haul the empty bucket in one hand. I thought the courtyard was empty, but a voice calls, “Alouette, where’s Ledger?” Zander’s eyes meet mine.

“I don’t know.” I have successfully avoided everyone for several days. I’m numb and it’s great not knowing where anyone is.

“We’ve found them,” Zander calls to someone entering from the royal hall.

“Who?” Swarley’s low voice booms through the courtyard.

“That tribe.” Intensity laces Zander’s voice. “I’ve found their camp. Where’s Ledger?”

I land near the dining hall and consider stopping to feign interest. I have no interest in getting directly involved in any of that.

“He’s probably below with his girl and the dragons,” Swarley says, catching Zander’s sense of immediacy.

Angus jogs down the north hall, probably from one of

the watchtowers. His eyes are wide with curiosity. "I saw you fly in. Do you have news?"

"I've found the savages," Zander says.

Angus stands up straight and raises his voice, "Well, let's go check them out."

"I was going to run it past Ledger. I think we should wait until nightfall." Zander's low voice keeps an even tone.

Angus frowns and puts his hands on his hips. "That would be a waste of precious time. We go now to scout them out. Sound the shofar, and let's get moving."

"Fine," Zander says and unties the ram's horn from his belt.

I slip into the dark dining room and down the back stairs before the blast reverberates through the air. Once. Twice. Three times he blows the alarm.

I step through the kitchen into the side room where the cistern collects rainwater. I use the pail lying to the side, scooping and pouring the cool liquid into the bucket I brought down with me. I'm lugging it back through the kitchen when a familiar voice stops me.

"It's too bad you didn't die like you were supposed to." Char's voice is quiet and tense.

A whimper escapes my lips, and my body tenses at the memory of him pushing me off Ellery as one of my executioners. I hold the bucket of water tight to my chest.

He is leaning with his elbows on the center worktable, hands folded together. He scrutinizes me through dark eyebrows, and I swallow hard.

"Muzzle yourself, Char," I say with a shaky voice.

"You're just like your tyrant of a father: a liar and a

manipulator."

"My father was a good man." I stand up straighter against his accusations, pushing out my jaw.

Char laughs.

My heart aches as I realize I don't believe my father was good. He was cruel, and all the things people say about him are true.

Needing to get away from Char and back to my quarters, I struggle to lug the heavy bucket up the narrow kitchen stairs. Water sloshes down the front of me. I come upon voices in the dining hall on the main floor. I consider standing in the dark corridor and waiting for them all to leave the island, but at any moment Char will come up the stairs and find me. I want to run away and hide from him.

"Whoever wants to go, can go," Ledger says. "We will simply spy them out."

"I'm in," several people say one after the other.

"I'll stay here," another speaks up.

"We need Bernhard or Ryllis to identify them. Which of you would like to go?" Ledger pauses.

"I'll go," a female voice says.

"I'm working on something amazing for evening meal," Terrowin says.

"Oh really? What is it?" Swarley asks.

Instead of staying in the dining hall, I keep my head down and walk out into the afternoon light.

"It's a surprise," Terrowin answers.

I decide to sneak up the stairs that zigzag up each level of the courtyard. I should just fly, but I don't want to be too conspicuous. I can't go outside, either; they'll see me. I step around the corner and head for the stairs.

"Hollis, if you're going," Ledger says, "we'll need an extra set of wings."

It is quiet for a moment.

"Alouette," Ledger calls, catching sight of me on the stairs. "Would you mind helping us out?"

Fear runs its cold fingers along my back, and I shiver. I don't want to go at all. But I can't say no to Ledger. After all, I'm here to help. I set the heavy bucket of water on the step and peer over the edge. I force a fake smile and say, "Sure."

A wave of guilt nauseates me as I realize Char is right; I am a liar.

***

Instead of darting through the sky, we glide along the orange, yellow, and brown treetops, following Zander's lead. He and Swarley carry Angus between them. I hold up one side of Hollis as Sybella holds up the other. She is considerably lighter than Ryllis. I could almost carry her on my own.

Behind me is Ledger. Belamy and Estefano always end up being his wings. I catch sight of Ledger. He's smiling with his face to the sun, the way he always did when we were kids. He loved when I would take him into the sky. My heart flutters at the sight of him, and I bite my tongue, telling my heart to stop it. He belongs to Hollis.

"We'll drop down here." Zander's quiet voice carries on the wind.

Each grouping lands gently between the colorful leaves. The wind follows us downward, sending autumn leaves racing us to the ground.

The last to land are Ryllis, Char, and Eljah. The chill in the wind makes the hairs on the back of my neck stand up. I try to shove down the dread. *I shouldn't be here. I should leave now.* But I can't leave Hollis behind.

Zander signals with a silent wave toward the south. Everyone follows him. We sneak through the woods for quite some distance. Periodically, Zander stops and crouches. We do as he does, except I'm sure he's calm inside. My heart is bouncing around in my chest, making me dizzy with panic.

We walk another long stretch, and the woods turn into a thicket. We sneak along the edge of the twisted vines, leaves, and thorns until he halts us mid-step. I pull my wings in tight to my back and squeeze my hands into fists. The landscape slopes upward, and he puts a finger to his mouth then points to the crest of the hill. He gets to his hands and knees and crawls to the top.

I let everyone pass me on either side. I don't want to see. I don't want to be directly involved. I am bad luck.

Ledger urgently whispers. "There they are! Look, three tents. Bonfire at the center."

I crouch and crawl to his side and investigate the small valley below. It's more like a basin. Smoke wafts up from the bonfire in the middle, reminding me of when we landed in Balfour and Ledger's Hundred Harvest Tree was a smoldering pile of ash.

Around the fire are three brown tents that come to a point in the middle like large, round, pointy hats. On the edge of the woods, awnings are fixed between the trees.

Zander's voice is barely audible. "They have sentries, so

we can't stay here long."

The people below are dressed in leathers and furs. Their billowing pants are tucked into wide boots. Knee-length tunics wrap tightly around their torsos.

Ledger peers over at Ryllis. "Is it them?"

Ryllis's face is etched with horror—wide green eyes filled with tears. She nods.

"They have sixteen horses," Angus says. "And they're unarmed right now." He points at several men milling about.

What is most unusual is their hair. Each one has silky, straight black hair, but some have it shaved on the top of their heads, revealing a pale scalp. A man stokes the fire, and his entire head is shaved except for a tuft on his forehead and small braids dangling from his temples.

A shout and a commotion come from the far side of the encampment in the woods. My heart hasn't slowed since we landed on these grounds, and it somehow beats faster as several men with red leather armor dart out of one of the center tents and into the woods.

"It's our men," Angus says under his breath. "Something's happening." He rises to his knees.

I frown. *How would he know what's going on?*

Ledger shushes him and grabs a handful of his tunic, attempting to pull him back down but failing. There is shouting in a different language, and a wail echoes through the valley.

"We have to do something!" Angus blurts, a bit too loudly.

"No," Zander says. "We must stay hidden."

"Those are our men down there!" Angus stands up and

pulls his sword from its sheath, and a man's voice shouts at us from the right.

An enemy warrior leaps out from the woods with two curved swords and steps on Zander's wing. Angus lunges, full of rage. Their swords clang together. Angus pushes the attacker back enough for Zander to get off the ground. We scramble from our hiding place as another man leaps out from the left. Swarley pulls his sword quick enough to keep the man from slashing Ryllis.

All at once, the whole camp awakes to our presence. Men with curved swords and riveted red leather armor dart up the hill toward us. Belamy, Estefano, and Eljah pull their swords. Zander puts the shofar to his lips and blows it louder than I've ever heard. It pierces my ear as Hollis pulls me down the hill.

"Go," Swarley says. "Get out of here! Grab the Balfourians and go!"

In the chaos, a man with a partially shaved head shoves Ledger to the ground. The man's face is full of intensity as he comes down hard toward Ledger's torso with his sword. My heart cries *No!* Estefano catches the attacker mid-swing, and Ledger rolls out of the way. They strike and parry as the hillside is flooded with enemy warriors.

As several barbarians break through the line of Ellerians, I loop my arms under Hollis's and shout, "Sybella!" She grabs Hollis's other arm, and we lift her into the air. When we reach the treetops, the swooshing of enormous beating wings fills the air. They aren't mine but Wilhelm's.

"Where are they?" Hellwig shouts from above. I point into the trees. "Baisser!" Hellwig commands the dragon to dive.

Sybella pulls Hollis higher. “Wait.” I can’t leave quite yet. *I must see Ledger make it out alive.*

The dragon folds its wings and drops between the trees. There are shrieks and shouts beneath the canopy.

Then Belamy and Estefano dart from the ground with Ledger. There are a few more clangs of swords when Eljah and Swarley tow Ryllis through the trees.

Then the rumble of the dragon’s call rustles every leaf. Two Ellerians joined together, without a Balfourian between them, dart into the sky. Zander’s white wings are doing most of the work to gain altitude, dragging Char toward Ellery.

“Where is Angus?” Ledger shouts from above. “Zander!”

Char’s hand is pressing on the right side of his chest over a patch of glistening blood. It drips down his arm as Zander lifts him higher and higher.

“Help me!” Zander calls.

“Can you take Hollis alone?” Sybella asks over the din. “Char is wounded!”

“Yes, go!” I scoop my other hand under Hollis’s legs and pull her out of Sybella’s grip.

“Oh my. Oh my,” Hollis murmurs and wraps her arms around my shoulders.

Hellwig and the dragon burst from the canopy without Angus. *Oh no! Angus must have been taken prisoner.* The air is thick with an impending storm. Thunder rumbles in the distance as the panic rises in my chest. I knew I shouldn’t have come. *I knew it.*

17 The Negotiation

LEDGER

"Where is Angus?" I shout as I run toward the edge of Ellery. Zander and Sybella soar over my head to the grand entrance of the castle carrying Char. I chase after them. *I can't believe what just happened. Zander left Angus there!*

By the time I reach the wide stone archway, they set Char gently on the steps and Sybella darts inside.

"Why did you leave Angus behind?" I yell at Zander.

He faces me with his eyebrows pinched together. "I didn't leave him," he says with more emotion than I've ever heard from him. "They captured him before I could get him out of there." He pants out of breath.

"But—"

"I'm sorry, Ledger." He shakes his head. "There was nothing I could do. There were six men dragging him down the hill."

Zander presses a hand below Char's right shoulder to help stop the bleeding. Soon, Sybella returns with her medical supplies and tends to Char's wound. It seems to be a surface wound, not deep at all. I think of Kava, then Tolliver, and how disappointed he would be in me for letting Angus get captured. Rationally, I know it isn't my fault. Angus was so hotheaded and refused to keep quiet or stay hidden. I shake my head.

Now we have to figure out how to get him back too.

Zander offers Char a hand getting up, but Char declines and stands on his own.

"What are we going to do?" Belamy asks.

I flip the question on him. "Do you have any suggestions?" As soon as I ask, I feel bad. If I'm supposed to lead them, does that mean I'm supposed to have all the answers?

Hellwig lands Wilhelm nearby and walks up the front steps alongside Hollis and Alouette. Hollis's blue eyes are wide and expectant. Alouette's brown eyes are scrunched and distant. They could not be more different.

"What were you doing out there?" Hellwig's tone feels like a reprimand.

"We were only supposed to be scouting out their camp," Zander says, rising from Char's side. "I didn't take everyone out there to make a haphazard rescue attempt. So don't blame *me*."

"You're not to blame," Swarley interjects. "Angus is." He joins the circle with crossed arms.

"It doesn't matter whose fault it is." I put my hands up, hoping to slow the conviction of Angus. "What matters is what we're going to do next."

Belamy jolts as if he were daydreaming and just came back to reality. "We could sneak into their camp tonight and get him back. Get them all back."

Swarley laughs loudly. "We blew the element of surprise.

They will be waiting for us."

Beside me, Char takes one step into the circle—a power move that makes me want to trip him. "We could send in a frontal attack. Then sneak a few around the back and rescue them."

Belamy reaches out a hand and pushes him back to the circle. "Absolutely not," Belamy says. "We do not have the manpower to force our way through their lines. They are *very* skilled fighters, and they outnumber us."

Zander to my left speaks quietly. "I've never seen the likes of their fighting capabilities."

The three on my right, Belamy, Estefano, and Char, nod their heads in agreement. Estefano's eyes are wide with terror. I worry Angus will be killed before we regroup and get down there again.

"There's got to be something we can try," I say.

"Well, since it's so easy to get captured, maybe we get captured and then fight our way out?" Swarley says it like it's a question.

Belamy laughs. "That's a horrible idea."

"What about a trade?" Alouette says. She stares at the ground as if deep in thought. "There has got to be something we have that they would want." She meets my eye from outside the circle. "Your father was smart. He saw that they were willing to make a trade. He traded himself and the other men for the women and children."

When her voice drifts off, no one says a word. No one balks at the idea. I consider anything we could trade them. Food. Water. Hodge podge furniture. Precious stones. Feathers. Saddles.

"A dragon," Hellwig says. "We could trade Wilhelm for your men."

Hollis gasps with shock. "You wouldn't!"

"You should be happy I didn't suggest Tristeh, Lassie." He runs a hand through his wild hair.

"That just might work," I say. The entire group perks up. I look each one in the eye all the way around the circle, winged and wingless. We work out our plan, then Hellwig takes off to secure Wilhelm until we are ready to go.

I swallow down the worry trying to invade my mind and stop me from making a good decision. *This is the best way. It's the only way.*

The six Ellerian men recede into the castle, followed by Sybella with her tan wings. Hollis and Ryllis follow along, deep in conversation.

Alouette is the last to pass me. I reach out a hand to ask her a question. She avoids my touch.

"Are you okay?"

"I'm fine," she says.

"I could pretend like I believe you, or you could tell me the truth, and we'd both feel better."

She gives a weak laugh with sad eyes.

I take the first step toward the castle, and she joins me. "Aside from the usual, I'm worried," she says.

"Me too."

"No." She shakes her head. "I'm worried they won't understand you. Their tongue is not native to yours. It's more western. Far west."

"How do you know?" I stop to look at her.

She frowns. "I speak a lot of different languages." She

glances away, as if ashamed. "My father taught me. He was Ellery's… mediator, the go-between to speak to other civilizations around the world. He was training me to step into that position before he—"

Before he killed the king and tried to take over Ellery is what she doesn't say.

"I heard the savages speaking," she says.

"You understood them?"

She crosses her arms. "I don't want to be on the front line with you."

"What did I do to you, Alouette, that you don't want to be near me anymore?"

"Nothing, you did nothing." She walks away.

"Then why do you keep saying things like that? That you don't want to be near me?" I follow her, hoping to keep her talking.

"I just feel so…" She swallows whatever words she was going to say, and a silent awkward moment stretches between us.

But I need to know what she was going to say. "You regret coming?"

"No."

"You don't want to be friends anymore?"

"No."

"You hate m—"

"No!" she cuts me off. At the threshold of the grand entrance, she puts a hand on the stone archway. "I ruin everything."

"What? No, you don't."

"I do." She turns around and meets my eyes. "When

I'm around, bad things happen. I can't let bad things happen tomorrow."

"They won't." I step forward and put a hand on her upper arm. "With your help, we can communicate with them. Please. Please go with us and talk to them."

"I don't want to talk to them, Ledger."

Then an idea hits me. "Okay. You don't have to speak. But can you at least be there to interpret? I really need you."

***

By the next morning, we are battle ready. Ellery drifted past their encampment overnight. We are northeast of their position by a few minutes' flight. Zander thinks we can make the trade and be back by midday meal. The only thing keeping me from losing my nerve is thinking about the roasted boar Terrowin has been preparing.

My body feels like it's floating down the dungeon stairs. Round and round in the darkness, passing a torch now and then, I stare into the flames as I clomp by.

Stepping through the entrance, I come to a halt overlooking the dragon's cave.

"It's about bloody time!" Belamy shouts from the other side of the dragon's cage. "We're all waiting for you."

My heart hammers out of control as I hurry down the stairs, around the enclosure, and join the Ellerians at the opening of the cave leading out of the underside of Ellery.

Belamy laughs. "You know I was kidding, right?" When I don't smile at him, he raises an eyebrow and says, "Nervous?"

I glower at him, and my head feels like it might explode.

He says, "Sorry."

"Ledger," Hollis calls from inside the cage. She reaches through the bars. "Be safe." She plants a kiss on my lips and says, "I love you."

I stand before nine winged people. Eighteen wings. "Char, you're here?" I address the bandaged Ellerian.

"I'm wounded, not dead." Char smiles. "Besides, with any luck, I won't have to swing a sword, just hold one up and appear terrifying. Right?"

Belamy laughs and says, "Right." Then he turns to me. "You sure you don't want to stay here with the other Balfourians?" Belamy is serious this time. "We can do this. You can hang here. We will get it done."

If I had wings, he wouldn't even be asking me this. It makes me feel inadequate and powerless. "I know you could do this without me," I say. "But those are my men down there. My *father*. I have to do this." I look around at each of them. "You know I appreciate your commitment and your sacrifice to bring these men back. Let's be smart down there."

They all nod, stand up straighter, and follow me down the cave to the outside. When I close my mouth and walk away, I realize I gave them an inspirational talk of some sort.

Hellwig is at the end of the long, twisted corridor with the green dragon. It is muzzled, saddled, and as soon as Hellwig sees us, he mounts up.

"To the sky!" he shouts, and the dragon leaps from the platform into the open air. Green wings spread wide and catch the air as they sail out of sight.

One after the other, the Ellerians leap into the air with

wings wide open. Burly Swarley has heathery gray wings. Sybella's are tan, and Eljah's are a darker brown. Most everyone else has brilliant, white wings. Belamy and Estefano scoop me up. One has black wings, the other has white, and I wish I had my own.

We are all armed with bows and arrows, swords, and spears. I wish I felt more confident in myself, but my confidence in the plan will have to do.

This time we don't fly in low. We come from high in the sky above the savages' camp so they see us coming... so they see the dragon coming. We put on quite an aerial display, descending slowly round and round with the dragon at the very top of the formation. Every wing is outstretched, swirling in a wide circle. The wind streams past my ears and in my eyes, making them dry out. I blink until they're normal again and watch the ground grow closer.

Belamy, Estefano, and I touch down first on the highest hill overlooking the camp. Alouette lands and stands directly behind me, lending me her white wings. She presses herself against me tightly, to stay hidden from sight. Her wings stretch above my head and beyond the reach of my hands. My heart thunders in my chest at the thought of temporarily having my own wings. I feel like an intimidating foe.

The Ellerians land on my left and right flanks. We take our positions along the ridge, swords drawn and bows pulled tight with arrows loaded. The men below are dressed for war, this time fully armed and wearing helmets with terrifying metal masks.

Their masks glint in the sun, making their eyes seem dark and hollow. The savage army of about fifty men comes together with ten horses at their center. There is a man with a wide-brimmed helmet, lined with fur, and a wolf tail protruding from the tip. He and several who flank him are without masks. His mouth moves, then his battle cry echoes across the wide space. They move together as one, marching forward.

Hellwig still circles the dragon in the sky above.

"Let's go," I call, and take the first step down the hill. We only descend halfway to keep our position of dominance.

From below, their front ranks part, and their leader and two horsemen ride forward and stop at the base of the incline. He shouts something in his language that I don't understand.

I'm hoping Alouette does.

"Alouette, what did he say?"

I feel her breathing at a quick rate. "I don't know."

My head throbs, and I grind my teeth together. "What do you want me to say?"

"Say cho'ngfu' and see if he will repeat it."

I speak in the lowest, manliest voice possible. "Cho'ngfu'."

The leader looks at the horseman on his left, then addresses me in his foreign tongue.

"Good, he slowed down," Alouette whispers. "He says, 'We have your man.'"

I nod so he knows I understand—sort of. As Alouette tells me what to say next.

I repeat the weird syllables that she says, hoping I said it right, but it's like I'm saying nonsense.

The men react with big eyes and mutter between them.

"What did I say?" I barely move my lips.

"You want to make a trade," Alouette says quietly. She tells me what to say next, and I repeat it for all the valley to hear. "You have asked for your man. Now point to the sky," Alouette says.

I lift my arm high and point at the dragon in the sky. I am lightheaded and terrified that at any moment they will charge and slaughter every last one of us.

"Breathe, Ledger," Alouette says.

Belamy, to my right, gives an encouraging nod. I should have had *him* do the talking. I breathe through the nerves that are choking me out.

"Put your hand down," Alouette whispers. "And say this…" Another string of strange words comes out of her mouth, then mine.

The men sit back on their horses. They speak sharply to one another. One agrees, the other obviously disagrees, pointing wildly at the beast overhead.

"They want Wilhelm," Alouette speaks with her cheek pressed against my back. "They also want the rider. They want Hellwig."

The leader leans forward on the horse, standing up in his stirrups. He shouts a strange demand at me, sending my heart into an uneasy rhythm.

"Shake your head angrily," Alouette says.

With a frown, I shake my head and repeat intense words at him, as my loud voice pounds against the back of my teeth.

The leader slams back on his horse, upset and seemingly put in his place.

"You said your dragon is worth fifty men without a rider. You want your man and all their other prisoners too,"

Alouette translated.

I consider the awesome strategy she's enacted without my knowledge. I want to cheer and howl, but the deal isn't done yet.

The men chatter quietly among themselves. The disagreeable horseman shifts his position. I wish I knew what they were saying. Then he shouts his consent to my terms.

"Okay, how do we get them and get out of here before releasing the dragon?" Her voice is panicky.

"Just tell them we will tie the dragon between two trees. And will leave it after he releases the prisoners," I suggest.

She nods against my shoulder blade, and I repeat several phrases one after the other, clearly and loudly, so there is no misinterpretation.

The leader asks something, and Alouette whispers a reply. I don't care what I'm saying, as one of the horsemen rides away. A few impatient moments later, a line of skinny, ragged men walks out from among the trees. With their hands tied in front of them, they are all secured together by one long rope.

On my left, Zander raises the shofar to his lips, alerting Hellwig that the deal has been made. I'm glad Hollis isn't here; she would be devastated to see the dragon go. But I catch sight of her father down below. His dirty blond hair is matted and nearly brown. His cheeks are sunken in, his eye is swollen and bruised, and there's a cut on his lip.

Panic rises in my throat, and I hold my resolve as Hellwig lands the dragon behind us. Zander meets up with Hellwig, who says, "Tie Wilhelm between two trees."

“He will rip them out of the ground in a snap,” Hellwig says.

“Doesn’t matter. He needs to be still long enough for us to get out of here,” Zander says.

Brilliant guy. That’s exactly what I was thinking.

The prisoners are led in front of the leader, who points up the hill. They are released. Relief brings a fresh air into my lungs.

When I nod to the Ellerians along the ridge, they leap into the air and scoop up one Balfourian after the other. I hold my position alongside Belamy and Alouette, overlooking the rescue mission.

As my winged friends return quickly from Ellery, they take another group of sickly, starving men to the island.

As each man is retrieved from the line of prisoners, I see him. *My father.* Estefano and Char land and take off in the same breath, hauling him off the side of the hill.

Then out of the center tent, two warriors drag a bloodied body through the middle of their camp. *Angus.* They sling him in a heap at the bottom of the hill and walk away. Terrowin and Swarley dive from the clouds and scoop him up in their arms. They turn northward and his back is covered with red stripes. I try not to tear up as I watch him go, dangling limply between them.

The leader gives a shout. Behind us, several men emerge from the woods, and the army at the bottom of the hill starts marching.

“Get us out of here,” I say. Belamy lunges at me, and I wrap an arm around his neck. Alouette slips her head under my other arm and we bound into the sky.

I glance below at the emerald dragon among the trees. A muffled screech spurts through the muzzle, but he stays on the ground. He grows more and more agitated as a group of leather-clad warriors encroach on his space. I lose sight of him as we soar over the treetops toward Ellery.

I don't know if it's the bobbing in the air or the adrenaline coursing through my veins. Or if I regret giving up Hellwig's dragon. But all the emotions twist together in my stomach and heave into my throat. Glancing up into the blue afternoon sky, I take long breaths until the nausea subsides.

Then a thought pounds to the rhythm of my heart. *We did it. We did it. We did it.*

Before we touch down on the surface of Ellery, I realize *We can go home now.*

18

Pink Moon Moment

TOLLIVER

It takes me three days to get time to approach Clovis. After laying the foundation of a third cottage, I take my leave and trudge through the evening light to the medical ward. Kava should have already left, and I will have a private moment with Clovis. I rap my knuckles on the knotty wood door several times. When no one comes, I knock again, louder.

"Enter," a weak voice calls from inside. I push through the door and find him seated in an armchair near a roaring fire. Healer Clovis is a small, bald, round man. His bulbous nose holds up tiny reading glasses. His clothes are a bit disheveled, as usual, but tonight, his eyes are glossy and tired. We greet each other with an obligatory, polite greeting as he closes his book and tucks it beside him in the padded armchair.

"Did you ask Kava to move back in with you?" I ask abruptly.

He raises his eyebrows. "I would never. She is a grown woman." He waves a hand in my direction. "And a married woman. She's your problem now." He smiles like he's being funny, but it irritates me.

"She asked if we could move in with you, and I want to know why." I put my hands on my hips and loom over him.

"This is the first I've heard about it," he says. "Take a seat, Tolliver." He points at the other armchair in front of the crackling fire. "I think I know why she's suggesting it."

I scowl, wondering what he's playing at. Sidestepping to the chair, I sit on the edge of the seat. I steel myself in case he is about to tell me what a terrible husband I am for Kava.

"Why?" I want him to get on with it.

"I am dying." His face shows no sign of emotion. He holds my gaze with all seriousness. "I have been ill for some time."

"Does she know?"

"Yes, of course. But I asked her not to tell anyone. I've been trying to find a cure for years." He looks down at his old, calloused hands lying in his lap. "I'm growing more and more tired. She sees me slowing down."

The corners of his mouth droop, and I can't believe I stormed through his door ready to yell at him. I stare at his hands and how they lie calmly in his lap. His whole demeanor is sad and weighed down. I thought it was because he was always standing over the concoctions and potions he makes. His table is filled with little bottles, mortar and pestles, scattered utensils, stacks of papers with endless scribbles on them. Drying herbs hang from the ceiling.

He makes a sound somewhere between a sigh and a chuckle. "I'm the healer of this village and I can't even heal myself. What a sad lot I am."

"Could Kava help? Maybe she can see if you missed

something in your tinctures," I suggest.

"She has helped, as much as she could."

"What ails you? Maybe we can talk with the Ellerian nurse to see if it's something she's seen before." An energy flows through my body, causing me to ball my hands into fists. Kava must be so devastated knowing he's been ill. I want to fight for him, for her.

Clovis shakes his head. "It's been done. Neelie is as perplexed as I am."

"What if we send the gatherers to find new herbs?" Adrenaline pounds through my head as more and more ideas come. I stand and pace from the back door to the fireplace.

"Tolliver."

"Now that they've brought all the medicines from Ellery, you can work your way through those—"

"Tolliver." The whisper of my name stops me. He sighs heavily and pulls the glasses off his nose.

"I'm sorry, sir." A revelation hits me. Maybe if Kava dedicates a little more time, she can help him find a cure. Moving in is exactly what we *should* do. Maybe this is why she wanted to in the first place. I feel like a fool for rushing in here and accusing him of manipulating her. I look away in shame.

"You are fine," Clovis says with a dismissive wave. "I'm sure no one wants to be forced to move in with their father-in-law."

"That is true."

He chuckles, for real this time. "I'm a lonely fellow, but you two need your space." Confusion clouds his eyes as I approach him and place a hand on his shoulder.

"I apologize for my rudeness. I didn't have all the facts."

He gives half a smile.

I gently squeeze his shoulder, then head for the door. "It might not be the worst thing in the world." As I head out the door, I frown at the fact that my life seems to be running me, instead of the other way around. I pull the door gently closed and step to the edge of the porch. But I would give anything for Kava's happiness.

Night has fallen. The world is gray, and it takes a moment for my eyes to adjust.

"Everything okay?" a man calls from the dark path. Tiberius walks along with glowing white wings. He stops at the bottom of the stairs as I descend. "Did you get some bad news?"

I pause. Clovis isn't telling anyone he is sick.

"No, no, nothing like that." It kind of feels like a lie, so I admit, "Nothing is going the way I want."

"Still troubled, are you?" Tiberius asks.

He was there when I got kicked off the council. My cheeks grow hot with embarrassment. Luckily, it's dark enough, it may not be obvious.

"*That* and Kava wants to move back in with her father." I wish I hadn't said it.

"Marriage is hard but worth every fight." He gazes at the moon. It is nearly full, lighting the path between the cottages.

"She thinks we'll get more time together." I laugh bitterly and hold back a sneer.

"You never know how long you will have together. If it were me… I'd give her whatever she wanted. Take nothing for granted. Your time together is a gift."

His words hit a nerve. My Ellerian mother died in childbirth before I could know her. He had a limited number of years with her. I could never imagine losing Kava, especially facing childbirth in the spring. She means more to me than anything in this world. *If I can stay in Balfour for her, I can move in with her father for her.*

And Clovis is dying. I shake my head. I should have known better than to fight it. I'm disconcerted with all the changes in Balfour. I thank him for his kind words and walk away with my mind made up, even though my head throbs and my eye twitches with frustration.

***

After a long, brisk walk with the bright moon guiding my path, I plod up our cottage stairs and through the solid wood door.

"Hey there," Merton, my housemate, says. He and Arla are eating some sort of hot soup or stew. The place smells like beef and cabbage. I hate the smell of cabbage, and I'm excited to tell Kava what I've decided. Most of us must share our homes anyway. We will be trading two housemates for one.

I give him a nod and keep walking to the back bedroom. I turn the knob and push through the door. Kava is making the bed and smoothing down the quilt's edges as I step into the room.

"Kava," I say sharp and loud with a big grin on my face.

She startles, throwing her arms in the air. Her head flails and her hair gets stuck in her mouth. I chuckle as she scrambles across the room to me.

"You scared me," she says with a happy tone and swats my bicep.

Laughing, I scoop her into my arms and plop her onto the neat bed. "Oh, no, I just fixed that!" she says as I dive at her.

"You only ever make the bed right before we get in it." I plant my lips on hers.

"I do not!" she says through my kiss.

I lean back and say, "Oh, do you make it in the morning before we leave?"

"Sometimes." She flashes a mischievous grin.

"Never," I answer my own question with the truth.

"Sometimes. Well, not today, anyway."

"Exactly. Never." I pull her close, halfway lying on the now messy blankets.

"You're unusually happy tonight." She runs her hands down both sides of my face.

"I have news," I say, feeling the seriousness return.

"Must be good news." She sits up, crossing her legs and folding her hands over her growing belly.

"Maybe." I stand and remove my tunic, making her wait as long as possible.

"Come on, what is it?" She pats the bed beside her. I sit in that spot and take her hands in mine.

"I'm ready to move into the medical ward."

She gasps loudly. "But you hated that idea. Are you sure? I don't want to make you do something you don't want to do."

"Yes I've thought about it, and you're right. It makes

sense."

"What? Say it again."

I scowl. "It makes sense."

"No, before that."

"You're right—" I stop short. Realizing what she's making me repeat.

"And that makes you…?" she asks, smiling and teasing me.

"Stop it, Kava." My brow furrows as she irritates me.

"This is such a rare occurrence, you saying I'm right. It's like a pink moon!" She smiles and runs her hands down my shoulders and along my bare arms. "Let me have my pink moon moment."

I shake my head and dismiss the irritation. *I love this woman.* Her brown eyes are brighter than I've seen them in days.

Silvery Tear 19

LEDGER

"Ledger, help me with him," Hollis calls as we touch down on the surface of Ellery.

I race over to Hollis. She presses a hand over a man's gut. He is wearing ragged clothing and is covered with grime from head to foot.

"They stabbed each one before releasing them!" Her voice is laced with panic.

It is my father lying on the rocky ground. I fall to my knees and drag him into a trembling hug. I pull back realizing what Hollis just said. *Stabbed.* My father's brown eyes are wide with pain, and his side is seeping blood. I don't want to lose him as soon as he's back in my care.

I take the rag from Hollis and press it over his wound. She scrambles away to another man lying several paces away. I gape at my father, frozen with fear, then I look around at each freed prisoner. They all have a gut wound. *How vindictive! How cruel. No wonder the savages let them go so easily.*

"Zander, blow the shofar," Hellwig shouts across the expanse of wounded Balfourians. I make eye contact with him and tip my head to the side with a silent question. He answers, "Call Wilhelm home."

I jolt. *We tricked them?* I thought the awful barbarians took the upper hand by wounding each of our men, but we're calling the dragon back. So many thoughts squirrel around my mind until one question consumes them all. *Will they go back to Balfour to exact vengeance?*

The shofar blares, long and loud behind me. Feeling chaotic inside, I need the craziness to stop. When the horn ends, a muffled shriek comes from the depths of the woods to the south.

Zander puts the ram's horn back to his mouth but stops. The dragon darts straight up in the sky and circles overhead several times. An enemy warrior dangles precariously from the lead rope and Wilhelm thrashes wildly, sending the man crashing to the ground. It caws again through the muzzle and lands near us outside the castle. Its giant clawed feet stir up a cloud of dust. I shield my father's wound from the particles on the wind.

Hellwig runs to the dragon. "You did great! Good boy!" He pets the beast along its front leg. Wilhelm prances in place as Hellwig praises it. "I'll be back. I need to reward a dragon!"

Hellwig's eyes are full of vengeance as he pulls the muzzle from the dragon's jaw. Wilhelm stretches and screeches loudly, nearly bursting my eardrums. Hellwig mounts the dragon and flies off the side of Ellery.

Zander stands a few paces behind me.

"What's he going to do?" I ask craning my neck.

"Probably scorch the savages to death," Zander says

with a blank expression.

I expect him to admit he is kidding. But he says nothing else. I search for Belamy; he will tell me the truth. He is bent over Angus's body. "Bel?" I ask a silent question and he shrugs at me.

I stare blankly. I don't want those vicious men to find out we are from Balfour. I tried to make sure they saw only the winged people among us, in hopes they would not make any connection. I don't want them to return to terrorize Balfour.

But I don't exactly want to wipe an entire tribe out of existence. That would be cruel and wrong.

The two feelings go to war inside me.

I consider asking Hollis to fetch Tristeh to catch up with Hellwig and stop him.

"Hellwig should *not* kill that tribe!" I shout to no one in particular.

"What?" Hollis asks, kneeling beside her father.

"Hellwig. He removed Wilhelm's muzzle. He's going to burn their camp—possibly kill them all."

"Who cares. Let's just keep our fathers from dying!" Hollis's father writhes in pain as she wipes the blood away and inspects his wound. "His cut is about two fingers wide," she shouts to Sybella.

"Yes, they're all around two fingers wide. It'll take some time to sew them up, but they'll survive. Let's start hauling them to the medical ward," Sybella says. She directs the Ellerians to bring them inside. She and Estefano lift Rylan and fly him into the castle.

My father is alive. Hollis's is alive. What about Angus's father? I search for him, glancing around to all our men.

Angus's brother lies beyond Hollis. He presses a cloth on his own stomach. His face is bruised and battered, but he is alive.

A thought hits me. *We did it. We actually saved our men.* I almost blurt it. Instead, I look down at my father. His face is gaunt.

"You're going to be okay." I give him a reassuring smile, even though I fear the worst. He bobs his head at me and holds my gaze for a long time.

"Sybella, Angus doesn't look right." Belamy's voice is strangled. Sybella has already gone inside.

"Ledger, come quick!" Belamy calls from across the expanse of craggy ground.

But my father— I shake my head over and over.

My father's hand touches mine. "Go," he says. He puts his hand on the cloth in place of mine.

I scramble over to Angus; his curly, red hair is splayed out between chunks of rock. I skid to a stop beside my cousin and take in the sight of his broken body and pale lips. His clothes are soaked with fresh blood. His eyes scrunch as they connect with mine.

My knees burst with pain as they hit the jagged ground. "Angus."

His mouth opens, trying to speak.

My insides begin to quake.

The world stops around me. The dust suspends midair. All noise ceases.

He moves his lips. Nothing comes out.

I lean closer, trying to listen.

His hand reaches out. I take it, feeling something between

our palms. I open our hands to find a small smooth stone. His lucky stone. Anytime he hunted, he'd carry it. Tolliver gave it to him.

A silvery tear seeps from his eye, trailing through blood and dirt. When it lands on the dry ground, his face goes slack, and his gaze grows distant.

My heart hammers loudly in my ears as the world starts again.

Touching the side of his neck, I wait and wait and wait. There is nothing.

I move my fingers to check the other side.

I lay my head on his heart. It is silent.

"No, no, no!" I hear myself shouting.

The quaking inside reaches my hands.

I shake his limp shoulders. "Wake up, Angus! Wake up! Why must you be so hardheaded? Why can't you stop and wait? I can't believe you would do this. I need you. I need you!" My body loses energy as the words flow out of my mouth.

I resist as someone tries to pull me away from him. Drawing his heavy body to me, I cradle him in my arms. I close my eyes and cry angrily over him for a long while.

Sometime later, a large, warm hand touches my shoulder.

"Let's bring him inside," Belamy whispers.

My muscles ache as I release my cousin into his arms. Angus's freckly face is a blur through my mess of tears. Belamy slides an arm under his neck and under his knees. Angus slides from my grip. I choke on the mucus in the back of my throat that mixes with too much dust in the air.

All the men have already been transported into the

castle. Someone helps me off the ground, putting my arm behind their neck and their arm around my waist, halfway carrying me behind Belamy and Angus's body. I feel like such a wimp. Why can't I function right?

I focus on walking and eventually look at who is helping me.

Hollis. My betrothed. My helpmate-to-be.

She already is my helpmate.

She nods at me but doesn't smile. I want her to smile and pretend everything is fine. But she doesn't. She simply helps me walk through wave after wave of grief. I can't let something like this ever happen again. If I had taken charge when I was supposed to, I could have talked to him and Angus might still be alive.

Inside the castle's medical ward, the Ellerians have hauled out mattresses, fabrics, and soft items to use as beds for our wounded. As we enter, I remove my arm from behind Hollis's neck.

Sybella stops working as Belamy carries Angus to her. She rushes to his side and searches for a pulse the way I did. A quiet sob escapes her lips and echoes through the stone room. Everyone silently watches her put her forehead on his. Her tan wings droop, and she hugs his lifeless frame.

We all watch as Sybella and Belamy lay Angus solemnly at the end of the line of wounded men.

She touches her lips with two fingers and presses them to his. When she rises, Belamy touches her shoulder. She acknowledges him and slowly goes back to work.

Hollis helps me sit on the cold stone floor beside my father. His wound is already stitched and bandaged. She sits beside me; and her father is lying beside her, bandaged as well. About a third of the men's wounds are already washed, stitched, and covered.

I turn to my father. His sad eyes cause my heart to ache all the more. He opens his arms, and I lean in for a hug. His chest trembles slightly—he mourns for our kin as well. As he releases me, I sit facing him.

"Where is Uncle Roan?"

He shakes his head and whispers, "Died in Balfour."

My throat constricts as I choke out a question. "Did you get to talk to Angus?"

"We never knew he was there."

I lean my head against the wall and stare at the smoothly carved ceiling. I draw in a breath through the searing pain in my chest.

"When are we heading home?" my father asks. I meet his dark eyes and my reflection in them. I look tall and strong compared to him, though I don't feel it. His beard is scraggly and there is dried blood at his graying hairline.

"I don't know, Father," I say. "We can't travel right now. They took a dagger to each one of you."

I place a hand on his. There is bruising around his wrists, dried blood, and rope burns.

"The longer we're up here, the farther we are from home." His voice hitches, as if the word *home* brings a lot of pain.

"I know, but we can't take the risk of being captured by the savages." My voice sounds confident. "We need to stay aboard a little longer."

He lays his other hand on top of mine and sighs. "Okay."

He closes his eyes and drifts off to sleep.

I made a decision, and he trusted what I said.

I compare my hands to his and consider the fact that I'll have to lead us home too. I swallow the lump of fear rising in my throat. I don't know what to do once our men can walk. *Do we ride Ellery for the next year? Or do we get down and risk running into the enemy tribe again?* Questions stir more questions as I sit beside my sleeping father.

***

Orange morning light floods in from either end of the long medical ward. The window shutters are pinned back at one end of the room, and the door is wide open on the other. I shiver from the cool breeze blowing between them, having slept without blankets. Stretching, I push myself up and sit against the wall. Hollis is already awake between her father and me. Brecken is eating from a bowl with steam rising from it.

My stomach growls.

Ryllis notices me, dips a cloth in a bucket, and walks over. She offers me the wet rag. I take it.

Her eyebrows pinch together. "I'm sorry, Ledger."

I nod but can't speak for fear of crying again. I put my face in the cold cloth, rubbing the angry sadness away. The rag is grimy by the time I finish with it; I feel refreshed and almost coherent. I glance at my father, who winces as he sets down his empty bowl. He struggles to lean on one elbow to reach over, and he pats my knee.

Everyone is gathered in the medical hall. Terrowin

ladles bowls of meat and some sort of boiled tubers with a spice I've never tasted before. He hands me a bowl. Each bite recharges me, wakes up my mind, and helps me think clearer. *It's time to take charge. It's time to make a plan.*

As everyone finishes, I ask Sybella if she thinks our men can make the trip back to Balfour.

"Ledger, they are all too weak to travel," Sybella says. She puts a hand on her cheek like she is overwhelmed by the idea. "If we make them walk home now, I can't ensure they will reach Balfour alive. Grier and Richah are still unconscious. Richah didn't even stir as I stitched him up. His wounds are far worse than any of the others."

Richah is probably the oldest among the wounded and is deathly pale. Grier had a deep slash in his back. Sybella said it was probably a week old. She scrubbed it out and sewed it up as well.

"If you move either of them, it's possible they could never wake. And we've lost one already." Her voice shakes. She pulls her wings in tight, pulling herself together. She and Angus grew quite close during their time in Balfour. I guess I didn't realize how close.

Silent sadness hangs in the room.

"I really don't want to stay here for an entire year. I never agreed to being away that long," Bernhard says. He sits cross-legged and hunched over his breakfast.

"If they can't travel on the ground, we may have no choice," Belamy says. He casually leans beside the doorway with his arms folded and one leg crossed over the other.

Many around the room voice their opinions to either stay on the island or make the trip home. Most of the Ellerians are up for staying on board, probably because they are accustomed to living on Ellery.

"Belamy, why do you think we should stay on Ellery?" I look up at him.

"First of all, living on Ellery is not difficult. Walking back to Balfour would be long and arduous." He plants his feet and talks with his hands, waving them from idea to idea. "Swarley could hunt for us, stock up before we hit the sea. Terrowin could keep us fed. We have enough guardians to keep people off the island." He pats his chest with a smile.

I look around at each person in the medical ward, sitting, lying, standing. Twelve wounded men have been starved nearly to death and beaten severely. Char is wounded, and Angus is—

I can't think about him.

That leaves only thirteen perfectly healthy people able to travel, ten of whom have wings. Not to mention two dragons. I'm almost convinced to stay, but I need to know if there is any hope of getting home faster if we get off now. "Does anyone, besides Bernhard, think we should get off now and travel on the ground?"

Around the room, none of the resting wounded say a word. Char shuffles from one foot to the other with a frown. "I'd honestly rather head back now."

"Me too," Ryllis agrees, appearing nervous.

Char stands up straight and clears his throat. "If we made a gurney for each who can't walk, we could fly them." His voice gets louder and louder. "I don't want to stay on Ellery for any longer than I have to."

The elevated tension in the room makes my head pulsate.

Attempting to think straight, I take a deep breath. "Anyone else?"

"Making gurneys is not a bad idea," Eljah says. "But I think you underestimate how many can't walk yet. Though that journey would be considerably harder, we *would* get back to Balfour before Ellery. It could take several months, maybe three."

I don't think we should risk the men's lives to get back sooner. I stand and pace for a moment. "How long until we reach the first sea?" It doesn't really matter what we decide today; we can always change our mind before we head out over the long expanse of water.

"Thirty days, maybe forty," Zander says, counting on his fingers.

"We should take a tally and do what the majority wishes to do." I inspect the eyes of each one listening. "Raise your fist if you think we should get off Ellery and journey back."

Only five hands move. Bernhard, Eljah, Char, Ryllis, and one wounded Balfourian, Rylan, wish to go.

"Raise your fist if you think we should stay on Ellery."

Exponentially more people raise their fists to stay. I don't bother counting how many. More than double. Most of the men lying on the floor, bandages on their guts—including my father—raise their fists.

"Oh, good," Hollis says with a dramatic sigh. "I'm not leaving Tristeh and her egg, no matter what. So I'm glad most everyone wants to stay."

I address the group. "Looks like we are staying."

"What about the others?" Char asks. "Maybe they want to go home now."

“There’s only one person missing. Hellwig.”

“Two,” he adds. “Don’t forget Alouette.”

I don’t make a move. “I’m pretty sure Alouette has no problem staying on Ellery. So even if Hellwig wants to leave, that isn’t enough to outvote those who wish to stay.”

“I’m here,” Hellwig says, joining us in the medical ward. “What are we talking about?”

Char opens his mouth to speak, and I hold up a hand, stopping him from answering his question.

I have questions of my own. I frown. “What did you do, Hellwig? Did you murder that whole tribe?”

He drops his hands and looks at me guiltily. “I may have burned all their tents and scattered them across the countryside. But murder them? Naw.”

I raise my eyebrows at him.

“Fine, I killed their leader and maybe a few others. Well, *I* didn’t, Wilhelm did. A dragon must eat.”

Disgust rises in my throat like bile, tasting bitter in my mouth. “Why would you do that? No one agreed to slaughter anyone!”

“It will take them days to reassemble. I was giving us a head start.” His eyes are wide, and his hands are in the air like he did nothing wrong.

I shake my head. “Never do anything like that again! We don’t go around killing people. They let our men go, and we stole our dragon back. That was enough. And someone should have told me we were going to take Wilhelm back. No more secrets!”

“Yes, sir.” Hellwig ducks his head and tucks his hands behind his back.

I grip my head with both hands.

I think of Angus, silent and still. *Did they deserve it?*

I shake my head. *No,* we *are not the savages.*

Their tribe being scattered across the countryside seems more like having stirred up a hornet's nest. They will be even more volatile and apt to attack us on the route back to Balfour. Not only that, if any of them have an inkling we are from Balfour, then our village is in danger too.

I turn to them all, stiffening my spine. "We are staying on Ellery, but I want to send a messenger to Balfour. Who is willing to make the trip back to tell them what has happened and warn them the tribe could possibly return? I need someone swift and willing to travel alone."

"I will do it." Eljah steps forward.

I expected Char to jump at the chance, but he remains quiet. Maybe Char is hurt worse than he's letting on.

"Thank you, Eljah. Gather what you need and find me before you go." I scan the room from one end to the other. "Let's focus on getting our men healthy. When we sail back into Balfour next harvest, they can walk through the square on their own two feet. Sound good to everyone?" Handfuls of them agree aloud or nod, so I walk out of the room.

In the hallway, I fill my lungs with fresh air. *I can't believe I just told everyone what to do.* I relive it in my mind. *What I do now, I do for Angus.*

20 Caught Up In It

TOLLIVER

Kava makes her rounds in the medical tent. I stoke the fire, kiss her on the cheek, and head to the build site.

The building team is in the rhythm of completing a cottage every four weeks. As the Ellerians discover their skill in constructing, we've gotten more efficient. The only thing slowing down the process is the felling and delivery of the logs.

Clovis gave us his bedroom in the loft because it is the only room with a door. He sleeps in the cove under the stairs, but he is most often awake before we come down in the morning. This morning he is sitting at his desk mashing something in a small bowl. Every time I look at him, I'm concerned this day could be his last.

Standing at the fireplace, I stir a pot of porridge. Footsteps thud across the front porch. As Kava makes her way down from the loft, there is a knock at the door. She yawns and stretches as she opens it to find Freya, a young pregnant mother whose labor pains have started.

While Kava takes her to the medical tent, I make her and

Clovis some morning stew like my mother used to make, adding bacon and beaten eggs to a bowl of porridge. I deliver the bowl to the tent and place it on the table beside Kava.

I linger in the doorway while her breakfast gets cold. Kava's attention is fully on Freya. The young mother pants through another contraction. *Is this how it's going to be? Never a moment to ourselves? Not even breakfast?*

"Tolliver, I need more rags. Can you fetch some from the cabinet beside the hearth?" Kava asks. I should have gotten out of the medical ward before she asked me to help out. I nod and hurry to the cabinet.

Inside I find a pile of neatly stacked fabrics. I grab two and carry them through the door. There are many men laying on different cots around the wide tented area. Terrif is almost fully recovered from the attack. I helped him get back on his feet last week, and he has regained enough strength to go back to his own cabin. He should go home today. Several others are down with a winter illness. Kava sent the first one home yesterday because it was only a four-day illness. The others still have a few more days until they are well enough to return to their families.

Several of the sick watch wide-eyed as Freya grunts and holds her breath. Most women birth at home, but Freya couldn't make it back to her cottage on the other side of the village. She shouted something when she first arrived about water breaking while she fetched firewood this morning.

Kava pulls a few freestanding curtains around Freya. They are wood frames with linen curtains tacked from top to bottom. I lay the towels at the end of the bed, and Kava asks me to assist her in changing out the padding underneath

Freya. I need to get to the build site, but I do it anyway.

After Freya survives another painful bout, she lifts her torso, and I pull the soaked blanket out from under her as Kava slides the fresh rags underneath. Freya settles back on the cot and rolls to the side, covered in a linen sheet.

"Toss them in that basket over there," Kava says and rubs Freya's lower back.

Tears pool in the pregnant mother's eyes. "I can't do this. I can't!"

"Yes, you can," Kava says. "You're strong and ready."

"It's coming! It's coming now!" Freya cries and jolts upright.

I swallow as the tension in the room rises. I need to get out of here before I get stuck helping again. I toss the soiled blanket in the basket and hurry toward the exit.

"Tolliver, I need your help one more time," Kava calls. I stand up straighter, feeling caught. She pleads with her eyes and an apologetic smile. I sigh loudly and join her on the other side of Freya, who is crying in loud sputters.

"Find her mother," Kava whispers. "And let Neelie know I'll need her today."

"I need Rylan!" Freya cries.

"Your husband's not in Balfour." Kava tucks several pillows under Freya's back so she is sitting up. "Breathe, Freya."

I dart through the cottage and out the front door. My legs carry me quickly up the dirt path. Kava said to fetch the girl's mother, who works at the mill. It broke my heart to hear the poor girl cry out for her husband who was taken prisoner. Hopefully, he is still alive to meet his child when

Ledger brings them home. Ledger's been gone for almost three weeks. I wonder if they've found them yet.

The mill sits neatly between the trees alongside the bank. "Laurid!" I shout. "Laurid, Freya is in labor!" I careen through the door into the large room. The turbine is moving with the power of the water. Freya's mother is holding a basket full of freshly milled flour. Her black hair falls in her face as she is startled by my entrance. "Laurid, come quick. Freya is in full labor. She couldn't make it home. She's at the medical ward."

Laurid shoves the basket into the hands of the girl next to her and follows me out the door. I begin to run alongside Laurid, but her stride is less than half of mine, so I slow to a jog.

Rhythmic sawing comes from somewhere off in the woods, then the crackling of a tree trunk breaking. Several men yell out a warning in the distance, followed by a loud thud when the tree hits the ground. A scream peals through the air from the direction of the downed tree.

I stop in my tracks.

"Go." Laurid waves a heavy hand. "Go give them aid. I can make it back on my own." She continues jogging toward the village. Without another thought, I scramble through the woods.

"Christian!" The men shout with panic in their voices. I race around the downed tree to a group of men with sawdust stuck to the sweat on their brows.

They scramble to the downed log and Elder Jubal says, "One, two, three, lift!" It only takes two of them to lift it. Luckily, it's not a massive tree, only as thick as my thigh.

Christian rolls out from under the tree, and they drop it immediately after.

"Don't you know enough to get out of the way of a falling tree?" Jubal shouts at the boy, then unties a water pouch from his belt and takes a long drink. "Tolliver, make sure he didn't break anything."

"I'm fine," Christian says with a dismissive wave.

I'm relieved that he seems fine. I'm not their healer. I'm not anyone's healer, for skies' sake. But the boy's eyes water as he touches his ribcage.

I grit my teeth and step over to him. "Tell me if this hurts." I run two fingers along his ribs on the left. He shakes his head. I run two fingers along his ribs on the right and he gasps. He might have a broken rib or two. "I'll take him to Healer Clovis."

Jubal jerks his head and the rest of the men walk away. I scoop the boy into my arms like a baby and pick my way through the trees toward the village. When we are a few yards off, he silently sobs, trying to hide his tears from me.

"It'll be okay. Clovis will fix you up nicely."

Sweat beads on my forehead and down the back of my neck. It tickles, and I can't do anything about it while carrying Christian all the way to the medical ward.

The tent comes into view, and a scream bursts from the flaps. Freya's next scream escalates and descends into a moan. I stop and wait, hoping to enter after it's all over. The girl's weeping continues. I walk slowly to the opening of the tent, and then there is a small squeak of a baby's cry.

"You did it, Freya," Kava says as I pull back the tent flap and enter. "You have a daughter."

I lay the injured boy on an empty cot on the far side of the curtain, blocking our view of the women on the other side. Now, I need to get back to the build site. I'm late again.

***

"This is why I suggested you apprentice as a healer," Kava says. She wraps her arms tightly around her abdomen, head sagging as she sits cross-legged on the bed.

Sitting next to her, I rub her back and stare at the wall of our bedroom. The mattress is old and needs fluffing. There's a chest of drawers beside the door and a trunk with a bunch of her mother's things inside.

"I'm not the healer type," I explain. "Especially after today. I know for sure I'm not a healer. I'm a warrior, a fighter, a leader. I can lead scores of men. But this?" Shaking my head, I hold up my hands. They carried a child with broken ribs today. Clovis inspected him and sent him home to heal.

"This is how it will always be," she says. "You'll be here, getting ready to leave, and I'll need you for a minute. It could turn into a morning-long assist. That's how it always was growing up in this house, which is the reason I asked if you would apprentice. I knew if we moved here, you'd be caught up in it."

So many worries and frustrations twist together in my gut. They churn and ache inside me. I want to fight her on it, but some part of me remembers what my father said about cherishing every moment with her.

I address her with seriousness in my eyes. "I will assist

where I can. But I'm *not* going to apprentice. You need to understand they will ask me to join the council again very soon. Then my assistance will be done."

"Okay," she agrees. "That is as much as I could have hoped for. Thank you, Tolliver." Kava kisses me on the cheek and wraps her arms around me.

It seems like she *thinks* I'm agreeing to a whole lot more than I'm *actually* agreeing to. I want to clarify and lay down the ground rules, but there's something about the way she hugs me tightly.

I decide to let it go, and simply enjoy her. *She will see. They'll call me for the council. They will need me soon.*

21

Orange Mess

ALOUETTE

I need to get away from Ledger's pain.

His grief on top of mine is too much, so I sneak away in the early morning hours and avoid him as long as possible. I can't even think about the loss of Angus or how I shouldn't have been there. None of that should have happened.

It's been thirty-eight days since Ledger declared we would stay on Ellery. The old man, Richah, passed away several days ago. As soon as we reach the sea, we will release his body to the depths.

Sadness reaches up and chokes me as I fly out to the eastern-facing lookout tower. The sun barely peeks over the horizon. I let out a long breath, letting go of all the painful feelings, and gaze at the morning display over the water. I knew we'd start across the Bettilliam Sea today. There is something in the air, the smell, the colors, the temperature. Everything. I take it all in, casting off worry after worry.

I step to one of the low spaces in the battlement wall and inhale the salty air. I hug my black cloak against the chill. The birds circle the shore while we approach the cresting waves. The edge of the water is white and frothy, blending into a gray-blue. The sun turns the distant surface a glittery gold, opening its eye upon the water.

Memories of my father fill my mind. He would wake me in early morning with a smile on his face and drag me out to this very tower. I look to the right, against the wall where he would stand, head leaning gently on the stone edifice. His face would reflect the orange-yellow light, and he would talk of Mother. It's the only place where he mentioned her name: Kimana. "It means butterfly," he said to my nine-year-old self. "But she was more beautiful than any butterfly." Tears would pool in his eyes but never fall. He lifted me into his arms, and we watched the sun rise together, heart to heart.

I sigh and lean against his spot along the castle wall, gazing out over the approaching water. It's been so long since I was in this spot. It has taken me a long time to allow myself to do anything I love.

The scrape of a shoe comes from the walkway along the outer wall of the castle. Hollis comes around the bend. I stand up straighter, preparing myself. I haven't talked to anyone for the past few weeks as they've cared for the wounded Balfourian men.

"Hi, Alouette." Hollis appears surprised. "I didn't know you'd be out here."

I nod.

"I came to see how close we are to the sea." Hollis climbs the last few steps into the tower and presses up against the low tower wall. Her face is full of warmth, and she inhales deeply. "I can't see much out of the dragon's cave with the opening pointed north. It would have been better for them to make the opening facing east, so we can see where we are headed from down there."

"No one made that opening. It was already naturally there."

"Oh, I didn't know. But they built the stairs, right?" She glances over at me with raised eyebrows.

"Yes. I was told there was a tunnel that went straight down, and they built those stairs to keep children from falling before they knew how to fly. They added the gate and lock only recently, though. To keep unauthorized people completely out of there."

"Hmmm, seems like stairs are pointless for those with wings." She tips her head toward my wings resting against the stone wall.

"Wings are like arms or legs. Sometimes wings were wounded or amputated, and some were born without them. So stairs came in very handy."

"I thought Ellerians banished the wingless from the island." She rests her hands on her hips.

I don't want to talk about this, but I smile and explain anyway. "That only started about three or four generations back in our history." I count on my fingers, remembering the succession of kings and queens on Ellery. "Yeah, four."

"Interesting." She faces the sunrise, which has revealed half of the glowing golden orb.

We stand in silence. I realize she and I have never been alone together. I peek over at her. She's wearing black leather pants, knee-high boots, a maroon tunic with a fur vest on top. The edges have spotted and spiky fur from some sort of wildcat. Her hair is pulled back from her freckly face. She leans on the waist-high tower wall and sighs.

"Well, I best get back to my egg," she says. "Don't want that thing to hatch without me."

"Do you know it takes many moons for a dragon's egg to hatch?"

"Really? How long?" She faces me with interest.

"I thought Hellwig would have told you by now."

She shakes her head. "I guess I didn't ask. I thought it would be like a bird's egg and take only one moon, maybe two."

"Oh. No, it's more like six or seven."

She gasps and puts a hand over her mouth. "I had no idea! I can't believe Hellwig never told me. What a goof!"

"So you don't have to stay by her side every day. Go relax, sleep in." I gesture to the rising sun. "It's going to take a while before the hatchling will be ready to emerge."

"Thanks," she says and reaches out to hug me. I jerk back, but the wall stops me short. "Oh, sorry. Not a hugger?"

My cheeks warm, and I tremble like a panicked bird in a nest. "I'm fine. I feel a bit… I don't know." I put out my arms and accept her embrace. She leans into me and gives me a short hug.

When she steps away, her cheeks are red too.

"I'm not used to people being nice to me."

Her jaw drops as she says, "You've been around the wrong people, then."

"It's not that. It's my father—" I clamp my mouth shut. What am I doing? I don't want to tell her this.

"Your father, yes, Roi du Ciel. He was… umm…"

"A bad guy, I know." I look away.

"I was going to say murdered," she says with a frown. She reaches out and takes my hands in hers. "And Dayson was killed as well. All of that must be really hard to deal with. If you want someone to talk to, I'm always available. I love talking and would be glad to listen, too. Whatever you need."

I look down at our hands as the pressure builds. I can't handle someone being this close. I shake off the wariness creeping up my spine. Gazing into her sincere, blue eyes, I wonder if it's okay to let her get close to me. I awkwardly smile, realizing she is already close, too close.

"I guess." I want to say *yes*. But I'm suspicious that anyone who gets close gets burned. I pull my hands from hers and back away. "I just need time."

"Okay." She shoves her hands in the pockets of her vest. "It looks like we will have all year long to become best friends." Her face gleams with a genuine smile. She heads toward the stairs and descends out of view. "Oh, Alouette?"

"Yeah?"

"It's not your fault." Her footsteps fade in the distance as I stare at the dusty stone floor. When I realize I'm holding my breath, I take in the cool salty air. Her words shake something loose in my heart, and it rattles around in my chest until it flings into my head in the form of words. Tears sting my eyes. I turn toward the sun's rays and let them fall as the words wash over me. *It's not my fault.*

***

Several days later, I take the chance that Hollis is right.

Maybe it is okay to need a friend. When I enter the dining hall to join the others for midday meal, many of them gape openly. I watch my feet until I reach them. They pulled doors from the upper rooms for makeshift tables and placed them in a large square so they all face the center. Someone must be handy with woodworking tools because they've made high stools and benches.

"Alouette, you can sit by me," Hollis calls from the far side of the table. One by one they all turn back to their meals as I make my way around the room. "Grab a bowl over there." She points at a separate table with an array of foods and a stack of bowls. I take one and fill it up with seasoned chopped meat, berries, berries, and more berries. They are blue, purple, and red.

I inhale the smell of cinnamon from what appears to be a pie. Probably pumpkin pie, being that there is a pile of pumpkins near the opening to the courtyard. I didn't think anything of it, but now, it seems odd.

"What's with the pile of pumpkins?" I take a seat next to Hollis.

"Belamy and Estefano found them yesterday." She glares playfully at them. "I think they forgot that there are considerably fewer people living on this island than before."

"What?" Belamy laughs. "I can't help that Swarley thought we needed twenty pumpkins. I was just doing what I was told."

"I could eat twenty pumpkin pies," Swarley says with his mouth full of food. A drip of orange dangles from his beard.

"But I'm not making twenty pies when over half of them would go to waste," Terrowin says. He is seated directly across from me. His wide smile gives it away that he's not mad.

"I'm serious," Swarley says after swallowing. "I would eat them all."

"No," Terrowin says, putting up a hand. "Get rid of them."

Someone enters the dining hall. Everyone stops talking. All eyes are on him as Ledger leaps from his seat. "Father, what's wrong?" Panic laces his voice.

"Nothing, son." Fergus waves a hand in the air as he limps over to the food table. Ledger gets up to help him. Fergus is sliver taller than Ledger with brown curly hair hanging to his shoulders and graying at his temples. His curly, dark beard with silver mixed in is neater today. It looks like Eljah gave him a change of clothes. He's wearing gray woven pants, a clean white tunic, and a black cloak with speckled wilderbeast fur around the neck. There is an obvious puckered seam in the back of the cloak where someone sewed up the hole used for wings.

Ledger introduced me to his father a couple weeks ago. It was an awkward moment. We didn't know what to say to each other, other than *It's nice to meet you.* I thought Fergus would dislike me because I was the reason Ledger left home. But he says nothing of it and behaves cordially.

Fergus joins us at the table. "I needed to get out of that room." His breathing is labored and it's obvious he is not fully recovered yet. Six of the men Ledger rescued are back on their feet and helping out around Ellery.

"Why is there a mule in the fountain?" Fergus asks. Belamy breaks out laughing, and the rest of the group laughs with him.

I jerk my head toward the courtyard. Sure enough, the mule is standing belly-deep in the water, nipping at the underside of the upper fountain pool.

Ledger laughs but watches his father carefully. When the howling subsides, Ledger says, "Our journey started out on the ground. I couldn't exactly leave Old Man Dudley's mule in the woods."

"That's Dudley's mule?" Fergus squints out into the afternoon light.

"Ledger wouldn't let us feed it to the dragon, either," Belamy says with a chuckle.

"Why is it in the fountain?" Fergus's features soften, and a smile plays at the edge of his mouth.

A smile sneaks across my face.

"Holy skies!" Belamy exclaims. "Alouette, you're smiling!"

All at once my guts wrench, and I scowl at him.

"Oh, I'm sorry," Belamy says, thinly veiling a smile. "I didn't mean to blurt that. I just haven't seen you smile in… well… forever."

Shrinking back, I don't want to smile again and give him what he wants. He didn't have to bring such attention to it. It's all I can do to keep myself from running from the room.

Ledger answers his father's question. "They don't have a place for livestock up here. Belamy tied it to the fountain so it would always have water." He casts a stern look at Belamy, hopefully for my sake.

"And the pumpkins?" Fergus points at the pile.

"Uh!" Terrowin groans. "Don't get started on the

pumpkins again." He gets up from his seat and swats Belamy on the side of the head as he strides toward the kitchen. "Get rid of the pumpkins—today!"

Spooning up bites as fast as possible, I swallow barely chewed food. Hollis is talking about something next to me. I nod along, hoping she doesn't need a more involved response. As soon as I'm finished, I gather my dirty dishes, say goodbye to her, and leave them in the basket near the kitchen door.

I take to the air and fly to the thirteenth floor, glad to get away before anyone stops me. My heart hammers an uneasy rhythm.

After a short time, voices fill the courtyard below. They get closer and closer. I consider opening the door to see what they are doing, when Belamy laughs.

He needs to be annoying somewhere else.

Then I hear footsteps outside my door. "This is perfect!" Belamy shouts. "High enough to get a decent splat. Bring them up here."

"Are you sure we shouldn't try farther down? Seems this is too high." That voice might be Estefano, low and serious.

"It will be fantastic!" Belamy howls. He drops something on the floor outside my door. "Hollis, you can do the first one."

Hollis cheers in a high-pitched squeal. "Give me the small one." Everything falls silent for a few long moments.

I frown. *What are they doing?*

They erupt with laughter and screams.

"Yeah!" Belamy shouts. "That was beautiful! Get a bigger one next."

The curiosity is killing me, and I can't resist it anymore. I stomp to the door and yank it open as Belamy releases a huge pumpkin over the side of the railing. I step to the edge. It spins wildly down and slams on the ground below. A belly laugh comes flying out of my mouth. I can't contain it, seeing the pumpkin bits splatter in an enormous, starbursting pattern.

I regain my composure and face them.

They're all wide eyed with shock.

"You want to drop the next one?" Belamy breaks the awkward silence.

Pausing, I shrug to compensate for my laughter. I really do want to drop the next one, so I nod.

He selects a medium sized one and puts it in my arms. His warm hands graze mine. The blood rushes to my head, and I swallow nervously. I can barely lift it over the waist-high stone railing. "Here," Belamy says, putting his hands over mine to help lift it to the railing. "Roll it off here."

He steps back. I lean forward and push it as hard as I can. It sails forward and straight down, twirling and twirling until… SPLAT! There is a loud yelp from below as we all break out in laughter.

"What the skies!" someone shouts angrily from down below.

I can't stop laughing enough to see who we peppered with pumpkin. My side aches as our chortles grow into giggles and groans. Hollis peeks over the edge first and gasps loudly, hiding herself from whoever it is down below. "Oh no, oh no!" She says. "It's Ledger. He's going to kill me!"

"I got this," Belamy says and leaps up on the stone railing.

He leans out and waves. "Sorry Ledg, we were disposing of the pumpkins."

Ledger groans in disgust.

"Seriously, sorry," Belamy says. He coughs, stifling a laugh.

"Are you going to clean this up?" Ledger shouts. I wonder what he looks like with my pumpkin all over him. I lean forward and peek down below. He steps over the largest part of the squishy slop and faces us with his hands on his hips. His entire right side is slimed with orange and specks of what I can only figure are pumpkin seeds. A laugh pushes its way up my throat, and I burst out laughing.

"Alouette?" he calls. "I can't believe you're involved in this."

I lean out farther and laugh loudly, my voice echoing around the courtyard. "I'm sorry I slimed you, Ledger."

He smiles and waves a hand. "No problem. I'm just not helping you people clean this up. Ugh!" He flicks some of the pumpkin goo off his hand.

I stifle a laugh with my hand over my mouth as I say, "Sorry."

Belamy leaps off the railing. "Now get out of the way, Ledger. The next one is coming."

Estefano lifts the largest pumpkin. "Is he clear?"

Belamy puts a hand across Estefano's chest. "Wait." He pauses. "Where's Swarley?"

"Probably in the kitchen with Cookie." Estefano tucks his hair behind his ears, preparing to push the pumpkin off.

Hollis scrambles from her seat on the ground. "You want to splatter him on purpose?" Her eyes squint mischievously.

My stomach aches from the amount of laughter bubbling out of my body. I sigh and press a hand to my belly.

"Swarley!" Belamy calls from thirteen stories up, eyes on the courtyard below. He waits a few minutes then shouts again. He waits a few moments more, opens his mouth to call again, stops, then exclaims, "Go!"

Estefano pushes the huge pumpkin, and all four of us lean over the edge to watch it fall. Shoulder to shoulder between Belamy and Hollis, my heart races. I worry Swarley will be hurt, but the thrill of making an absolute mess of the courtyard and startling Swarley surpasses all worry. It's been so long since I've had fun.

The pumpkin whirls through the air and lands right in front of Swarley as he exits the dining hall.

"Whaaa!" Swarley bellows and flails back awkwardly. Orange muck splatters him from face to foot.

We can't contain our laughter as he shouts and wipes his face and beard.

"It went up my nose, you ninnies!" He points at us and shakes his finger. There's even stringy orange goo in his gray wings; he flaps furiously.

We laugh and laugh, lying across the edge of the balcony, watching Swarley blow pumpkin out of his nose onto the ground.

"Here's your twenty pies!" shouts Belamy. He tosses another off the balcony, and Swarley takes to the air, flying toward us. "Run!" Belamy says before the pumpkin even hits the ground.

Hollis scurries to the right, and Estefano takes off to the left. Belamy pulls me away from the edge, and I push him through my door. I shut it and slap the bar down to lock it. We laugh together and lean against the door.

A few tense moments later, Swarley reaches my door and pounds on it. "Belamy! Get out here so I can smash you into pumpkin mush!" He laughs and hits the door again. "You can't stay in there forever."

"Yes, I can!" Belamy yells back. He faces me and blurts, "Will you marry me?" He smiles and faces the door, as if he's holding it shut. His biceps flex. He chuckles and says, "I can't leave this room, or I'll die. We might as well marry now because I'm going to be here for a while."

I pinch my lips together with my teeth and try not to laugh at his joke. But so many confusing feelings are flying around in my heart as Swarley pounds on the door and Belamy gazes into my eyes.

He leans close, and I breathe him in.

He gently touches his forehead to mine.

I don't look away. I don't shut my eyes.

My heart rattles in my chest, and the temperature rises, until I pull back with a gasp and shove him away with both hands.

Winter Solstice

22
Flurry of Wings

TOLLIVER

"I didn't call you here to argue with you," Grandmother says. "I care and wish only the best for you. Please sit, Tolliver."

The flames flicker as I skirt by and sit across from her in the armchairs before her hearth. Winter is nearly here, and fireplaces are being used for more than meals. Settling into the chair, I want her to understand how upset I was for getting removed from the council all those weeks ago, but it came out like an attack. It's taken me weeks to cool off. But I guess I'm still hurt over it. I know there's no need to be disrespectful to her, especially because we've both been too busy to have a sit-down together until now.

I try again in a softer tone. "Queen Huyana, I simply wanted to say I was blindsided by the removal."

"Don't do that," she sighs. "I'm your queen, but we are family. You can still call me Grandmother. I know I'm not your blood, but I have been your grandmother all your life."

Something about the way she speaks to me draws me down from the height of my offense. "I would like that very much," I agree.

"And though you've found your birth family, it doesn't void the family you grew up with." She settles back in her seat and folds her hands in her lap. "You know, I grew up with a second family too."

I remember the story she told about being hidden away on a sailing ship and not returning to Balfour until she was grown. I've never given any thought to what might have happened to her in those years. "You grew up on a ship. Who raised you?"

"Her name was Piper, wife to the ship's captain," Grandmother says, eyes growing distant. "She was silky sweet and used her charm to get whatever she wanted. I still dream of her because she was as much my mother as the Queen of Ellery was."

I stare into the flames and listen to the soft ups and downs in her voice. I feel a commonality with her I've never realized was there.

"Two families formed my life," she continues. "I wouldn't be who I am right now if it weren't for both of them. Not many people get that privilege. You too have that honor to be loved a double portion. Therefore, I ask you not to pull away from your adoptive family. I speak from experience when I say life is fragile, and you never know when you will lose a part of your family at any moment. Cherish us all, Tolliver."

I nod and thank her. We chat for a long time about the council. She graciously tells me what her plans are for the future of Balfour. She is a brilliant and creative woman.

"Please do not speak of the council's business outside of this room," Grandmother asks.

Before I can agree, someone pounds on the door, startling

us. “Your Highness, a message has arrived,” a man calls from the porch.

Her eyes light up. I’m at her side in an instant, helping her to her feet and shuffling with her to the door.

She flings it wide. “Message from whom?”

Tiberius stands on the porch alongside Jubal. A handful of people gather at the foot of the steps.

“Ledger sends a message,” a young Ellerian man says. He bows slightly and his dark brown wings flatten out, parallel with the ground.

Tiberius stands outside the door on the porch and asks, “Do you wish a private audience?”

Grandmother waves him off, stepping out onto the porch. “Tell us your news. All will hear in time. Might as well get it started.”

Eljah adjusts the long bow hanging from his shoulder and stands up straighter. “Yes, ma’am. We successfully rescued the men of Balfour.” He pulls a small piece of parchment out of his pocket and glances at it several times. “There are several who were not among them and died before we could find them: Cullen, Tovias, and Brooks. We used Ellery as a base as we traveled east. When the men were rescued, it was discovered that not only had the enemy beaten and starved them, but the savages tried to sabotage our rescue efforts by stabbing each one on their way out.”

Grandmother and Tiberius exchange glances. I frown at the audacity of such a deceitful enemy.

“We will prepare for the arrival of our wounded. How soon until they arrive?” Grandmother asks.

“They sent me to tell you, the men were too badly

damaged to make the journey back to Balfour. They've decided to stay on Ellery and will return next harvest."

A crowd gathers around Grandmother's cottage, young and old, winged and wingless. They take in the information, muttering between them. She reaches for the rough wood railing at the edge of the porch. She bows her head for a second.

"There was also one other tragedy." Eljah glances at the page, then at me. "Angus was wounded and killed during the rescue."

The words club me across the chin as I'm taken aback by the news. I press my back against the cottage and hold my head in my hands. *Angus, my cousin, my best friend.*

I close my eyes as grief and guilt burrow into me. I should have known better than to send them on that mission. I knew something terrible was going to happen.

Eljah interrupts my punishing thoughts. "I also come with a warning. As much as we could, we disguised ourselves as traders and opportunists so they would not know we were from Balfour. But there is still a chance the tribe could return to attack Balfour."

The harsh autumn wind picks up around me and chills me to the core. I imagine that detestable tribe returning. I would slaughter them all. I would avenge my cousin with iron and justice.

"What else is written there?" Grandmother holds out her hand.

Eljah hands her the page. "All the names of survivors and the fallen."

"Thank you, young sir." Grandmother nods to Eljah.

She scans the page and addresses Jubal. “Tell the families of Cullen, Tovias, and Brooks. Go to Ria—let her know of Angus and her husband.”

“Husband?” I step toward her with anger in my tone.

“The message says Roan had fallen in Balfour, south beyond the river. Tillman, go bury him where he fell.”

Grandmother plants her feet and addresses anyone within earshot. “It seems our Ledger has been successful. Let us spread the news of the liberation of our men. They will rest and recover while we expand our village.”

Several scurry away. *Angus can't be dead.* We thought we lost him once before. I refuse to believe it.

I reach for the page in her hands. She lets it slip away.

Grandmother turns from the railing. Her brow is stern, and her nostrils flare. “Tiberius, gather your guardians. We have need of their skills. Prepare them for battle. I know they have been on sentry duty, but they must also be ready for this vicious enemy at any moment.”

“I will gather them,” he says with a nod.

In a flurry of wings and feet, everyone is dismissed.

The paper in my hand says Angus died in Ledger’s arms. I crumple it violently, punishing it for telling the truth.

23

Love Their Sugar

LEDGER

Sitting in my favorite spot on the balcony of the Ellerian royal suite, Hollis and I stare into the tumultuous waters of the Bettilliam Sea. The last time we were over this ocean, I was worried about survival, about finding Alouette, and about having left my family. This time, I'm aware of so much more, such as the names of different lands and the name of the churning waters far below the floating island of Ellery.

Hollis smiles. "Are you happy?"

We are seated between the gaps in the stone wall. The low portions are about waist high, and the taller sections are just over my head. There is enough room between the high parts for us to sit face to face, legs extended with our feet touching.

I consider her question, watching the glow of the sun's midday rays on her beautiful face. "I guess I am."

She smiles. "You never say anything definitive."

"What does that mean?"

"You *guess* you're happy?" She shrugs. "It's not very convincing."

I turn my legs toward the balcony and scoot closer to her. “I’m happy I’m with you and that my father is safe. It’s just…”

“Just what?” She copies my actions and slides next to me, putting her hand in mine.

“I want to be home already. I don’t want to be on Ellery anymore. I wish we hadn’t agreed to stay.”

I’ve changed my mind six *stinking* times since we rescued our men, only I didn’t tell anyone. I’ve ignored and tolerated the decision for months. “We could have arrived home by now. *That’s* what will make me truly happy.”

An image of Angus flashes through my mind. How we buried him at sea. I don’t like that we couldn’t bury him on the island. It felt like we threw him away. I can’t think about the sadness sitting deep in my belly. I only want to go home, but it will take another eight or nine months.

Hollis smiles and lays her head on my shoulder as someone walks through the royal chambers and out onto the balcony. I look up to find an old man, my father. He seems to have aged a lot while I was here on Ellery this last year. There are wrinkles around his eyes and more gray hair on his head and in his beard than I remember.

“I’m going to go check on Tristeh.” Hollis squeezes my hand and leaves me alone with my father.

“How are you feeling?” I ask. He isn’t limping anymore and is gaining weight back.

“I’m doing well,” he says in a low voice. “I came to check on you. I realized something.”

I tip my head in curiosity as he leans against the stone wall beside me.

"Last week was the second new moon since winter solstice," he says. "Your birthday." He pats me on the back, and I perk up. I forgot my own birthday. He pulls something small out of his pocket. "I made this for you. Carved it out of wood. After having been tied up for weeks, I needed to make something with my hands."

He places a small, wooden open book with tiny etchings on the pages into my palm. I'm so honored that he thought of me. But I'm confused why he made me a book. I don't exactly read or write much. Mother does, a lot. She would love this.

"It's you. A ledger, a book. When you left Balfour to find your winged friend, I was so angry at you, enraged you would leave your mother like that. As she shared with me about your yearly visits with Alouette, I realized I was being selfish. I didn't want you to grow up, and I didn't want to share you with the world. But you are a book with endless pages. Enough for everyone."

I am frozen in shock at being directly praised by my father. I soak in every word.

He meets my eyes and speaks solemnly. "I was holding you back, thinking you were too weak and immature to be a good leader. But look at you. You've harmonized us all on this island. When something is lacking, you find a solution. You've always been a hard worker, and I may have overlooked you for Tolliver because he was outwardly strong and ambitious. But not everyone is the same. You are not your brother. You are diligent and courageous."

I sigh, wishing I were a little more like Tolliver. "I don't feel very courageous. I'm often afraid."

He lays a heavy hand on my back. "Courage is doing things in the face of fear. It's not fearlessness. You *are* courageous, son."

"Thank you," I say as my cheeks warm, embarrassed to be about talking so much about myself. "It feels like I'm pretending to be brave."

"Everyone is faking it, Ledger. No one is fully confident in what they're doing. Not Jubal. Not Tolliver. Not even your grandmother—who is apparently a queen." He shakes his head and chuckles under his breath. "Not even me."

I perk up and raise my eyebrows at him. "Really?" I can't believe he would admit this.

"I doubt myself all the time." He tucks his hands into his trouser pockets and glances at the castle walls extending high in the air. "When I submitted to be their prisoner, I instantly doubted. When they forced Cullen and Berthold to fight to the death, I blamed myself."

"They forced them to fight?" I close my eyes against the idea. "I didn't know that."

"That's what they used us for. Entertainment. We were barely fed. We were constantly bound together. They would cut two of us loose, gather in a circle, and throw us at each other. At first, Berthold refused to fight Cullen. I only caught glimpses of how they beat him and forced the knife into his hand. Eventually, they beat him until he was unconscious and tied him back up with us. Then they cut Rylan free—Jubal's son." My father looks at the ground, shaking his head. "Rylan will never forgive himself for what they made him do to Cullen. That's how we lost Brooks and Tovias too."

"I'm so sorry, Father." I put a hand on his back, the way he comforted me. I don't want to know who was forced to fight Brooks and Tovias. I worry he was one of them by the way his shoulders slump and his eyes close.

We sit in silence for a time as I imagine what it was like being forced to fight your own countrymen. My thoughts flitter to Balfour. I worry that vicious tribe will return to exact revenge.

Somewhere above, a shofar peals through the air and someone shouts the word, "Land!"

We both sit upright and look at each other, then gaze across the wide waters. Sure enough, there is a tiny strip of land across the horizon, barely visible. All the memories of my last trip come rushing back. The joy of seeing land, sailing over beaches, and into the tallest mountains I've ever seen. They towered over Ellery. In some places you can leap off the island's surface. Men in bushy fur coats flood my memory, and I groan. "Oh no."

"What's the matter?" my father asks.

"I just remembered what comes next on this journey."

"What?"

"Last year at this time, mountain men boarded Ellery, kidnapping Hollis and Tolliver."

He pounds a fist in his hand. "Well, this time, we will be prepared."

I stand up straighter and realize he's right. I consider every danger we faced last time. We can be ready for every single one because we have several advantages now. "We also have Ellerians who understand what they want. Let's go make a plan."

"And that's courage, son!" He follows me through the door in search of the others.

***

"You'll be fine, Ledger," Alouette says.

Standing in the throne room of Ellery, my legs begin to shake. I can't hold myself still at the thought of confronting another dangerous people group. The throne behind me is a harsh reminder that I'm a nobody from Balfour, pretending to know what he's doing. Every Balfourian who is willing to wield a sword stands at the ready around the cavernous room.

"I'll do it." Char has an intense expression in his eyes.

"No, Ledger can do this," my father says, pushing Char away from the foot of the throne.

My father gives me a confident nod. I glance at the other Balfourian men, armed and ready to defend if something goes badly. They steel me enough to stop my shaking.

Alouette says, "The Waya tribe should understand most of what you say. Keep it simple. Don't panic." She turns to walk away, and I grab her arm.

"But you have this way with words, and you understand other languages, even if you've never heard it before," I explain. "It's not only that I'm afraid. *You* can handle this better than me."

She faces me. "You're our leader. You need to talk with them."

"Just because I'm the leader doesn't mean I do everything like make all decisions, have all the ideas, lead the battles, feed our people, *and* negotiate all the trade deals." I throw up my arms. "Will you please do this?" I hush my voice as Belamy and Estefano escort two strange men into the throne room.

I let go of Alouette's arm and face them. Thankfully, Alouette doesn't run off. She straightens her stance and takes a step back, forcing me to take the lead. I'm so irritated, my head pounds behind my eyes.

The men from the mountains come to a rest at the foot of the three steps to the throne. They are clothed in coats made entirely of fur, with hoods covering the backs of their heads. The one on the right is wearing a hood made from the head of a wolf. I remember him from last year. He kidnapped Hollis. Blood courses wildly through my veins. *Maybe I am a bit scared.*

The man next to him wears a necklace full of teeth and little tufts of hair in between. He is the one who hacked off Hollis's hair. My hands shake, so I slide them behind me. I avoid looking directly at the teeth-collector's necklace. I don't want to know if any of that hair belongs to Hollis.

The two men nod, and the wolfman speaks. "Who is you?"

I stand up straighter and say, "I am Ledger."

"Where is king with wings?" he points at Alouette and gazes around the room at the other Ellerians.

I pause for an awkward moment, not knowing how to respond. It's a long story. *What do I say? Do I start at the beginning? Do I skip to the end? What is the end?*

Then my mind goes entirely blank.

Alouette whispers, "You're in charge now."

"I—I'm in charge now," I repeat, my eyes widening and

pleading for her to do the talking.

"I no idiot," the man yells. "Something wrong here!" He stomps his foot on the ground and walks away.

Finally, Alouette steps forward and says something in a language I've never heard. The words stream out of her mouth in choppy, harsh syllables.

Wolfman nods and faces her with his hands on his hips. He responds in his language quite positively with his eyebrows raised.

Alouette steps forward again to my side. "We have grain and sugar to offer."

"Sugar?" Wolfman perks up.

Fergus and Berthold haul two sacks of grain and a medium canvas bag to Wolfman's feet.

"We want coal and iron ore," Alouette says.

Wolfman replies in his native tongue loudly and apparently angry.

Alouette speaks harshly back and points at the grain and sugar, holds up two fingers.

Wolfman's response is thoughtful and deliberate. Around the room, my people are intently focused on the conversation they don't understand, but every single one has their sword in their hand, and some have a dagger in the other. I pull my shoulders up, letting their confidence strengthen me.

Alouette holds up two fingers again repeating the same words, more intensely this time. That's the girl I remember. Fierce about what she wants. I miss seeing her this way: bossy and strong-willed. I grit my teeth against the tension in the room.

Wolfman gives the teeth-collector a command only he

and Alouette can understand. Teeth-collector walks away, and Estefano follows him out the throne room door.

Wolfman asks her a question and Alouette gives a lengthy reply. She holds her chin up high and eventually puts her hands on her hips. I don't know what she is saying, but whatever it is, it elicits a curt bow from Wolfman, then a deeper bow at me.

A short time later, Teeth-collector and another tribesman enter, carrying a bag over their shoulder. Estefano is joined by Terrowin. They escort them to the foot of the throne where the men lay their heavy loads and pick up our two grain sacks and bag of sugar.

"Thank you," Wolfman says to Alouette and me. "Next time… more sugar." He points at the medium bag.

Alouette nods with a kind smile.

He takes his leave with the rest of his men and marches out the door.

When they are gone, Alouette relaxes. "That's their weakness. They love their sugar."

I blow out a held breath. "Do you see what I mean?" My voice is more stern than I intend. "You are a natural at negotiation. If I'm the leader of this mess, then you are officially the ambassador. Ambassador Alouette, everyone!" I shout and wave my hand at her in introduction.

When no one cheers, I glance at her with a goofy grin, scrunching half my face.

She rolls her eyes and says, "Fine, but we need to stock up so we have something to trade next time. Wasn't that our last bag of grain?"

"There doesn't need to be a next time," I say. "We're

going home, remember?"

She takes a step down the stairs and says, "Yeah," over her shoulder.

I frown. She is not a dismissive sort of person. I want to ask her what that's about, and I want to ask her what she said to Wolfman, but after what she just did for me, I've asked enough of her for today.

24

Snowy Ride

ALOUETTE

"I'm pretty sure you just gave away the best thing on this island." Char's lip curls up in a sneer, and hatred radiates off him in waves.

I spin on my toes away from him and keep walking out of the dining hall where we all ate evening meal, celebrating the successful trade agreement with the Waya tribe. They usually provide much more for Ellery. Because we had very little to offer, I was forced to pull out the provisions I had stashed in my closet.

"Alouette," Char calls. "I'm talking to you." He catches up with me in the courtyard. "You shouldn't have been hiding all those provisions in your quarters. You should have shared them with us!" His voice echoes in the wide courtyard in the brisk winter air. "You may be even more selfish than Ciel!"

At the mention of my father, something inside me is crushed. I hang my head, resisting the urge to scream in his face and tell him to never say my father's name again.

Char's footsteps stop right behind me. "You're just as evil as him. You're so evil, it got Dayson killed," Char blurts for all to hear.

My heart withers at his words. I can't breathe. I can't stand. Hot tears flow down my cheeks. This is what I get for coming out of hiding: an attack from Char.

He pushes my wing to the side and whispers in my ear, "I'm sure that's why Ciel died. Because you're so privy-scraping evil."

"Char!" Belamy shouts from the doorway of the dining hall. All at once Belamy bounds into the air and lands in front of me, shouting in Char's face. "Shut your vengeful mouth! How dare you say something like that to her—or anyone for that matter. What is wrong with you?"

"Stay out of this, Belamy," Char growls. "This has nothing to do with you."

"It does now." Belamy steps closer to Char, pushing him away from me. I want to close my eyes and fly off to my quarters, but I'm surprised Belamy is sticking up for me.

Fergus emerges from the hall leading from the blacksmith shop. He scowls at us, and I'm embarrassed at the commotion. He rushes over, eyes stern and lips tight.

"Ciel was a cruel tyrant of a man—not even a man—a monster, who didn't deserve to rule Ellery," Char spouts back.

"You better shut your mouth, Char." Belamy balls his fists.

Fergus puts an arm between them. "Stop this."

I take a step back, worried punches will be thrown. I back up against the fountain and scoot around it to the mule tethered there. I brush its fur with my hands, and it calms me down a little. I step around it and put the mule between Char and me.

"I will not!" Char's wings flap as he jerks toward Belamy. He takes to the air out of Fergus's reach. Belamy bounds into the air as Char throws a fist. Belamy dodges it with ease. Char's face grows redder with rage as Belamy slips out of the way of two more punches.

Fergus stands beneath them, out of arm's reach. With his hands on his hips, he shakes his head. Balfourians and Ellerians alike step out of the dining hall to see what the commotion is about. Ledger and Hollis watch me with concern. Fergus walks over to me.

"Are you all right?" Fergus asks.

I shrug and gape at the aerial fist fight.

"We've done this before, Char. You can't beat me," Belamy taunts, whisking back and forth.

Char takes another swing, and Belamy catches his fist, twists it around Char's back, and slams him to the ground face first.

"Why are you going after Alouette? Why?" He yells through Char's white wings flapping in his face.

"She's—" Char groans as Belamy twists his arm harder.

"She didn't do anything to you."

"Ciel killed my wife!" Char's voice cuts through the frigid air as flakes of snow begin to fall all around us.

Belamy's arms flex as he drags Char off the ground, standing him upright. "You were never married. What are you talking about?" Belamy's dark eyes are intense, and his bottom teeth are bared.

"I was betrothed. She was *going* to be my…" He whimpers quietly as Belamy releases his grip. Char rubs his shoulder with embarrassment all over his face.

"*He* murdered her," Char says to me.

"*She* is not Ciel." Belamy steps between us again, with his hands on his hips. "Do you want to be punished for every awful thing *your* father ever did?"

Char looks him full in the face with his eyes wide. He doesn't answer, but we all know what his answer is.

"Leave Alouette alone," Belamy demands.

Char takes to the air through the flurries, like he's rising through the falling sky. I watch him disappear over a balcony several stories up.

Belamy approaches me like I'm a traumatized animal needing to be calmed. He tiptoes around the fountain and stops on the other side of the mule from me. He runs his hands along its haunches.

"You okay?" he asks.

My heart still races in my chest, but at least I am breathing. I feel publicly judged and found guilty. It's as though I'm falling from Ellery all over again, pushed off by Char's accusations. I look at Fergus then at Belamy. Instead of sharing any of the wreckage inside me, I lie. "I'll be fine."

"I can't pretend that's true. I saw the look on your face." Belamy touches my hand entangled in the mule's mane.

We are joined on all sides by the others.

"What was that about?" Ledger asks.

"Char is a mean slop-sucker." Hollis rolls her eyes.

Sybella steps up beside me. "Are you all right?"

The attention is like I'm reliving another humiliation. I stroke the mule's back, trying to calm down enough to speak.

"Char said some things that were very hurtful." I clear

my throat, hoping to avoid the tears welling in my eyes. Belamy brushes his fingers gently over mine. I meet his eyes and say, "I need some time to recover. Excuse me."

I step away from the crowd and stretch out my wings. They carry me through the air, into the falling snow.

I think of Belamy and wish I didn't take off so suddenly. It's nice to have friends, to find comfort in them. In him.

I inhale the crisp air and let the chilly flakes wash the embarrassment from my face.

***

Sometime later, there is a soft rapping on my door. Feeling like a cornered fawn, I wait for whoever it is to leave. Another knock is joined by Belamy's soft voice. "Alouette?"

The way he says my name draws my heavy body from the bench toward the door. I lift the latch. He pushes the door open, and I stop it with my foot. Only one of his eyes is visible.

"Hi," he says.

"Hi." I wait for the reason he's here.

"We came up with a new game," Belamy whispers. "I thought you might enjoy it."

Hiding my trepidation, I blink as he continues.

"The snow is really piling up. First time in years…" He smiles and squints. "Anyway, I was wondering if you'd like to go for a snowy ride?"

I frown more out of confusion than rejection. "What are you doing?" I'm unable to resist the curiosity.

"I can't tell you. It's a surprise."

I open the door so I can see both his eyes. *Is he joking me?* His face is sincere, eyebrows up, eyes bright.

"You'll love it, I promise." He holds out a hand. "Come on."

"I need to…" I consider what I'll need.

"You don't need to do anything. You've had plenty of time to mope over Char's idiocy. Now it's time to have some fun."

"I was going to say I need to get my boots on."

He notices my stocking feet and smiles. "Of course."

I leave the door gaping open and walk to the bedroom. He follows me and chatters on and on about the snow and how it's piled up against the outside of the castle.

As I sit on the edge of my bed lacing up my leather boots, I watch his facial expression flip from wildly excited to boldly focused and back again. His brown eyes are big and intense. When they look at me, it's like he can see everything I feel. I pull my long, black leather skirt down over my boots.

"You ready?" he asks as I pull on my thick fur cloak.

"I guess." I shrug.

He holds out a hand and says, "Trust me. This is going to be great."

I take his hand and let him pull me from the edge of the bed.

Out in the courtyard, the beauty of the sparkly white drifts fills me with awe. It sticks in the cracks of the tan stone along the walls, on each balcony going up sixteen floors, and covers the entire courtyard below. We step off the ledge together and wing our way to the ground. His feathers are so black against the snow, they stand out in contrast to everything around us. They are quite the opposite of my pale wings.

Happy voices fill the courtyard as we land in the fluffy snow. From the grand entrance, Swarley, Estefano, Zander, and Hollis come sauntering in. Swarley calls out, "Bel, we smoothed it down so we can slide on our bums. Come on!" He waves a hand at us and leads us through the Grand Hall and out the front entrance.

Outside, there is an enormous hill of snow against the north-facing wall of the castle. They've carved steps up the side. Each of these grown men climb one after the other. I find it amusing they don't act like guardians at all. More like children. An intrigued smile peeks at the edge of my lips as Belamy passes me to climb the snowy stairs.

I stand at the bottom and watch Swarley take the first ride. He slides down, gray wings flailing awkwardly behind him. He ends up rolling the last few paces and coming to a stop three quarters of the way to the edge of the island. He stands up, shakes snow from his wings, and pumps his fists in the air. He yells something about sliding the farthest.

Zander goes next. For such a serious guy, he is having a lot of fun. He doesn't go as far as Swarley, who hasn't left his position.

Then Estefano sits and gives a shout as he slides down the hill out of control. His dark hair flips wildly around his face, preventing him from seeing where he's headed, and he nearly crashes into Zander.

"Watch out!" Hollis yells. Belamy gives her a hard push. She keeps her feet up, screaming all the way down, past Zander, Estefano, and surprisingly past Swarley. His eyes are wide with shock, and he stomps after her, shouting something.

She stands up and raises her hands in triumph.

I quietly laugh to myself as Belamy calls me. "Alouette, give me a push." I climb the frozen steps and kneel behind him. He says, "Give it all you've got. I need to at least beat Swarley."

I shove as hard as I can against his wings. He sails away from me, down the crystalline hill, and past his friends. Belamy doesn't quite reach as far as Hollis but zooms past Swarley.

"You can't use your wings, Belamy. That's cheating!" Swarley yells.

Belamy's laugh echoes off the wall of the castle. They playfully argue for a minute, then turn their attention to me. I gulp at the attention and realize it makes me quite nervous. I shake it off and sit, tucking my smooth leather skirt tightly between my knees. I push myself as hard as I can down the hill toward my friends, realizing that's what they are to me.

Cold air whips against my face, chilling me to the bone. I slide wildly down the packed snow, keeping my boots from touching the ground. I make it past all of them and don't slow down when I pass Hollis, who leaps out of the way.

The edge of Ellery comes up quickly and without anything to stop me, I sail out off the edge of the floating island. I flail my hands and feet out as my wings catch me in midair. Without warning, memories of my execution and being pushed off Ellery come jolting back.

"Alouette!" a voice reaches me as my wings work the air. Belamy dives from the surface, his wings filling with air.

He swoops around me, his feathers brushing mine. "Holy skies, are you okay?" He gives a half-hearted laugh with his eyebrows pinched together.

Tears escape my control, and I cover my face, feeling vulnerable and ridiculous. *I have wings—falling shouldn't matter.*

He touches my hands and pulls them from my face. "Hey, you're okay. You won the farthest slide," he jokes, trying to lighten the mood.

I don't pull away from him. I hold his warm hands. I want to let him into my dark world. I want to let him lighten me up. I really do. I attempt a moment of honesty.

"I was executed right here," I say, glancing up where I slid off the island. My wings keep me level with him.

He sighs and draws me closer, putting one hand on my back, like we are dancing in midair. "I know."

"It jarred me for a second."

"Let me take you home," he says.

I inhale sharply and gaze into his comforting eyes. He is taking responsibility for my panic. I shake my head. I draw on his lightheartedness and let it warm me.

"Please, let me take you back to your quarters." His wings work the air, drawing us upward.

"No, Belamy." Everyone stands at the edge of the island gaping at us. Their concern makes me feel accepted instead of humiliated. "I want to go again."

"Go where?" he asks.

"Sliding."

He chuckles. "Really?"

A smile warms across my face, and I look deep into his

eyes. "Really."

He holds my hand as our wings shoot us upward, past the edge and high in the air above our friends. They cheer for us as I recover from my fall. I give a timid smile to Belamy as we soar toward the snow-covered castle together.

Spring Equinox

Poppycock 25

TOLLIVER

When Jubal sends for me, I wonder if they are ready for me to join the ranks of elders and advisors. It's about time. I've waited months for their call. Spring has sprung and we completed eight new cottages over the winter. The first blooms emerge, pink pearwood trees and trailing wisteria. The buttercups yawn toward the blue skies as pine pollen dusts everything in a hint of chartreuse. Even the air is hazy as I follow Jubal's youngest daughter, Myst.

I'm confused when she leads me back to their home, not the elder's meeting place.

Myst opens the back door and smiles. I enter to find Jubal sitting on a bench at their family table. His hand is covered with a blood-soaked cloth.

I stop short.

This is the third time in the last week someone has asked me to help with a wound.

"No." I turn back toward the door.

"Please," Jubal says. "Kava is busy with someone else."

I groan and slam my hand on the door frame. Swallowing

any pride I have left, I take one step back inside.

"I… umm… crushed my thumb," Jubal says while clearing his throat. He is obviously embarrassed. He should be. What a clumsy oaf. I stomp over to him and not so gently unwrap his thumb. A snorting chuckle sneaks out of me.

"Don't you dare laugh at me, Tolliver," he says with a scowl. "It was an accident."

He groans as I take a closer look.

"I just need to know if I need stitches or something. And if I should clip the nail right off." He groans as I turn it back and forth in the firelight.

His thumb is swollen almost twice its normal size and his thumbnail is completely smashed and hanging precariously to the side. I never considered what it would look like under a fingernail.

"What did you hit it with?" I ask.

He purses his lips in anger. "Stacking the logs."

I stifle a laugh. "Stacking firewood?"

"No!" He yanks his hand out of mine. "Stacking the logs for the cottage we're building. What do you think I am, some sort of soft egg with ears?"

"Yes, yes, I do," I say with a smile. "I'd clip the nail off; you can't save it now. But it'll grow back."

"It will?" His eyes brighten.

"Yes. A couple months ago, Kava treated Cecil for a broken hand, and he lost a fingernail in the process. Now there's a strange little black bump of a fingernail growing back." It doesn't matter how much I have tried to not be Kava's apprentice since moving into the medical ward; it seems I am.

"Cut it off. Wash that blood off, and put a clean bandage on it. You'll be fine." I leave him to suffer alone.

I stroll back to the medical ward to see if Kava is ready to go to midday meal together. I enter through the tent flap. There is no one around except an old Ellerian man asleep in the far corner.

I slip in the back door of the cottage and find Clovis coughing into a bucket sitting on the edge of his makeshift bed beneath the stairs. A drip of blood taints the corner of his mouth. I hurry to him. "Clovis, are you okay?" I sit beside him on the bed.

He draws a wheezing breath. "I can feel my insides slowing down. It's time."

"What? You can't know that." He hands me the bucket, and I lay it on the floor.

"I've seen enough men on their death beds to know."

"Where's Kava? She needs to be here." I start to get up.

"No." He holds weakly on the side of my tunic. I let him pull me onto the bed beside him. "It's better if I'm gone before she returns. You can't erase the memory of someone's last moment."

I want to tell him he's crazy and fetch Kava. But he's right. There are things that haunt you for all your days. I put a hand on his back to comfort him and touch a strange mound of flesh and bone. A bone pointing the wrong direction for a wingless man.

"What is this?" I touch his back, rubbing my hand on the mound.

He sighs. "That is a secret I thought I would take to my grave."

"Is it a cyst?"

"Wings." His voice is so quiet, I wonder if I misheard him.

"Wings?"

He nods and leans back against his pillow in exhaustion.

My mind races. Of course. We are all Ellerian. Most of us are wingless. I've never thought about it before, but if we descended from winged people, surely there would be a few here and there born with wings.

He shivers, and I pull his blankets up to his chest. His voice is barely above a whisper. "My healer father removed them before I was two weeks old."

I keep a straight face, but the horror of a baby having his wings removed disgusts me.

"Were you the only one…" I raise my eyebrows. "… born with wings in Balfour?"

"No. There were a few before me. And a few after me. Kava."

"Kava what? Had wings?"

My heart jolts in my chest then races faster than my thoughts. *Kava had wings?*

He closes his eyes, and his mouth descends into a frown. A remorseful tear streaks down his cheek. "I removed hers. I did a better job than my father did." He reaches for the mound on his back.

Shock closes in on my throat as I struggle to believe it. My darling Kava was born with wings, in a village where the winged are the enemy. I shake my head. I've been so concerned with fitting in somewhere, wingless from a winged family. I didn't consider it could have been the same in reverse, winged in a village of wingless.

Calming myself takes more energy than not asking him a hundred questions. But one question refuses to stay hidden. "Does she know?"

He opens his cloudy eyes and they connect with mine. "No."

"Can I tell her?"

He frowns again with a nod. He's either deep in thought or drifting off; I'm not sure.

I sit with him for a long time.

Instead of sitting wordless waiting for him to die, I fill the silence. "I just got back from Jubal's cottage. He exploded the end of his thumb while laying the logs of a cabin. Lost his thumbnail."

"You are one of the best apprentices I've seen in my time, besides Kava, of course," he whispers.

"What? I'm not—" I stop myself short.

He thinks I've been apprenticing. No need to disappoint him now.

"Rylan was terrible. He cried at least once a week that first year." Clovis smiles with his eyes closed.

"What a ninny." I pull the handkerchief from his hand and dab the drying blood on the corner of his mouth.

He lets out a heavy breath. I assume it's a laugh. "He cut himself a lot, too."

"Really? On what?" I'm actually interested.

Should I hold his hand? He doesn't seem to need comfort. He doesn't even appear to be afraid to die. I guess he's had a lot of time to prepare.

"Washing tools. Carrying buckets." The old man

smiles and adds, "He could hurt himself walking through a doorway." He chuckles with a gurgle in his throat, and starts a long, strained coughing fit. He sits up, and I hold the bucket.

I hold up a finger at him like he's a child. "No more funny talk."

"Oh, poppycock," he almost rhymes.

I laugh and he gives a half smile, lying back on his pillows. I enjoy that he can be such a sassy old goat, even now.

For a long time, he doesn't move or say anything. His breath becomes shallower.

His face fades to gray, ashen and still. His bald head no longer has a shine to it. His body is entirely still, including his chest.

I lay two fingers on the side of his neck. He is gone.

Tears well in my eyes. I let them fall. No one is here to see me weep over my father-in-law. He was a kind and caring man. A loving father. And a winged Balfourian.

I reach for Clovis and move his hands so they rest peacefully on his chest. *Goodbye, Clovis.*

***

Soon the front door swings open, and Kava waddles in with an armload of cut plants in several baskets over her eight-months-pregnant belly. "I got those herbs you needed. Which ones did you want me to hang, and which did you want me to chop straight away?"

I meet her eyes. My tears give the secret away.

"Oh no!" she cries and bustles to my side. "No, no, no he wasn't supposed to go yet. He sent me to get a few things. I told him it could wait, but he insisted."

She drops to her knees at his bedside and lays across his chest, large pregnant belly in the way. She weeps for a long time as I run my hand along her back, half in comfort and half in search of remnants of wings. There is nothing there, unlike Clovis's back.

The last few moments of his death flash through my mind. After she falls silent, I caress her long brown hair.

When she sits up, her eyes are red and there are wrinkles pressed into her skin. I pull her to me and hold her. "Did you talk to him?"

I nod against the side of her head.

"What did he say? Did he tell you anything?" She pulls away and sits beside his pillow. A thousand words scatter from my mind. I can't tell her she had wings. I can't even wrap my own mind around it right now. It's too many shocking things at once. She folds her hands into his and waits for me to answer.

"He said you didn't need the memory of his last breath."

Her eyes darken as more tears fall. "Oh, Papa. That was *my* choice. Not yours." She shakes her head at him. "What were his last words?"

I consider it and realize he said the stupidest thing. "It doesn't matter."

"It matters to me. Please, Tolliver."

I slump and reiterate the story of Rylan hurting himself all the time and his laughing. "I told him no more funny talk. And he tried to rhyme with me saying, 'Oh, poppycock.'"

Kava blurts a strange laughing cry that I don't understand. Tears stream down her face as she chuckles. It is so strange. She is laughing and crying? Pain and joy at the same time.

"That was a rhyming game we used to play when I was little. I would say something, and he would reply with a rhyme." She wipes the tears from her cheeks and sits up a little straighter. "I guess he won that round."

Her sad smile is so beautiful it makes my heart ache. I love her glassy brown eyes, rosy cheeks, smooth pale skin, and rounded belly.

I guess it doesn't matter what happens. As long as we're together, we can do anything. And I guess I should stop denying the fact that I'm Healer Kava's apprentice.

26

Distinct Crack

LEDGER

"Ledger? Oh, there you are!" Hollis squeals. "It's happening!"

It's early morning, and Hollis is dragging me from my comfortable bed. I am groggy, and my right eye won't open all the way. "What happened?"

"It's just starting; you didn't miss anything. Come on. Put a shirt on. Wake up your face. Let's go!" She bounces in my blurry vision.

I'm confused by all the words, sorting through them in my mind. *What is she so excited about?* She flings a tunic at me and it slaps me across the face, jolting me wider awake.

I groan as I slip it over my head. "What's going on?"

"The egg—the egg is hatching!" Hollis presses her little white teeth together in an overzealous smile.

"Oh." I stretch and yawn as I pull myself off the mattress on the floor.

She darts around behind me, and before I can resist, she is pushing me toward the door. I squint at the morning sunlight as she drags me through the courtyard and past the fountain where the old mule's manure is piling up. A pale yellow flower blooms in the middle of the muddy, nasty mound.

It takes me until we come around the bend of the last few steps down to the dragon's cave to wake up all the way. Her excitement is infectious and my heart races with delight as I follow her down and around the cage. Tristeh is curled up in the corner and Wilhelm is missing.

"Where's the green dragon?" I ask.

"Oh, Hellwig took him out so he doesn't eat the baby. Papa dragons are known for eating their young. Sometimes. I don't know if it's all the time. But he wanted to be sure it didn't happen." She yanks open the cage door, and we slip inside.

A hiss emanates from the corner. Hollis says, "Tristeh, you're fine. Ledger won't eat your baby. Not all boys are mean."

I chuckle to myself and follow her to the back wall where Tristeh's red, scaly body is wrapped around the pile of rocks. Her egg is nestled among them.

The only other animal I've seen birthed is a cow. It is disgusting and messy. I wonder if this will be disgusting and messy.

"Look, Ledger." She points at the egg. "There was one crack, but now there's two!"

It is a gray, stone-like egg with lighter and darker parts, but there is a distinct crack down the middle and another branching out from it.

I'm surprised it has taken until spring to show any signs of hatching. "Interesting," I say. "How long until it comes out?"

"Hellwig says a couple of hours." She kneels down and

gets settled in view of the egg. Seems I will be here a while. My stomach rumbles, and I wish I had grabbed something to eat on the way down.

"Hellwig has been teaching me what happens when the baby is here. How to raise it. He says I can help train her—or him." She giggles and claps her hands.

I smile at her excitement. I love seeing her this way. The energy rolls off her as I sit cross-legged next to her on the cold stone floor.

There is a strange scratching inside the egg, and Hollis gasps. "Did you hear that?"

I shush her so we can listen for it again. Then another crack forms, branching out from the biggest one down the middle. It too gets larger, almost wrapping around the back side.

We sit in the quiet for quite some time. Hollis bursts with words, chattering about all the stuff Hellwig told her about raising dragons and training them. My stomach growls loudly, and she looks at it. "Whoa, are you okay? Are you eating yourself from the inside?"

"Yes, I'm very hungry," I say. "Want to go get some breakfast? Although it might be midday meal by now."

"Naw, you can just bring me something." She changes sitting positions on the floor.

I kiss the top of her head and walk toward the gate. Someone enters the cave above. It's Brecken, Hollis's father. "I came to check on my girl."

"Papa, it's almost time," she calls from beside the beast and her egg. Tristeh whines. Hollis says something encouraging until something distracts her.

"Oh my lands!" her voice stops me in my tracks. Another crack spreads around the egg, and I scoot back to them. Another crack, and another. "It's happening, it's happening!"

Something slimy protrudes, then it separates and opens like a tiny lizard mouth. Tiny white teeth glow in the darkness of the cavern. As I step closer, Tristeh puts her nose to the egg and inspects the emerging baby.

"Should I help it?" Hollis asks.

"No, they should know what to do." I take my position next to her as the egg cracks again, this time fully in half. A front claw stretches forward.

"Is it a black dragon?" Hollis marvels at the creature. "I can't tell. But when they're wet, they always look darker."

The other claw emerges and pushes the top part of the egg off. Hollis sighs, and I notice there are tears in her eyes. The baby dragon stretches again and pushes itself forward. A little pink tongue slithers out.

Hollis crawls forward on her knees and snuggles up against Tristeh's tail. She slowly reaches over with her hand and brushes a few pieces of the shell off the baby's head. "There you go."

Its tongue flicks out, and she lets it lick her hand.

"I'm your grandmother, little darling," she says.

It leans forward at her touch. She rubs her hand over its smooth head and through the slime. "Come on. You can come out now."

It holds its head up shakily and jerks toward her. Releasing both of its front legs, it rests for a moment, breathing in and out very quickly. I scoot closer and notice its eyes are sealed over with some sort of white patch.

"Is it blind?"

"They are born blind," she whispers. "Tristeh has to lick that off." Then all at once, the baby dragon spurts from the egg into Hollis's lap. Its gossamer wings unfold, and its tail uncurls twice as long as its body.

"Oh my, oh my!" she sputters in between giggles. "Oh, it's red!" She lifts to show a faint glow of red along its back. "Tristeh dear, your baby is red! Red is the best!" She snuggles with the slimy dragon and kisses it on the head. It takes up all the room in her lap, and I bet if she stood up, it would be as tall as her chest from nose to tail.

It pants as if it's expended all its energy. Hollis brushes off the goo and rubs the white over its eyes. It comes off easily in her hand. "Gah!" she exclaims. "I didn't know it would do that." She holds out her hand unsure what to do with it, and the baby licks it out of her palm. She giggles. "I guess it's my baby now. I fed her first, Tristeh!" She wipes off the other eye and feeds it to the newborn.

"How we doing in here?" Hellwig calls as he walks in without Wilhelm. He joins Brecken, who is now standing at the gate of the cage.

"It's here!" she calls. "Look!" She reveals the baby dragon in her lap. As the light hits the drying scales, it appears more and more red.

"That is dandy!" Hellwig cheers. "I sent Zander out with Wilhelm so I could check on you."

"How do you know if it's a boy or a girl?" Hollis searches its body.

"Bring it here," he says with a wave. He saunters toward the wall and retrieves a torch.

Hollis struggles standing up with the hefty beast in her arms. I help her stand by putting my hands under her arm. Tristeh stirs restlessly behind us. I cringe with worry that she will sneak up on us.

Hollis walks boldly to the gate, and Hellwig hands me the torch. "Give me the tail, and hold this behind it. We are looking for bulges behind the vent."

He lifts the tail and holds it up to the light. "Males have two, females have one," Hellwig explains, then points to the spot.

"It only has one." Brecken points with a smile.

Hollis cheers, "A girl!"

Hellwig drops the tail as Hollis shuffles back to Tristeh and the broken egg. "You have a baby girl!"

"Do you realize how rare that is?" Hellwig calls after her. I hand him back the torch. "We only have a female once in every ten births or so."

"Why?" I ask.

"Females are more aggressive. There can only be one in a group of males. They'll eventually kill each other." He gives me a look, like he's seen it before.

"How long does she have before that happens?" Brecken asks.

"Months. Maybe a year, if we're lucky."

"They won't kill each other," Hollis says like she's talking to a baby. "You won't try to kill your mum, will you?" She stops next to Tristeh. The mother dragon's head is high, nostrils flaring. "Come here, Tristeh. Kiss your baby."

"Hollis!" Hellwig shouts. "Tristeh is taking an aggressive stance. Get out of there!" Before he finishes his warning,

Tristeh lets out a hiss and jolts to her feet.

Hollis's eyes are big, and instead of darting for the door, she runs toward me as I race to her. I help carry the little lizard away from her mother. Tristeh caws loudly and prances in the corner. With how untrained she is, I'm surprised she has the will to not attack Hollis with the baby.

As we scramble out the door, Hellwig slams it behind us and latches it tight. Tristeh fills the room and our ears with a terrifying screech. Hollis screams, startled by the noise. It rattles me to my core, and I have a hard time catching my breath.

Brecken rubs a hand on her back in comfort, while gazing at the scaly infant.

"I guess not all mothers and daughters have a good relationship," she says, panting and holding the baby tight to her chest. "But Grammy will be your best friend."

Her resolve is shocking. I can't believe she can be so carefree and playful. I swallow back the fear that chokes me and soak in her lightheartedness.

"I'm going to call you Ruby," Hollis says. "That was my grandmother's name. Right, Papa?" Her father nods with a proud smile. "And her name matches her red scales."

She beams at me. I can't wait to see the look on her face when we have our own children. I ache to be back in Balfour, to start our life together. I wonder if her father would allow us to marry on Ellery.

"We'll have to keep Ruby upstairs," Hollis says to Hellwig.

"Yes, but my only advice is to keep her in a closed room, and do not—under any circumstances—sleep in the same room with her. You could end up being her breakfast," Hellwig says without a trace of a smile. One fluffy white eyebrow raises.

Hollis laughs, and he clears his throat.

She shakes her head and wipes the grin off her face. "Yes, sir."

***

Hellwig leads us to the tavern on the main floor of the castle. It is directly across from the main dining hall and slightly smaller. It's about eighteen paces long and probably ten paces wide. The main difference is there are three windows with shutters and a door. It can be secured with a little work, turning it into a home for a hatchling. My father joins us with a hammer and a handful of nails.

"This is the perfect place to keep her, as long as the windows and door stay closed." Hellwig pushes a pair of shutters over the first window overlooking the courtyard.

My father hands me the nails as he gets to work nailing the first set of shutters closed. The metal-on-metal pounding echoes through the empty stone room. The only distinguishing feature is the stone fireplace built into the far wall to the right. Last year, I sat in this room near the fire, sewing the holes in my flying contraption. A lifetime ago. I wonder what happened to it. The Ellerians probably threw it out or burned it when they imprisoned us.

Hollis stands near the door, cradling the red dragon. Its tail hangs past Hollis's waistline, and its wings lay against her chest, almost touching her chin. It's about as big as a full-grown rooster, but definitely more dangerous. It licks its sharp teeth as Hollis pets its scaly head.

Alouette steps through the doorway, with her wings folded tightly behind her. She looks at Hollis with curiosity. "What are you doing in here?" Before Hollis can answer, Alouette notices the hatchling. "The egg hatched?"

Hollis offers the dragon to her. "Her name is Ruby. Do you want to hold her?"

The little lizard squirms and nearly falls out of her grasp.

"Shut the door so she doesn't escape," Hollis says.

Alouette steps through the doorway. But before she can push the door shut, Ruby wriggles out of Hollis's embrace, lands, and scurries out the door. They both squawk and race after the little red dragon.

I dart to the door, wondering if they need help rounding her up.

Ruby runs straight for the mule, who hee-haws in alarm. It thrashes, pulling on the lead rope tied to the fountain. Its back hooves flail in the air.

Hollis dives and catches Ruby, a few feet from the mule. "No, no, Ruby. We don't eat friends."

Alouette catches up with her. "You caught her in time. There's no telling what she would have done to him."

"Yes, let's make sure that doesn't happen ever again." She turns, heading back to the tavern gulping air and red-faced.

"And let's send someone to fetch her something to eat." Alouette reaches out to pet its red scales.

"Yes," Hollis says and whispers something to Ruby. "Thanks, Alouette."

Alouette smiles and dismisses the thank you.

"I'll probably need a lot of help caring for this wild, little thing. Would you like to help me?"

As they enter the tavern and push the door shut tightly, Alouette says, "I'd be glad to help."

"Ledger, nails?" my father asks.

I snap to attention and walk briskly back to his side. He takes several metal nails from my hand and hammers the last shutter closed. When the task is complete, he gives his attention to the fireplace at the far end. Belamy delivered several armloads of wood before we arrived.

"Would you like this lit?" My father glances over at Hollis.

"Not yet." She sets the dragon on the floor in the middle of the room.

Alouette kneels next to it and runs her fingers along Ruby's spine. Hellwig joins us around the hatchling, watching it squirm and crawl in circles around our ankles.

My father kneels beside Alouette. "What else do you need for her in here?"

Hellwig scans the empty space. All the tables and chairs that used to crowd this room were removed in Balfour. "She'll need water and meat," Hellwig says. "A lot of meat. A growing dragon eats endlessly. Never turn your back or assume they're not hungry."

"Good advice," my father says. "I'll fetch a basin. I have one in the smithy shop. I'll need an extra hand carrying it though."

"Can I help you?" Alouette's brown eyes connect with his. I smile at the fact that she and my father have been spending time together.

“That would be great,” he says and rises from the floor. He holds a hand out to her, and she takes it.

Her wings spread out as she gets up and follows him to the door. It’s interesting how her wings show her emotion. The wider they are, the happier she is. I am glad to see her happy.

Delineation Day 27

TOLLIVER

Delineation Day, the ceremonial retelling of Balfour's history and spring festival, comes quickly. The trees are in full bloom, and the spring breeze flicks petals in the air and wafts the sweet smell of cherry blossoms as I stir a pot on the hearth. Kava comes down from our bedroom dressed in a sky-blue dress over a crisp white underdress. Her pregnant belly protrudes beneath the gathers of fabric. The sleeves are short, and the skirt touches each step as she hobbles down. Though Kava is not done being sad, her cheeks are rosy, and her eyes are bright.

We buried Clovis next to his wife last week. Kava is handling his death with grace. As I stare at her and my unborn child, I realize I'll have to help deliver our baby without Clovis around. The weight of the thought makes my chest tighten. She is due in a couple of weeks. I need to make sure Neelie will be ready at a moment's notice.

"That should be done by now," Kava says, waving a hand. "Pull it off the fire." She snaps me out of my worries.

"I know what I'm doing." I put on a smile and kiss her

cheek as she walks toward the tented medical ward out back. "No, no. I've already checked on them. Everyone out there is fine. We must leave for the festivities."

"I just wanted to say good morning." She pulls open the back door. She stops to gaze at her father's empty bed under the stairs.

Lost in thought, she frowns.

With a sigh, she steps out the door and greets her patients one by one as though they are all her children. *She will be a great mother.* A nagging feeling in my chest heightens; many women haven't survived childbirth.

I pull the iron pot from the fire and set it on a pad on the table. Steam wafts in my face when I remove the lid. I wipe my hands on a nearby towel, tuck in my tunic, and slip on my pastel-green longcoat before heading out the back door. "Ready?"

The morning sun lights up the tent and her face. "Ready." She gathers the basket she packed last night for any just-in-case situations. I pull it from her grip and carry it for her.

We walk arm in arm out of the medical tent and along the paths crisscrossing through Balfour. It is a brisk morning, and she shivers. Before I have the chance to give her my longcoat, we are approached by a girl with white wings.

"Good morning, Kailani," I greet her.

My father arrives shortly behind.

"Good morning," Kailani says. "I thought we would walk with you for our first Delineation Day." She swishes around in a pale pink dress with no sleeves and a neckline that rises high at the nape of her neck. Ellerian formal wear is interestingly different than Balfour's.

Tiberius gives a short bow. He too is wearing a longcoat, but his is light gray over black trousers and a pink tunic, matching neatly with our springtime event.

"You two look lovely," he says, nodding at Kava.

Kava thanks him, and we make our way to the village square. There is an unbelievable number of people milling about. There are more wings than I've ever seen in one space.

The four pillars of the village square are adorned with spring foliage and flowers. At the center, various musicians play together: drums, lute, a viola with bow, and several flutes and flageolets. Their song is a call to ceremony.

Suddenly, a loud dissonant tone clashes with the music, and the musicians to stop. A shofar blast carries loud and long. It blares three times. Guardians leap to the air.

"Is this an exercise?" I ask Tiberius.

The worried expression on his face gives me the answer before his words. "No." He lets Kailani's hand go and darts in the air after all his men.

"Kailani, take Kava back to the cottage," I say in a rush to follow. "I'll be back." I dart between startled well-dressed people through the square. The guardians all fly southeast, and I follow them on foot through the paths out of Balfour.

By the time I reach the edge of the last cottage, I catch sight of a gathering of men on the crest of the eastern border across the river. They are dressed in red leather with metal masks over their faces. *They've returned.*

I put my hand to my side, where my sword should be. But it's not there.

I cannot hear what is being said as half the guardians land before them, and the other half keep to the air with arrows poised, aggressively protecting our village. The guardians on the ground bear swords and hold their position as Tiberius lands behind them. Someone hands him a weapon and speaks to him with rushed words.

The tribesmen on the knoll hold their ground. There are only two on horses and two on foot. They hold their swords out, ready for a fight. Who knows how many there are on the backside of that hill? I worry our Ellerian soldiers won't hold them off. *I need to protect Kava.* As I turn to find her again, there is shouting on the hill.

The four enemy warriors advance, and Tiberius raises his sword, shouting the word, "Fire."

The guardians let their arrows fly. A dozen arrows buzz through the air. Both men on foot fall, as well as one horseman. They crumple and stop moving.

Tiberius raises his sword again, declaring something I can't hear. The guardians on the ground move forward swiftly.

They encircle the tribesman on the horse, and no one comes over the hill. I stand up straighter.

No one else is coming?

The man on the horse swings his sword as several guardians overtake him. The clang of metal on metal rings out until a silence falls on the valley. Tiberius commands several companies of guardians to search for more enemy warriors throughout the woods. He sends the rest of to set up a perimeter around the village.

***

Hours later, we are called from our homes to the village center by the dinging of the bell. Music fills the square once again. I have the sensation that I've already lived this same moment as I walk beside Kava, her arm looped in mine. This time her eyes are full of questions.

Once the people have gathered again, the flageolet trills high and then stops.

"Welcome Balfourians and Ellerians," Jubal bellows above the din. As the people hush, he announces, "I bid you a good Delineation Day. As you know, the savages returned this morning. We conquered them quite swiftly. There were only four men left. They were bent on avenging their kinsmen. No doubt due to the damage exacted by those we sent to rescue our men."

So many thoughts rush through my mind, and I'm suspicious that this isn't over. There couldn't have been only four of them. They must be hiding deep in the woods waiting for a weakness in our defenses.

Tiberius steps onto the platform. He catches my eye as he connects with everyone around the wide space. "If I may, Elder Jubal."

Jubal waves a hand at him, like he is getting his toes stepped on.

"Thank you." Tiberius's wings spread wider and wider as he speaks. "We have searched the woods on all sides. There is no sign that there are any more of this tribe for at least a day's march. We will continue to hold the line to make sure we are all safe." He tilts his head at Jubal and exits the platform.

"Let us get back to our festivities," Jubal announces.

"There are no weddings this season but several of our children will receive their names. Take a moment to find your family members, and we shall follow the path to the Hundred Harvest sacred grounds."

A drum begins, calling us to order, and the musicians play an upbeat marching song. We follow the path of pink, white, and red petals leading westward out of the village. The trees are varying shades of green with budding leaves and white flowers. The sky is clear blue, and the morning sun is at our back, pointing the way with our shadows.

We enter the Hundred Harvest sacred grounds to find it still beautifully decorated. Tables are adorned with white cloths. Lanterns hang all around. Though the sacred tree is dead and gone, the grassy clearing is beautiful and welcoming. But after this morning, I feel like something bad will happen again at any minute, and I don't trust the peacefulness.

The afternoon drifts by as we share a delicious meal of Balfourian and Ellerian dishes alike. Our people are becoming more of one people with each passing moon. Ellerians are incorporated in almost everything we do in Balfour. Building houses, protecting the village, even helping in the medical ward.

Sitting with our combined families, we eat together. I think about Kava to going into labor. A heaviness spreads from my chest to my shoulders. Her very life hangs on whether or not I can deliver my own child.

Kava squeezes my hand. "You're tapping," she whispers. "Are you troubled?"

My heel stops tapping against the leg of my seat. "I'm

fine."

I don't want Kava to worry about me when she's lost her father and is about to bring a child into this world.

I feel disjointed. I jumped to action this morning with the perimeter battalion. I knew exactly what to do, and it felt good to run toward the action. But deep down, I know I didn't belong there.

It doesn't take long for the evening to set in. We all gather around the large pile of wood and kindling for the evening bonfire. Grandmother—Queen Huyana—promised the true version of the ceremonial retelling of Balfour's history. She has been busy over these months organizing the council and expansion of Balfour.

Elder Jubal and Advisor Tiberius walk through the crowd, each with a flickering torch. They raise them together, then toss them on the massive stack of wood. People settle in the grass beneath the starry sky as the last bit of light fades from the horizon. The growing flames spread throughout the bonfire and cast an orange glow on everyone's face.

Smiling, Grandmother pulls a stool beside the bonfire overlooking the people. The majority of Balfourians are seated on the ground, with some Ellerians scattered throughout. Many remain standing or pull a stool over to sit and listen.

Grandmother clears her throat and explains to the Ellerians our tradition of retelling Balfour's history today. "Now it is time to tell the true story. It is true that it began with Balfour and Laurel. Their love was beautiful, but they did not come from the west to settle with twelve families. During the reign of King Lazarus, my great-grandfather, he made a decree banishing the wingless from the floating island of Ellery. He decided they were no longer suitable to live in the sky with their kinsman. Laurel, being wingless, was forced from her home and away from her winged husband, Balfour. He fought to keep her aboard the island, but no one crosses a king. And because the winged Ellerians were not permitted to leave the island without permission, he was not allowed to join her on the ground."

Sadness is etched in the corners of Grandmother's mouth and between her eyebrows. "So, he chose to have his wings removed and live on the ground with his wife. They called it Ellery's colony. But the truth is, it was a wingless prison colony. The Ellerians have been a very exclusive people, never allowing ground-dwellers to join them in the sky. When children without wings started being born on Ellery, the king believed there was ground-dweller blood infecting his people. He decided to eradicate it."

Grandmother sighs and folds her hands in her lap as she continues, "They created this colony and forced the wingless to leave their families. Wingless mothers, taken from winged children. Families were torn apart."

Around the grassy area, tears reflect the light of the bonfire. I can't believe our history has been kept from us. It's hard to believe our beginnings were this terrible. It is a far cry from the beautiful story told every Delineation Day for as long as I can remember.

Her voice fills the clearing as hundreds of people listen in. "The colonists were forced to work the ground and supply Ellery with the crops they could grow in this fertile soil. The Ellerians would return during harvest, and they'd feast in the colony, then take what they needed." Her disgust shows as she points southward, where our freshly tilled fields lay.

"But everything changed the year I was born. I was the first wingless princess. My parents loved me dearly, that I do remember. My grandfather, King Rayven… I was his favorite." She chuckles and a few people take the chance to laugh with her as she eases her way through her story. "King Rayven tried to fight his father's law—for me. He wanted to keep me on Ellery, but the people began to rise up against him. During that year's harvest feast, my mother sneaked me away. She hid me in the belly of a boat that left the village when I was four. The captain of the ship didn't return me to where I belong until I was nineteen."

She sighs and looks up at the starry sky. "In those years I was gone, there was fighting and bloodshed. From the stories I heard, it was the worst fifteen years this village had ever known. King Rayven went mad and declared war on the colony.

"But from that time on, this was no longer their colony. As the older generation passed away, the parents were telling their children a different story. A story of lies about Ellery and the origins of the Balfourian people. As the previous generation died, so did the truth." She pauses for a long while. The fire lights only half her face. My younger siblings listen in. Killian is enraptured by the story. Mila has tears in her eyes as she holds little Hazel. I touch my mother's arm, and she gives me a somber smile.

"In all those harvests, Ellery would dispose of their wingless children. I would meet a midwife out beyond the lake. We would bury the dead. For the rare few who survived,

I'd carry them into Balfour."

A glistening tear streaks down her cheek. "Today is the day of forgiveness. We can mourn the past, but we must not hold a grudge. We were all victims of cruelty in one way or another, whether under the law or the rule of a king. But the time of cruelty is over."

I stare into the wildly flickering flames of the bonfire as she describes how they are developing a better system of community on the council and will implement it soon. I see the benefits of both, but knowing Grandmother, she's planning something different. Something unusual.

I swallow all the worries about the council, the perimeter battalion, and my child coming into this world. I will do what I must do: deliver my child, and when they call upon me, I will join the council, delivering our village into the next phase of its life.

Family 28

ALOUETTE

Everyone is buzzing around Ellery, getting ready for Hartwynnian Day. My most favorite day of the year. I put on the beautiful dress made by the Hartwynnians. Their tailor supplied us with a delightful change of clothes to be able to join the celebration in style. I was given a pale green dove-down silk dress. I love the dark green swirls around the bottom of the floor-length hem.

I pin my hair up in a twist and let it spill onto the top of my head in organized ringlets. My mother used to wear her hair this way for Hartwynnian Day. I smile at the thought of her.

"Come on, Alouette. We're missing the parade!" Belamy calls out from the courtyard.

I slip on my shoes and grab my winter cloak, stopping short. I don't need it anymore. It's plenty warm, and it should be considerably warmer on the ground. Everything bubbles inside of me with joy, nervousness, and trepidation. I'm not exactly sure how to feel.

I step out on the balcony and inhale the warm, spring air.

It is full of pollen and possibilities. I step off the balcony and into the open air. My wings carry me to the courtyard below.

Belamy's eyes light up as he watches me descend. I can't believe how my heart flutters. I never felt this way toward Dayson. Belamy has shed his winter garb and guardian weapons for a bright white tunic tied neatly at the nape of his neck and pale gray long pants that look as though they have been pressed. His bronze skin and black wings contrast strikingly against his clothing. He reaches out a hand with an elegant bow.

"You look beautiful."

I take his hand, blushing. "Thank you." The butterflies in my stomach intensify.

He escorts me out the front entrance of the castle, down the long path of stairs to where the last few Balfourians await a ride. "Who are we taking down?" I ask.

"We are not working today. We are celebrating. Swarley, Zander, Estefano, and Terrowin are taking care of them." Belamy winks at me as we reach the last step.

I wave at Ledger and Fergus as we walk off the edge of Ellery and descend to the ground together. My heart hasn't stopped its excited rhythm, and I take a few deep breaths to convince it to calm down and to not get its hopes too high.

I notice Hollis waiting below with her father along with several others.

"Would you save me a dance this evening?" Belamy asks.

"Yes," I reply, before our voices are drowned out by the celebration.

The smell of lilies wafts in my face as we descend toward

the flower-lined path winding toward the city of Hartwynn. The music gets louder the closer we come. Below, there are enormous mattress-sized drums with two Hartwynnians at each, pounding out an exciting, anticipatory rhythm.

We touch down and fold our wings back. A Hartwynnian on either side of us receives us with a hug and a flower necklace. Due to Belamy's height, he must bow low to accept his welcoming gift from her. I recognize one of them immediately. It's Clementine. For many years we attended the Hartwynnian Ball together. She pined over Mathias, and I encouraged her to dance with him. I wonder if she married him.

"Welcome back to Hartwynn, Miss Alouette," Clementine says, who adorns me with a necklace of plumeria and carnations. Her skin is a deep blue and hair a dark brown. The dress she wears is a lighter shade of blue with white lace along the bodice and bottom hem. I adore everything about how the Hartwynnians dress.

I've never known why their skin is such unusual shades. I've seen many of the civilizations around the rest of the world; we are all some shade between my pale pink skin and Belamy's deep umber. But here in Hartwynn, they have blue, red, yellow, or green skin with dark brown or black hair. *Are they born like this? Do they dye themselves for the celebration?*

Clementine takes my hand and leads me forward, as does the red-skinned man who leads Belamy. They wave to the people lining the streets, encouraging their cheers. Our names are announced loudly somewhere down the parade route. "Welcome Alouette of Ellery! Welcome Belamy of

Ellery!" The crowd raises their voices in an excited roar. I smile at the beautiful, colorful people and wave at a blue child with a small, solid-blue flag in her hand. She jumps up and down, waving back.

As we pass the first set of drums, my heart matches its rhythm. I walk in step with it all, with the drums, with Belamy. He is soaking in the praise and joyful welcome. He lifts his black wings, making himself appear taller and more radiant than I've ever seen him. I blush at the thought.

We pick up the pace as more names are announced, "Welcome Ledger of Balfour! Welcome Fergus of Balfour!" Then Hollis and Brecken join the procession alongside Ledger and his father.

"Welcome Zander of Ellery! Welcome Swarley of Ellery!"

The cheers reach deafening heights and gradually taper off. The drums pick up their beat and lead us down the path between them. We reach the dancers, twirling in bold colors matching their skin. My heart fills with their joy and acceptance. They spin and spin around us, ruffles brushing our sides. They clap and dance and wave large colorful flags in the air. The amount of color all around is more vibrant than I remember.

I catch a glimpse of Hollis and Ledger walking hand in hand several yards back. She is wide-eyed and happy. Her jaw drops, her hand goes to her cheek, and she says something to Ledger. His easy smile and gentle nod tell me he's enjoying the performance as well.

The rhythm picks up as we head toward the castle on the hill. The voices rise in the Hartwynnian anthem. I know the words, but I don't sing along. Their harmonies dip and rise through the air.

We leave the twirling dancers behind as we make our way up the sloped walkway. The sky fills with petals falling all around us.

We reach the castle gate where there is a platform set up in the middle of the road. The King of Hartwynn, Nivek, stands with his hands folded across his chest. He is an elderly man with crinkly blue skin that is quite faded compared to the younger blues along the parade route. His kingly robes are a brushed golden velvet with a thick, white fur hem. His vest is a midnight blue with golden buttons down the front and gold stripes from neck to waistline. They shimmer in the morning sun. His slender pants are tucked neatly into calf-high boots that are shined to a blackish-blue gleam.

He is flanked by his red son, Nicholae, and red Queen Riyah. I avoid eye contact with her because the last time we were here, she was quite vicious to my father. I sigh and push my irritation aside.

We've caught up with the rest of the Balfourians and my countrymen as we stop at the foot of the platform. Ledger and Hollis approach to our right, then Zander and Swarley join us on our left. The drums escalate, then come to an immediate halt with a loud boom.

All the people around the castle gate bow toward the platform. I too hold my skirts and curtsy. I notice Ledger gaping in awe and reach over, pulling him downward. He comes to with a jerk and bows before the King of Hartwynn.

"Welcome, Ellerians," King Nivek says. Cheers go up all around us as people rise from their respectful positions. He raises his blue hands to shush them. "I am curious as to what has happened to your people over these years. The last we saw you there was a new king, the next you were missing, and this year you are down to a humble few, some of whom do not have wings. What, my dear ones, has happened?"

Out of the corner of my eye, Ledger turns toward me expectantly. I clear my throat and step forward. "Your Majesty. Much has happened, and I would love to tell you the entire, long story. But for the sake of brevity, you must know our people have decided to settle on the ground."

King Nivek smiles wide. "I was worried you had been conquered or worse, slaughtered. I was going to ask who this enemy is so we may avenge you and vanquish your enemy."

I place a hand to my heart. "You are gracious and kind. I am honored—*we* are honored to have your allegiance."

"If your people have moved to the ground, then why are you and these wingless ones still on Ellery?"

I haven't yet said this in a language Ledger understands. He doesn't know what I've been doing when I've spoken to the different people we've traded with. The Hartwynnians speak our language, so now Ledger will hear the full truth. "We are ambassadors and merchants between our new home on the ground and the peoples of this world. We will continue to trade our goods and bring back the commodities to which we are accustomed."

"Ahh, yes," the king says. His eyes brighten. "We have our tribute ready for you, but if it is too much, we can divide it among our people."

Something shifts. I don't know if it's his tone, or the way he says it. *Are his people starving? Are they giving away too much?*

I plan my words carefully. "Your Majesty is correct. We do not need such a generous tribute this year. May we have a private conversation to make the necessary adjustments?" I give a short curtsy.

"What a delightful idea." He flicks one finger at the man standing off stage to his right. He then signals the flag-bearers. They lift their flags in the air and swirl them over their heads. The drums pick up, and the petals begin to fall around us.

Ledger touches my elbow. "What is happening? We're merchants now?"

"We've always been, Ledger. It was the only explanation that would keep other people off the island, knowing we are still willing to trade with them. If we are going to keep Ellery to ourselves, we must keep this up."

Leaning away, his eyes dart here and there in thought. The king descends the backside of the platform. One after the other my people ascend, wave at the Hartwynnians, and follow the king to the castle. The Balfourians follow along with our performance. When it's my turn, I wave and blow a kiss, my usual salute to my favorite city in all the world. I worry these big changes on Ellery will ruin what we have in Hartwynn.

Hopefully, they will continue to honor us for saving their people all those years ago. I remember the stories as I take the steps off the back of the platform.

It was before I was born. King Paxton of Hartwynn was a young king, new to power. An enemy to the north tried to take the throne from him and chose the wrong time of year to attack. My people helped defend their fortress and outlying towns. They were losing ground before we arrived. As the story goes, Queen Vasilia jumped to their rescue without even being asked. She sent out guardians in groups of ten to defend their small villages and nearly a hundred around their capitol city. The king was grateful, and she didn't stay to lay claim to anything—land or otherwise. Every year since, we've been given this celebration and extravagant gifts.

A thought stops me. *Vasilia must have been Queen Huyana's sister*. I watch Ledger following Hollis through the front gate of the castle. *He will be my king one day.* Tears sting my eyes, and I don't know why.

I blink them away and lean into Belamy, sliding my fingers between his. He squeezes my hand and meets my eyes with a wide grin and a raised eyebrow.

***

After the feast and the dancing, we climb the stairs of the castle's keep, the tall fortress at the city's center, and the best view of the night sky. Clementine takes each step at my side. She hasn't stopped talking since I asked her about Mathias at the ball. "We've been married for two years, and our daughter is one year old now. It is all thanks to you."

I shake my head, but before I can object, she continues.

"Yes, it was you who made me brave enough to talk to him. Ever since that day, we've been inseparable." She turns to him on the stairs and smiles at his green-skinned face.

By the time I emerge from the stairs ahead of the rest of my friends, the sun has dipped beyond the western horizon.

The sky is fading from purple to orange. Clementine's words fill my mind and heart with hope.

The Keep is the innermost and highest part of the palace inside the castle walls. There is another castle gate to the north built in a tall square with jagged gaps to defend the fortress. The stone outer walls extend between three circular flanking towers until they reach the front gate. I glide my eyes along the western wall. Crowds of people stand all across the top of the walls and the towers to get the best view of the sky for the pinnacle of today's celebration: sky flames.

I stand against the stone railing when someone approaches. Figuring it is Belamy, I turn to say *hello*.

My eyes fall upon Ledger. He is giving me a gentle smile. "It's nice to see you so happy."

I consider how I feel, and he's right. I am happy. "Thank you, Ledger. I'm glad to have you as a friend." I peek at our friends behind him, who are gaping at the castle below and the open sky above. "I'm grateful for all of them too. It's nice to have so many friends."

"Alouette, we are your family," he says and guides me to face them. "By blood or by choice, we are family. And we chose you."

I smile at each person. Hollis giggles and is counting the stars as they start to appear in the sky. Belamy, who competes to count the stars before her, is smiling and pointing, unaware of how much I love him. The thought sends a thrill through my soul.

Swarley, Zander, and Estefano stand side by side, hands in their pockets and chatting about something funny Swarley said. Ryllis shivers and threads her arm through Bernhard's.

Behind them, several sets of wings mingle with the rescued men of Balfour.

Standing beside me, Fergus holds my gaze for a long time until he wraps an arm around my shoulders in a short, fatherly hug. I feel cared for, protected. Their acceptance surges through me, and tears well in my eyes.

I gaze up at Ledger beside me. "I'm so sorry for what I said to you in Balfour," I confess.

He gives me a quizzical look.

"I said you didn't know me. That was harsh of me to say."

There is a silence between us for a few sad moments.

He sighs. "I forgave you for that while we were still in Balfour. But you were right. I didn't know you. Everyone grows and changes. But you must continue to let people in so they can know the newest version of you."

I raise my eyebrows and smile. *How can he be so forgiving?* "Thank you, Ledger. I not sure I deserve your goodness."

As the others overhear our conversation, they step closer in a tightly knit circle one after the other.

"It doesn't matter what you think you deserve. I love—*we* love you. And we'll never let you go," Ledger says, as Hollis ducks her head under his arm and snuggles close to him. "Thank you for allowing me know you better."

"Me too," Hollis says.

"And me too," Belamy says, stepping beside me as the first sky flame soars through the sky and bursts loudly over our heads.

Ledger is startled by the explosion and squeezes Hollis

tight. I let Belamy wrap his arm around my shoulders as the sky fills with brilliant, colorful explosions. Brilliant red, regal blue, cheerful yellow, and refreshing green.

I want to feel settled and peaceful, but with every boom and crackle, my heart rate speeds up. I resist the urge to cry.

Ledger has given me a family. Something I only ever had with one person: my father. There's a tremendous weight on my chest. I don't want to let them down. I can't shake the feeling that the tide could turn at any second. Maybe if I pretend there is no tide. Maybe if I pretend as though nothing bad could ever happen again, everything will be fine.

29
Wild Beast

LEDGER

With torches lit all the way around the Tavern, I sit in the windowsill against the closed shutters watching Hellwig train Ruby. The firelight reflects like glass off Ruby's red scales. Her green eyes contrast brilliantly against her cherry exterior. The dragon has grown to twice its size in the last four weeks. Its haunches reach Hollis's waist, and its wings stretch over her blonde head.

Each morning, I meet my dear Hollis in the grand dining hall, we eat together, check on Tristeh—who is sulking in the dragon's cave—then return to the Tavern to continue Ruby's training. I've never seen her stick to working on the same thing over and over. Usually she gets bored with tasks within a day or two and must find something else more interesting.

The routine is the same nearly every day. We arrive. Hollis pets Ruby until she's touched every scale, every spike, and every talon. Then Alouette takes a turn petting the dragon, then Hellwig.

"She will learn we are not a threat and to trust our care," Hellwig says.

Hellwig introduced the lead rope several weeks ago. Today, he pulls a muzzle from his satchel.

A nervous thought hits me. "When are they able to breathe fire?" I rise from my seat. "And when are they taught *not* to breathe fire?"

Hellwig arranges the straps of the muzzle as he approaches me. "They are always able. They don't figure it out until they feel threatened. Luckily for us, we can control her surroundings. She won't have to learn about that for quite some time. Next lesson, the muzzle." He winks and struts toward the dragon. He lays the crisscrossed leather cone on her shoulder. He rubs it on her side, like he's cleaning her.

"Can I do that?" Hollis folds her hands in front of her.

"Sure, step to her other side."

Hollis steps around to Ruby's right side, and Hellwig slides the muzzle underneath its folded wings. She rubs Ruby all over with the muzzle, following Hellwig's directions down each leg, down its tail, along the underside, up its neck, and finally near its nose and mouth. Ruby's talons clink on the stone as it gets anxious when Hollis slides the muzzle in place over its closed jaw.

"One. Two. Three. Four. Five." Hellwig counts how long Ruby allows the muzzle to stay in place. Then when it flails back, Hellwig pulls the leather from its mouth. "Good. It took Tristeh months and months to get to five. Ruby is proving to have a better temperament than her mother."

"When can we try to get them together again?" Hollis leans against Ruby, stroking her outstretched wing.

"Never," Hellwig says bluntly. "They should never even be in the same sky together, let alone the same room."

Hollis frowns at him.

Alouette sidles up to Ruby's left side, pulling its other wing out and running her hand the way Hollis is doing. "Sorry, Hollis." They pet the dragon in silence for several long moments. Hellwig packs the leathers in his satchel. He opens the door and pulls in a makeshift cart, hauling Ruby's daily meal through the door.

The dragon jolts but doesn't dart forward. Hellwig pulls the cart to the far wall, near the water basin. Hollis and Alouette tuck its leathery wings against its scales and step slowly away.

Once they are clear, Hellwig whistles once, long and loud. The dragon's wings claw at the air, lifting it from the ground as it flies to its meal. Hellwig steps away from the cart, and Ruby devours the meat like an overly hungry dog.

We exit, leaving the dragon to its treat for a job well done.

"Good work today, lassies." Hellwig waves and saunters off toward the dining hall. "I'll be taking Wilhelm out to hunt today. Would you like to see if Tristeh is ready to leave the cage?"

"Sure," Hollis says, skipping off behind him. Alouette and I watch them go.

"She is really good with dragons," Alouette says. "It's like she's been working with them all her life."

I smile at the thought. "She never met one until she nursed Tristeh back to health last year."

"Has she worked with horses, mules, or anything needing training?" Alouette asks.

I shake my head and give a silly smile. "Just me."

Alouette chuckles. "I would have thought you were the trainer and she the wild beast."

We laugh together for a moment. I do love my little wild cat.

***

"I don't think we should be doing this," I say, feeling anxious and walking slower and slower down the stairs to the dragon's cave. "Tristeh wasn't even ready to leave the cage yesterday."

Hollis descends several stairs ahead, holding Ruby's lead rope. The rope is attached to a harness around her forelegs and back. None of this feels right.

Hollis sighs. "What if Hellwig is wrong? What if they only needed some time to get used to each other. We won't take Ruby into the cage, just to the edge and see what Tristeh does. Hellwig is still hunting with Wilhelm, so it will be fine." Hollis loops the rope in her hands over and over, a sign of nervousness.

My insides are all jumbled together in an anxious hodgepodge. I'm headed into conflict, and I should stop it now before Hollis walks us into an inescapable predicament. But curiosity reduces my logic to a speck. *What if there's a chance?*

I decide to enter the cave before Hollis and the baby dragon, so I scoot alongside them, and down the stairs ahead. I pick up the pace and enter ten or so steps before them. I hurry across the overlook to the edge of the cage and gaze down below. Tristeh is on her feet, hackles raised, and eyes flashing with what I can only figure is alarm. Tristeh opens her powerful jaws with lines of razor-sharp teeth, and a loud hiss emerges.

Then Hollis walks the small red dragon into the room. She has a tight rein on the lead rope, pressing the dragon's shoulder against her hip. She slowly walks to the edge of the platform beside me, with Ruby between us. When Ruby sees her mother, her wings splay out to the sides and her hackles raise, matching Tristeh's stance.

"Ruby, this is your mother. Be a good girl." Hollis keeps one hand on the rope, and the other across Ruby's back.

Down below, Tristeh rears up on her back legs and caws louder than anything I've ever heard. My hands shoot to my ears to block the painful screech.

Hollis leans toward the bars. "Tristeh! Stop it," she reprimands. "This is your baby."

Tristeh beats her wings, and she springs into the air. She flies directly toward us with her talons directed at us. She looks like a falcon coming in for the kill. I flail away from the bars, praying they hold her back. I've never seen her so violent. My heart beats so hard I can barely stay upright.

Tristeh lands on the bars with all four legs clawing at the cage. She screeches as Hellwig enters the other side of the dragon's cave with Wilhelm. "Tristeh!" he shouts. I can barely see him through Tristeh's battering wings. "Hollis? What are you—"

"I'm sorry. I'm sorry. I'm sorry," she cries, yanking the baby dragon away from her mother with the lead rope. Ruby resists and holds her ground beneath the giant mother dragon attacking the bars of the cage. "Ruby, come!"

I dismiss my distaste for touching any animal, let alone a fire-breather, and help Hollis. I push on her shoulder and against her outstretched wing, and so does Hollis. But Ruby doesn't budge. What a strong little beast. She's only the size of a small mule, but the two of us can't move her. Her eyes stay fixed on Tristeh. The only thing that moves are her nostrils, flaring in and out.

Hellwig opens the cage and lets Wilhelm inside, who strides to the water trough in the far corner. Hellwig yells something unintelligible over the racket Tristeh is making. When he flies up the outer stairway, his face is beet red, and his eyebrows have never looked more vicious. "I told you they will never tolerate each other! When will you listen? After you lose a limb? Or your life?"

Ruby holds fast to her position as Hollis and I push her away from her mother.

Hellwig lands in Hollis's breathing space. He joins our plight, yanking the lead rope from Hollis's hand and elbowing her out of the way. He slides a calloused hand around Ruby's shoulders and under her forelegs. "Ledger, grab her around the gut. Hollis, get her tail."

We obey and lift together, pulling her from her statue-like stance. Hellwig nods toward the stairs, and we shuffle around for him to go first. Her muscular body stays frozen in place for ten or twelve steps. As we head up the blackened staircase, she loses her tension and becomes limp in our grasp. I am at the point of dropping her when Hellwig stops and sets her on the stairs. "Never disobey me again. I know you have not committed to being my apprentice, but you might as well have. If you want any contact with these dragons, you will do as I say."

Hollis's eyes well with tears, and I reach for her. "Yes, sir," she says.

As he turns to go, Ruby's throat rumbles, and she yanks from Hellwig's grip. She darts up the stairs, away from us, away from her mother screeching in the cave below.

We all scramble up the stairs behind her. Hollis and Hellwig shout for her to stop. The tink of talons on stone fall silent as we hurry to catch up. I'm out of breath as we emerge from the stairwell.

"I'll check outside, you check the courtyard. Give one whistle, and she should come to you," Hellwig yells as he takes flight toward the grand entrance of the castle.

Before we can make it into the courtyard, there is a terrible ruckus. The mule hee-haw-haw-haws over and over. We dart into the courtyard to find Ruby chasing the mule round and round the circular space. It must have broken free in fear of being eaten. Dudley's mule thrashes its back hooves in the air as Ruby chomps after it. Hollis whistles once, but barely loud enough for anyone to hear.

The poor mule escapes the red dragon's reach for a few moments more as Hollis gives up whistling and darts toward them. I race after her. She should *not* get in the middle of this dangerous pursuit.

People emerge from their daily routines to gawk at the chaos.

Hollis can't run fast enough to catch up with Ruby or the gray mule who puts up its last fight in a fit of loud hee-haws and cambering hooves. Ruby dives for it, talons bared, and her jaw clamps down on the mule's jugular. They both tumble forward in a red and gray swirling mass of scales and fur. Hollis screams. I grab her by the shoulders and stop her from getting any closer.

Hellwig flits through the grand hall and lands beside us. "I should have seen that coming." He walks away shaking his head, reaching for the lead rope. He stands and waits for Ruby to have her fill.

Alouette flies down from her quarters and puts a hand on Hollis. "Are you okay?"

Hollis stands watching wide-eyed in shock. I put my arm around her and kiss the top of her head.

"Alouette, get the door," Hellwig calls.

When Ruby lifts her head from the mule, he tugs on the rope with one whistle. Responding to his training, Ruby walks to the Tavern with Hellwig as Alouette opens the door.

"Hollis, you are no longer permitted to handle Ruby," Hellwig says with a frown. He leads the baby dragon into the room and out of sight.

"You can't tell me to stay away from my own dragon!" she yells back. Her face reddens, and her fists ball up. She races in after him.

Alouette starts to close the door. I push through as Hellwig snaps at her. "Let's not do this in this room."

He removes the lead rope and drags it out of the room. Hollis follows closely behind.

Outside of the Tavern, Hellwig turns on her. His wings whisk air in Hollis's face, causing her hair to blow back. Hellwig says, "You are reckless and thoughtless. Alouette will finish Ruby's training. You can stick with Tristeh; you two are exactly the same." He stalks off.

Hollis whirls around and cries in my arms for a long time. Alouette says, “I’m sorry.” I’m not sure what she has to be sorry about.

30 Not Normal

TOLLIVER

I jolt awake to a quiet whimper. In the dark of night, I reach for Kava. She is not beside me, and I sit up to discern the shadows in the room. The window lights a figure at the end of the bed.

"Kava?"

After a few short exhales she answers, "I'm here."

"You okay?"

"I'm…" She moans trying to get the words out. "The baby's coming. Soon."

My heart responds first, shooting blood straight to my head. I jolt out of bed and scramble around in front of her. Kneeling before her, I put my hands on her belly. It is tight with a contraction. "How long have you been up?"

She lets out a slow breath. "Only a little while."

"What do you need?"

"I need to catch my breath long enough to get downstairs."

"Oh no you don't. We agreed you would deliver up here. Tell me what you need, and I'll get it."

"I'm just so thirsty."

"On it!" I dart from the floor and down the stairs. My body is buzzing with adrenaline as I turn the corner. I grab a cup and before I pour the water pitcher, I decide to bring the whole thing. Otherwise, I'll be running up and down the stairs. I open the cabinet beside the back door and grab a mound of towels and rags. Outside the back door window, the roof of the medical tent glows with morning light. I need to fetch Kailani. She agreed to assist.

Back up the stairs, I set down my armload of stuff, hand Kava the cup, pour the water, and say, "I'll be back."

Before I make it out the door, pitcher in hand, she calls, "Where are you going?"

"I'm fetching my mother."

"It's still early, Toll. I could be laboring for another couple hours, or even days." She winces, either at the contraction or at the thought of laboring for days. "You can get her later."

"No, she should be here from the start." I set the pitcher next to her on the floor and kiss her forehead. "I don't want anything to go wrong. I want you to survive this. I want our son to survive this."

"Oh, you think it's a boy, do you?"

"I have a good feeling." I smile, for real this time.

"Can you light the oil lamp before you go?"

"Anything for you, my love."

When the lamp is lit, the pain in her eyes is evident as another contraction comes. She tenses her whole body and leans away from the pain.

"Breathe, Kava."

She inhales deeply then lets it out slowly. Once the contraction passes, I race all the way to my mother's front door.

I knock and try the door. It is locked. I knock louder and call, "Mother!" After a few silent moments I knock more vigorously, Mother, Kava's in labor!"

The latch on the other side of the door clanks, and the heavy wooden door flings open. My mother's sleepy face is crinkled on one side, and her hair looks like a cat slept in it.

"Kava's in labor," I say, quieter this time. "She's been going good for a couple hours now. Can you help?"

She scowls.

There's no indication that she understands I need her to hurry. "You understand what I'm saying?"

She nods and waves a hand at me.

When she pushes the door shut with a yawn, I stick my foot in the way. "Come to the medical ward as soon as possible."

"Okay," she mutters and shoves the door shut.

I want to burst in and help her wake up more, to make sure she understands to hurry. She makes me think of Ledger and how long it takes him to wake up. If it was him, I'd have to dress him and shove him out the door.

But I must trust her and get back to Kava immediately. A punch of guilt pushes me off the porch, and I run back to the cottage. The sky is filled with pink light. The clouds across the horizon are streaked with red.

I take the stairs two at a time to our bedroom. Kava is lying on her side of the bed and a raspy snore emanates from her. I pad quietly across the room and kneel at her side. Her eyes are gently closed, and she might actually be asleep. I raise my hand to touch her, but another snore comes out.

Maybe I should let her sleep. She'll need it.

Downstairs, I consider what we need in order to bring our child into this world. I light the fire and fill a pot full of water, hanging it over the small flames. Soon enough it will be a roaring fire, and it will boil the water. I step out the back door to check on the last person in our care. Meyer is fine, but he seems to think his cough is some sort of ailment that warrants a three-day sleepover in the medical ward. Instead of arguing with him days ago, Kava welcomed him. "Good morning, Meyer," I call.

Sitting up on his cot, he salutes me. "Good morning, Tolliver."

"Kava's in labor this morning," I warn. "You are free to go when you're ready, but she won't be down to check on you."

"Oh, don't mind me, youngster. I'll read my book and stay out of your way." His round cheeks turn a shade of rose as he smiles. He pulls a book in front of his face, and I head for the door.

As I cross the threshold, a scream comes from the second story. Throwing myself forward, I make it up the stairs without a thought. Kava is on the floor beside the bed with her arms on the mattress, writhing in the pain of another contraction. Her face is becomes a deep shade of crimson. "Breathe Kava, breathe."

She obeys and inhales.

"Let it out." I kneel on the floor beside her.

She blows it out slowly as a tear streams down her cheek. Another inhale, another exhale. Another, and another.

As the contraction subsides, she says, "That was a big

one."

I notice my hand is in a puddle of something on the bed. I lift it, and the stuff drips from my fingers. She laughs at my surprised expression.

"My water broke," she says, breathing normally now.

"Could have warned me." I fake a laugh to seem as lighthearted as she's being. But my insides are churning about the fact that I left her alone. I put my arm under hers to help her off the floor. "Come on."

"This actually works for me," she says.

I rub her back. "What can I do for you?"

"Can you clean up the bed?" She smiles at me like I'm going to yell at her for asking. She must not know I would do anything for her today. Anything.

"No problem." I untuck our blankets and sheets, scoop it all together, and throw it down the stairs.

"I need a towel or two," she says as I pull out fresh sheets from the trunk.

I was about to ask why, when another contraction starts, and she puffs heavily. I hand her several towels, and I make the bed. She piles the towels on the floor like a cushion for her to sit on.

The next contraction begins as the front door opens and booms closed. Several voices chatter as footsteps echo on the stairs.

I tuck in the last corner of the sheet as several people walk through the door.

"Good morning," my mother says with a smile. Her face is more awake than last I saw her. "I brought Neelie and Kailani to help out." Her voice is like oil on my wounds, soothing and relieving. It's as though she is sealing the fate of this day.

When Kailani's white wings clear the doorway, Neelie steps into the room.

"I'm feeling much better today, and Adaya said you were desperate for help," Neelie says.

"Thank you, thank you, thank you," I say to the three women coming to my wife's aid.

Neelie pushes her wavy, silver hair behind her ears and shoves her sleeves up. "Let's see how far along she is."

As she brushes by me with her tan-feathered wings, another person steps into the room. "Excuse me," Elder Jubal says. His lips are pursed and eyes are shifty, like he is uncomfortable being here. "A council meeting has been called."

My mother looks at me with surprise.

I touch her shoulder. "Go. You brought the help I need."

She gives me a kiss on the cheek before stepping out the door. "I'll return as soon as I can."

"Tolliver, you are needed as well," Jubal says.

I step toward him, and he backs out the door, and down one step. His irritated countenance doesn't change as he speaks.

Kava whimpers loudly.

"She is ready right now, Tolliver," Neelie calls.

I turn back to my wife, who is grunting through the pressure in her abdomen. Another cry bursts from her lips. My heart sinks. I should be at her side, not dealing with Jubal's issues. "What do you want, Jubal? Get to it quickly, I need to get back to her."

"That's just it," he begins. "Huyana wants you at the meeting this morning."

"Now?" I ask, my eyes wide.

"Yes, now."

Everything within me pulls toward Kava, and now the moment I've been waiting for, my invitation back into the council has come.

Kava lets out a scream and Jubal winces like it's a blow to the face. His skin goes pale beneath the neatly combed beard.

My wife sits on the other side of the bed in pain. Neelie is kneeling beside her, encouraging her to breathe. Kailani uses a wet rag to wipe Kava's forehead.

"I can't come now. Kava is about to deliver!" I shout. "Can they postpone until this afternoon, at least?"

"I don't know, Tolliver. If you want in, now's your chance. Leave her to the women's work and let's go."

From Jubal's mouth it sounds like a harsh judgment. For a fleeting moment, I realize these two women could take care of Kava, but I vowed not to leave her ever again for any reason. I learned that lesson a long time ago. It's *her* above everyone else.

"Toll!" Kava cries out.

"I can't. I can't come with you," I say to Jubal.

"You know what you're giving up, right?" He smirks like he's won. I want to punch him in his curled-up mustache.

I point down the stairs. "Get out of here. I have work to do."

My heart is racing, and I can't even begin to care what he will say to the council. I must take care of Kava.

***

"Take another breath and push, Kava, push," Neelie says in a calm voice.

I'm missing it!

Kava obeys and bears down. Her face reddens as she groans and cries out. "I can't. Something's wrong. I can't."

I have no way to reach her with the women on both sides of her. I climb onto the bed and crawl over to her. Crouching down, I pull her chin up. "You can do this. Rest until the next one starts again."

She purses her lips. "Here it comes."

"Push. One, two, three, four, five—" Neelie encourages.

"Holy heavens!" Kailani blurts.

I can't see what she's seeing. "What? What's the matter?"

A baby's cry emerges from the floor. Kava lets go of my hands and slumps against the wall, exhausted.

"A boy!" Neelie lifts the tiny baby as he sucks another breath into his new lungs.

"And he has wings!" Kailani shouts. Her eyes are wide with joy. She laughs. "How is that possible?"

"Wings?" Kava tries to move, but she is tired and weak. I wave Kailani away, and I slip my hands beneath Kava.

Neelie wraps a small blanket around the baby. She rubs his chest as he screams and grows pinker by the moment.

Kailani lays a couple layers of towels down as I lift Kava onto the bed and cover her with a blanket. I sit beside her as Neelie places the baby in my wife's arms.

"Kava, I have something to tell you. I guess it cannot be hidden anymore." I take a clean rag from the bedside table and wipe Kava's face with it. I pull her chin up to meet my eyes again. "Your father told me something before he died that you need to know. He was born with wings."

Her eyes widen, and she starts to look away, at our child. But I hold her chin and her gaze.

"He told me his father removed his. But that's not all. You too were born with wings. And he removed yours."

I assumed she was going to argue with me. But she merely lets out a sigh and tips her head toward our child.

"*That's* why he has wings," I say with a smile.

I glance at Neelie, who is cleaning up the floor. Her expression is blank. I want to know what she is thinking.

Kailani leans in and sticks her finger in the baby's hand. He grips it, and she giggles. "What will you call him?"

Kava and I speak different things at one time.

I say, "We don't name them for a year."

Kava says, "Liam."

I look at her, confused.

"It's the name my father was going to give me if I were a boy. I think it fits him."

"But what about tradition?" I ask.

"Nothing we do is traditional. We are not normal. I cannot bear calling him 'the baby' for an entire year. Let's call him who he is. He is special. The first winged Balfourian: Liam."

I caress her hair and kiss her on the forehead. I take him from her arms, holding my son for the first time.

"And he will keep his wings," I say aloud. He will be allowed to grow up in a family with and without wings. And he can be whoever he chooses to be.

Then a revelation hits me. *I am a father.*

Tears pool in my eyes. I will never allow my family to be torn apart the way I was torn from my parents.

I turned down joining the council. Looking at my wife, then at my son, I know I made the right choice.

"Hello, Liam." I kiss his warm, fuzzy head. His pale hair is starting to dry. It is wavy and blond. Like mine.

Summer Solstice

Overpowered 31

LEDGER

As Ellery drifts over the shoreline, I don't remember this place. It is densely wooded over rolling hills and deep ravines. Almost jungle-like. I wonder what I was doing this time last year when a memory hits me. After the second stretch of ocean, I had given up on being coherent. Last year, I was in the depths of sadness, sleeping all the time, avoiding everyone, and not watching the horizon.

That's when *they* attacked. The men dressed all in black boarded Ellery and overtook us easily. We have a plan already in place in case Lianmin attacks again.

As the meal-bell rings in the castle somewhere, my heart hammers in my chest. I rush indoors. It's time to activate the plan.

Everyone is gathered in the dining hall for midday meal. When I arrive, I get their attention with a loud whistle. "We are approaching the place where we were boarded and taken prisoner last year."

"There's no way anyone boarded Ellery here. We are way too high," Char argues. He frowns and looks at me like

I'm an idiot.

"Excuse me, Char. You were not here." Anger causes sweat to bead on my forehead. *Why does he always doubt me?*

"It's true." Hollis cuts the tension. "Ledger and I were the only ones here last year. They shot metal hooks out of some sort of crossbow, and they scaled the island."

Char sits back in his seat, corrected.

I suppress a smile of satisfaction "Let's implement the plan we decided on and stand watch on all the towers." I catch my father's eye. He acknowledges me as I continue talking. "These are the same people who attacked Ciel's castle and drove us off. They are extremely good fighters."

The moment I stop talking, Belamy makes a suggestion, then Swarley throws out another idea, and Zander disputes it. The debate makes my head spin.

Then my father stands. "We already have a plan."

Char stands up, speaks over everyone, and unsheathes his sword. "I say we take the fight to them, none of this hiding-in-wait foolery."

Several Balfourian men loudly voice their agreement to his suggestion, pumping fists in the air. One is Berthold, Angus's brother. Another is Baer, who was the leader of the ground troops against the Ellerians for all the years I've known him. Baer's face is scarred from years in battle, with a fresh scar from the barbaric tribe that took him captive. He nearly lost an eye. They throw ideas back and forth on how to overtake the Lianmin. They're attempting to change the plan we've already agreed upon.

No. I shake my head. I can't let them lose their heads

over this. I walk to the center of the room, raise my hands, and speak loudly, "The Lianmin are like no enemy Balfour has ever known. They may not be vicious and bloodthirsty like the savages, but they are skilled in combat, quick, and clever."

"We cannot fight brawn against brains." I address the whole group. "We must match their smarts. That is the only way we will win. Our plan is well-crafted. This time we will be ready for them. We will outwit them. That is how we defeated the savages and struck a trade agreement with the Wolfman's tribe."

My father stands up straighter. "I agree. Let's stick to the plan. If we can keep them from boarding the island, that is the majority of the battle right there."

"We must control *every single* avenue onto the island, day and night," Zander says.

Baer's countenance shifts. His eyes light up as his gruff voice emerges. "In addition to the watch towers, the Ellerians should fly around the bottom side of the island, scouting for anyone trying to climb."

"Good idea," I say. "Let's designate guard shifts. Who will take the lookout towers?"

Everyone volunteers for a shift at one of the four lookout towers on the outside of the castle, the dragon's cave opening, and flying the perimeter of the island.

I scan the crowd, making eye contact with everyone as I finalize the plan so we are all clear.

This year, we are prepared. I smile at the thought. We will not be taken prisoner on our own island. We will survive, and we will return home to Balfour.

At the far end of the table, Alouette's countenance is dark, like she is holding back tears. I raise my eyebrows at her with a question in my eyes. She shakes her head, gets up abruptly from the table, and slips out of the room.

***

Dressed in the armor my father made, I stand on the north-facing lookout tower at the end of a long nighttime shift. I yawn and think about how nice it will be to crawl into bed and get some sleep. I think about Hollis and how a day has not gone by where she has obeyed Hellwig. He and Alouette train Ruby in the morning, and Hollis watches everything through the cracks in the shutters. Later, she returns and does the same training without Hellwig around to stop her. I joined her a few times, but I couldn't take the sneaking around and disobeying Hellwig.

The eastern horizon begins to glow a faint purple. I stare at it and wonder if I'm imagining it. The blast of a shofar from the east sobers me up. It blares four times, telling our people to organize on the east side, outside the castle. I lean as far out as I can over the edge of the tower. A figure dressed all in black climbs onto the surface of Ellery. *They are here.*

"He must have made it past Swarley circling the base of the island," I say to no one. I run through the castle, catching up with many of our Balfourian men, who are arming themselves with the many weapons we were gifted by Hartwynn.

Thank the skies for Alouette, who negotiated that deal. She reduced the amount of food they gave us and asked for weapons, armor, precious metals, iron ore, and more. It was surprising, the amount of supplies they gave us.

Each person darts down the Grand Hall, and I follow them out the only ground floor exit from Ellery's castle. The sky is getting brighter with each racing moment.

As we run into the action, three more masked men have scaled the island of Ellery with grappling hooks and long ropes. I can't believe they all made it past our flying scouts. Perhaps they are hard to see, dressed all in black, blending in with the dark stone on the belly of Ellery.

One intruder swings his sword at Belamy, who then flies over the man's head. Another masked man ducks a strike from Swarley. Another swings his legs in the air at Zander, landing a blow square in his chest. Zander catches himself from falling backward by putting out his enormous wings. The fourth intruder clashes swords with Estefano, who overtakes the masked man, driving him toward the edge.

A screeching cry of a dragon emanates from off in the distance. I scan for Hollis. Hopefully, she is staying hidden like I asked her to.

Over the surface of Ellery, a gray dragon darts over our heads with many ropes dangling from it. I remember that dragon from Ciel's castle. It belonged to Ellery. Six men dressed in black rappel down the ropes and land on the island. The dragon flies away when another dragon calls. A familiar call. *Tristeh.*

Hollis had better not be on that dragon!

I grind my teeth as the intruders draw their swords. Several of my winged friends fly toward them. Father draws his sword and leads a company of men on foot. I charge toward the battle alongside him. My heart thrashes out of control.

Before I reach the fray, I stop when Tristeh caws again from somewhere below. My father leads the men onward. The gray dragon darts over our heads with Tristeh in pursuit. I spot the white saddle on her back, but no Hollis. *Thank the skies!* And no muzzle.

Tristeh catches up with the gray dragon. They are equally matched in size. She clamps down mid-way up its tail. She yanks her head to the side and pulls it out of its flightpath. The gray dragon dives downward, curling up on itself, and grabs Tristeh's underside. Their large leathery wings flap faster, sending them in a spiraling death roll midair. The two ferocious beasts attack and take bites out of each other as they descend toward all of us.

Hollis screams. She's frozen in shock on the stairs of the castle, sword in hand.

No! She needs to get out of here.

"Tristeh!" she cries.

A masked man breaks through our line and dives at me. I defend myself, stopping his sword from jabbing me in the gut. Behind him, Berthold slashes his back, and he whirls around to face him.

Above us, Tristeh and Gray separate, flying away from each other and gaining altitude. Tristeh circles back for another attack, and the gray dragon does the same.

I glance around for Hollis. She went back inside; I sigh in relief. But in the next breath, she appears in the grand entrance, face flushed with anger. "Attack!" she shouts, pointing to the sky as Ruby soars over her head out of the two-story doorway and into the morning light. Ruby darts into the violent mass of scales, lands on the gray dragon's back. All three dragons fight each other, suspended in one dangerous moment.

Tristeh draws blood as she yanks her head back with a jaw full of silvery scales. The gray dragon wails in pain. Tristeh and Ruby claw at Gray. Blood and scales rain down.

I throw myself into the fight my father is having with a tall, bulky Lianminese man. We come at him together, overpowering him. We push him back toward the edge of Ellery, swords clashing. The man scrambles away, and Father pursues him. I notice there are at least two of us for each one of the masked men.

Suddenly, a loud screech stings my ears as I catch sight of Tristeh falling out of the sky. A dark, bloody slice stretches the length of one of her wings. She falls backward as her wings fold in on her, slams against the northern edge of Ellery, and falls out of sight.

Ruby crawls up the larger dragon, clinging to its hard exterior. She swings her head under its neck and makes three violent strikes at the underside, scales ripping off. She then sinks her teeth into its jugular, the way she did to the mule. Gray goes rigid and its wings stop flapping. Ruby keeps them suspended for only a few minutes more with her small wings but stays clamped to its neck until it goes limp. As they descend, I catch sight of Hollis running toward where Tristeh hit.

I can't go to her, as another masked man swings at me. I fight him off, then he takes a jab at Alouette beside me. She attacks with ferocity. Her cheeks are flushed, and her jaw is set. Estefano dives into the middle of us and forces the enemy back.

Alouette whirls to the next man in black, who strikes Char across his right shoulder. Char is stunned momentarily as his armor absorbs the blow, and Alouette slashes the masked man across the back. He goes down, and she runs him through. Char's face is as white as a cloud.

"You okay?" Alouette asks with fire in her eyes.

He bobs his head in shock, and she stalks away, dark hair blowing back from her face.

A moment later, Hollis exchanges blows with another Lianminese. My first inclination is to defend her and get her out of here. But Hollis has more fight in her blood than I do. Her lips are pinched tightly, and there is rage in her eyes, no doubt fueled by the horrific sight of her beloved dragon going down. Estefano joins her fight, and I lose sight of her behind his white wings.

A shout comes from across the surface. Belamy's voice echoes off the stone, "Yield or we will throw you from the island!"

Several Balfourian men back him up, and I realize our plan worked. The masked men stop as they notice how close they are to the edge.

My father holds his heavy sword to the throat of one. Baer and my cousin, Berthold, stand side by side holding another hostage. Several lower their swords, seeing they are trapped.

The sky is empty; the dragons are gone.

"I want to speak to Jin," I call in a loud voice. I put some depth to it and frown. "I demand to speak to Jin!"

One intruder jerks and lowers his sword slightly. He peers around as if assessing our group until his eyes fall on me. He raises a hand and pulls the mask from his face. *It's him.* Pale face, dark eyes, and long black hair in a braided ponytail that falls to his waist. "I am Jin."

"I wish to make you a deal." I stand up straighter.

"More are coming; we will defeat you," he says in choppy sentences.

Out of the corner of my eye, I notice Alouette with a revengeful look in her eye, warning me she is about to make a foolish move. Her sword arm tenses, and I leap for her before she reaches Jin. I grab her arm and stop her short.

"He killed my father!" she screams. Angry tears stream down her distorted face.

"I know," I say. "But killing him won't bring your father back."

She yanks her arm from my grip.

I turn back to Jin, who is flanked by my father and Brecken, Hollis's father. They hold their swords at his neck, and I approach him. "What was Ellery providing to your people?"

Jin scowls from me to Alouette. I hold her back as he realizes what I'm asking.

"Ellery gave black pearl, jewels, gold."

"You showed me mercy once. I know your people are strong. But we want peaceful passage over your land on Ellery." I wave a hand at the castle behind me.

"You have gold?" he asks.

Alouette crosses her arms with defiance. I stare at her until she softens.

“We do. Will you grant us safe passage?” I have another idea and step forward. “And we wish to visit the castle we abandoned on the ground. Will you escort us there?”

He stands up straighter and shouts something to his men in their strange language. The men slip their swords into their sheaths one after the other, as well as Jin. He puts his hands flat together in front of him and bows to me. “You have deal. Show gold.”

We wait outside the castle as Alouette and Belamy fetch the precious metals and gems. They mutter argumentatively between them as they approach. She holds a book-sized bag and he holds a fist-sized one.

Alouette’s voice is deadpan as she says, “We will give you the small amount now.” She points at Belamy’s small bag. “And we will give you the rest along with your man, after we’ve visited the castle.” They both glance at the Lianminese man Alouette killed, lying between them.

I’m surprised at her gall.

Jin makes his decision. Not much happens in his facial expression, but he puts his chin up as he says, “Agreed.” He accepts the small cloth bag, pulls it open, digs around in it, then cinches it shut. His men crawl off the side of Ellery and rappel down the ropes.

Jin holds his position for a moment more, then nods curtly and follows his men.

The morning sun glares in my eyes as I look for Hollis. I glance from person to person standing in front of the castle. My father, Berthold, Belamy, Alouette, and more. But no Hollis. I must find her and make sure she doesn’t race off to find Tristeh. I shake my head as I bound up the stairs to the grand entrance of the castle.

Goodbye 32

ALOUETTE

After Ledger flees into the castle, I follow him down into the depths of the island. I clear my head in the swirling dark passage, shaking off the fury and vengefulness still clinging to my skin. My fingers tingle as I squeeze them and shake them in front of me. *Did I avenge my father by killing that man?* I swallow hard. I thought I would feel better if I could kill one of them myself.

But I don't.

I enter the dragon's cave and head for the stairs along the outside of the cage.

"Alouette!" Hollis shouts from inside the dragon's enclosure. "Tell them. Tell Ledger and Hellwig I have to find her. You know how it is to lose someone. I *have* to go." Wilhelm is muzzled and saddled. Hellwig waits with his hand on the gate's latch next to Ledger. She wants me to convince them to let her go.

My heart sinks. She is using my pain as an arguing point. I blink and refuse to give her what she wants. "You should not put yourself in harm's way."

She flinches. I've never seen her speechless. I descend the stairs into the dragon's cave, step by step. When I reach the bottom, she's found a new argument.

"I sent a scout to find out what happened to her. He is less conspicuous than Wilhelm," Hellwig says reasonably. He settles his wings closed and leans on the bars with his arms crossed.

"Where is Ruby? She didn't come back. We have to find them both and bring them back. Maybe Tristeh needs help getting back up here. Wilhelm can pick her up and carry her back."

Hellwig clears his throat with a grave look on his face. "Wilhelm may not be able to do that."

"I thought he was the trained one, Hellwig!" Hollis screeches. She breathes heavily and her voice comes out shaky and panicky. "I'm not ready to lose her! She can't be dead. She's just… hurt!"

Her pain wounds me deep. I turn away from her and hold my hands over my heart.

"All we can do now is wait," Hellwig says, pulling the large metal gate open slightly. "Come now." He waves her out the opening.

Silence falls on the dragon's cave, leaving only the crackling of flickering torches. Wilhelm lets out a breath. I make my way around the outside of the enclosure and stop in front of the gate next to Ledger.

Hollis finally gives in and walks out of the cage with shoulders drooping and head hanging in defeat. I understand loss and the uncertainty of survival. It's only a dragon, but to Hollis, Tristeh is everything. The emotions rolling off of her pick at my old wounds. They press and press, and I'm not sure if I should be here. I should go, but I can't leave Hollis, my hurting friend.

Ledger puts out a hand to Hollis. She pulls him in and crushes her face into Ledger's chest. She weeps over her missing dragons, and my own grief rises to the surface alongside hers. It chokes me, and tears threaten to fall. I press on my eyes and wipe away any evidence. I can't lose it here, in front of everyone.

A gust of air comes from the tunnel leading outside, carrying with it a scuffle of footfalls. Belamy emerges around the corner, walking this way with his large black wings outstretched behind him. He face is alarmingly solemn.

When Hollis notices him, she runs toward him. "Bel! Did you find Tristeh?"

Hollis is halfway to him when Belamy says, "Tristeh is wounded. There is a tear all along one of her wings."

She grabs hold of his forearms. "We have to go get her!"

He keeps walking forward, forcing her to walk backward. "She's here."

"What?" She halts his forward movement. "Where? How?"

"When I reached them, Ruby was trying to carry her by herself. Not that I did much, but I helped fly her home." Belamy leans forward with his hands on his knees, his exhaustion showing.

"Impossible," Hellwig whispers.

"Heaviest thing I've ever carried," Belamy says, out of breath.

Hollis bounces on her toes and darts down the tunnel.

Ledger races after her. Hellwig grabs his training satchel and lead rope before taking flight toward them. I watch them go as Belamy steps up beside me.

A warm hand touches my back. "How are you doing?" Belamy asks.

I take a deep breath before I meet his gaze. I'm held together by mere twigs and crumbling ash. I decide to give him an honest answer instead of denying anything's wrong. "I don't know. I feel very… unsteady."

I put a hand on his forearm for support and realize he deserves the same care no matter how I feel. I gaze into his deep brown eyes. "How are you?"

Belamy puts his hands on both sides of my face. My heart flutters, and I don't resist it.

"I am fine—a little exhausted. Nothing a few moments with you won't heal."

I smile as the tone of his voice sooths my wounded heart. I pull him to me and wrap myself around him, strong and stable. I let a tear fall as I tuck my face against his neck. One little tear won't matter.

***

It takes six days from the time we struck our deal with the Lianmin to arrive at the castle on the ground. The time is consumed with caring for Tristeh and Ruby, the valiant dragon who saved her mother despite their instincts to destroy each other. My heart aches as I remember Tristeh's pitiful cries as Sybella stitched her wing back together. There were about twenty people holding her down with ropes and linens. But eventually, Sybella was able to put her back together and tie her wing closed. When Sybella said, "Who knows if she will ever fly again," Hollis fell apart.

I shake the memories from my mind as I land before my father's half-built castle. My whole world is gray and cold. I shiver as a chilling rain begins to fall, prickling the skin on my arms and face. The stone structure is mostly torn down and in ruins. I bypass its meaninglessness and walk to the place where I watched my father die.

The only things left are piles of ashes and charred remnants of logs with bright green stalks of grass growing all around the area. The pain of his death shoots through the depths of my heart into my gut. I wrap my arms around my stomach.

One little tear turns into more. And more. I let the tears fall down my face as I kneel in the weeds. After everything that's happened, there is only one thing left to say.

"I forgive you, father, for being so cruel to our people." I barely speak the words so Ledger, Belamy, Hollis, and the man who cut down my father cannot hear me.

I sniffle, and someone brushes along my wings. Belamy kneels beside me and holds my hand. I search his eyes for judgment. But there is none.

"Ledger has something for you." Belamy jerks his gaze toward the castle.

I push my wings to the side and glance behind me. Ledger is holding a large flat rock.

"I thought we should mark his place," Ledger says. "The way my grandmother marked the children's place."

I wipe the tears from my eyes, pull myself from the

ground, and go to him. I accept the heavy stone and walk to the spot where Dayson and I placed my father's body into the flames.

I set it into the ash. Hollis hands me her stone with a gentle smile. It's the size of a book. I stack it on the first.

Char, of all people, hands me the last stone.

"What are you doing here?" I snap, feeling attacked by his mere presence.

"I…" he stutters. "I wanted to apologize for being so harsh to you." He sighs and hands me the stone.

I take it, confused and drained of any energy to keep resisting.

"I blamed you for your father's cruelty, but you're not to blame."

Holding the plate-sized rock, I formulate something to say to my friends—my family.

"I forgive you, Char. And I'm so sorry for what he did to you. To all of you," I say to the whole group of them. "I'm sorry I didn't stand up to him. I didn't stick up for you, or myself."

Belamy puts his hand on the small of my back. "It's not your fault. I was one of his guardians. I knew what he was doing was wrong, but I did nothing. I was so glad to get off that island. I saw him as the lesser of two evils. But it's not my fault either. Ciel made his choices, regardless."

I nod. I'm not sure if it would have helped anything if I did speak up.

What he did was not my fault, I decide.

I turn back to the grave of my father and lay the last stone on top. "I forgive myself for not speaking up." My chin quivers, and warmth fills me. *I forgive myself.*

A cool breeze blows in from the west, and the sky opens up. The afternoon sun shines on us. I take a deep breath as a weight lifts from my chest. I can breathe again.

Preventative 33

TOLLIVER

With the onset of the autumn weather, I am preparing an enormous batch of elderberry syrup. With the cold comes sneezing and coughing. According to Kava, this preventative has saved many a man, woman, and child from full-blown sickness.

The eighth weak and achy person this week walks through the door. Neelie takes young Christian by the hand and walks him to the medical ward. Over the summer, our building team raised an addition off the back of the cottage, replacing the old tent. Now it is sealed up nicely and holds in the heat. Not to mention it is roomier—enough for eight sick beds. Christian will officially fill that last bed.

"We should have built a bigger medical ward," Kava says with a smile. "I guess we need to do some preventative medicine too. I'll take care of the sick if you can start handing out doses of elderberry syrup in the square. We'll pass the news and get everyone covered."

"That's a good idea." I wrap my arms around her slender body. She recovered quickly from the birth of Liam, who is still asleep in his bassinet under the stairs.

Kava steps to the curtain and silently pulls it back. He must still be asleep because she closes it and walks to the shelves along the back wall. Another new addition to our medical needs: shelves built all the way around our living area. She organized Clovis's containers of herbs and medicines and medical journals with room for more. My goal is to have them all read by the end of the harvest season, achingly filling my brain with every discovery Clovis made. If I'm in this for life, I might as well get all the knowledge available to me.

"Let this cool for a little bit, then take it to the square, I'll start the next batch straight away." Kava hands me a ladle and a box of wooden cups. "The perfect dose. Everyone should get one each day for the next three days."

"I'll take Liam with me," I say, taking the box.

"He's fine. He's still sleeping."

A small squeak comes from under the stairs. Kava's eyes light up. "Wow, you're so intuitive."

"He would love being out with all the people."

"He does love people, doesn't he?" She opens the curtain, and his chunky five-month-old legs stick up from the bassinet. She coos at him and lifts him into her arms.

She takes some time to nurse him and dress him warmly. Neelie taught us how to bundle his little feathery wings against his back so he's comfortable and they aren't in the way.

When we revealed to the rest of the village that Liam has wings, there were wildly varying reactions. Most Ellerians found it to be no big deal. Some Balfourians were offended that this truth wasn't revealed by the queen on Delineation Day, but she was unaware of this phenomenon. They demanded to know who else was born with wings, but of course, Clovis only told me about himself and Kava.

I described the small scars above Kava's shoulder blades and told them to check each other for signs of a surgery. There was only one who reported signs of scars. After that, the outcry faded to nothing. This village has grown tired of surprises.

Kava tucks Liam into the sling across my chest. He faces her, and she kisses his rosy cheeks. "I love you, little man," she says. Then she leans up and kisses me. "I love you, large man."

I haul a box in one arm and a giant iron pot in the other out the door. My brow is sweating by the time I reach the village square. The sun is nearly at its peak, and I wonder if I should wait to administer everyone's dose at midday meal. I set the pot and box on the platform in the square and notice several elders and advisors heading to Tillman's cottage. Must be meeting day.

"What are you doing?" a woman asks from behind me. I turn around to find Kailani.

I set down the pot. "Giving out some preventatives. A terrible cold is starting to get around. Would you like to help?"

"Sure." She touches Liam's head with a smile.

"Can you ring the bell?" I ask. "Only two rings—it's a nonemergency."

With a nod, she makes her way to the bell hanging from the southwestern post and pulls the rope, clanging the bell twice.

My ears are still ringing as I lay out a long row of cups on the top step and ladle the syrup into each one. Folks emerge from their homes and make their way over. Grandmother ascends into Tillman's house and the door shuts behind her. Curiosity chips away at my sense of duty, and I can't stop myself from heading toward the cottage.

Kailani hands folks a cupful, explaining how it will keep them from getting sick. They drink and leave.

"Where are you going?" she calls to me.

Before I get too far, I realize they will never let me in without a reason. "Oh, I think I should bring them their doses at the council meeting. Can you take Liam?"

"Yes!" she says with delight. I slip the sling off me and over her shoulders. It hangs awkwardly on her wings.

"Is that going to be okay?" I ask.

"It's fine," she says and waves me away. She cups one hand under him and reaches for the next dose with the other. "See?"

I fill eight cups, group them in fours, grab one group with each hand, and stride toward the council meeting. My heart races at the thought of being in on something again. Several speak at one time, like they are in an argument. I wonder what it is about as I take a breath and push the door open.

The room falls silent as soon as I enter. I smile and explain, "Elderberry doses. There's a nasty sickness going around, and we'd like to prevent it from spreading."

No one says a word.

My mother is seated on the far side of the table between Elder Chasen and Elder Jubal. Chasen has his hand on her back, like he is comforting her. I want to ask her if she is okay because she looks like a startled jaycoon found eating someone else's drying jerky.

I set the cups on the wood table and those nearest me take one: Advisor Gabriel, Advisor Cabot, and Advisor Tiberius.

My queen grandmother sits calmly with no expression. Her short white hair lays neatly around her face. Her cheeks have no color, and her eyes are glassy.

I scrutinize her. "Are you feeling well?"

"I *am* well. Thank you." She gives a strained smile.

I hand her a cup. "A preventative."

"Thank you." She drinks it slowly and hands it back.

After everyone has taken their dose, silence falls again. I gather the cups and head out the door. Shutting it behind me, I wait for them to start speaking. Someone mutters something and Jubal responds. "He had his chance."

The comment drops like a rock into the bottom of my stomach. Why does it bother me so much when this is what I chose? *I want to work alongside Kava. I want to care for my son and for the village.* I chose this.

***

The second morning of handing out doses of elderberry syrup goes by quickly. I remember yesterday and Grandmother's eyes. They were glassy. Not from emotion. And she was pale.

She must be ill.

"Kailani, can you take the rest of this back to Kava? I need to deliver a dose."

She gives me a kind smile. "Can I take Liam too?"

In my head, I'm already halfway to Grandmother's house. "No, I've got him." I walk away with two full doses. Liam is sleeping soundly in the sling as he bounces gently to the rhythm of my steps.

At Grandmother's door, I knock three times.

"Come in," a quiet voice calls.

Inside, I find Grandmother bundled up in a cushioned chair close to the roaring fireplace. The table has been pushed aside. She turns her head and raises her eyebrows. "Oh, Tolliver, come in."

"Good morning." I set the two cups on the hearth and kneel in front over. Her eyes are watery. "You don't feel well, do you?"

"No, I don't." She frowns.

"You weren't well yesterday either, were you?"

"No, sir," she whispers like she is a child who's been found in a lie.

I smile at her and put a hand on her head. It is hot and dry. "Have you been drinking any water?"

She shakes her head. "I can't get warm." She shivers.

I pour her a glass of water and tell her to take small sips until it's gone. I give her the first elderberry dose. She complains that her feet are frigid, so I put some water over the fire to heat. I spend most of the afternoon caring for her, doing what Kava's been doing for the sick folks in the medical ward.

Eventually, Liam wakes up and starts getting cranky. I take him out of the sling and pull a stool up next to Grandmother in front of the fire. "Could you imagine Kava and I having a winged child if the truth of our lineage was never revealed?"

She watches me with my chubby-cheeked Liam. I change his diaper on the rug at my feet. His little white wings splay out to either side. I could not even imagine removing them. What a painful process it must have been for Clovis and Kava.

"These truly are changing times. And more changes are coming." She meets my eyes. "We are heading into the next and biggest transition Balfour and Ellery have ever known. You are the oldest in this royal family." She drags in a breath.

I interrupt her. "Don't ask me to be who I am not, Grandmother. I have found my place."

She smiles and reaches for me. I take her frail hand in mine.

"You've chosen to follow Kava's family's path, and you are suited to it very well."

I blink at her words. *Kava's family's path?* "It seems it is in my blood as well. I have learned my birth mother was a skilled midwife and healer."

"Well, you are a wonder," she says with a smile. "I am proud of the man you've become."

"Are you sure you want to pass this to Ledger?" Her eyebrows rise, looking serious.

"Yes," I answer truthfully. "Though I fought leaving the council last harvest, I know where I belong."

With a nod, she releases my hand and lies back against the chair as if the effort of this conversation tired her out. "Ledger will arrive any day now, and I need you to bring him to me as soon as he arrives. Don't let him sit down, even for a moment." Her voice is strained and it's obvious it takes a lot of energy to speak.

“Then I will bring him to you as soon as he arrives,” I agree. They could be here within the next couple weeks.

“Thank you, dear one. Bring our entire family.”

Liam squawks, and I lift him in my arms, bundled tight and warm. I stand, tucking him back into the sling. I thank her and direct her attention to the mantel. “I left another dose for you. Please take it at nightfall.”

“I will,” she says with a half-smile and a wheezing breath.

I leave her to heal. She may not survive until Ledger returns; I must keep her alive for as long as possible. I plan to check on her morning, midday, and night until he arrives.

Autumnal Equinox

True Leader 34

LEDGER

Standing outside of the enormous cage, I watch Sybella remove the binding from Tristeh's wing for the last time.

"I think six weeks is plenty of time for her wings to mend. Now she needs to start stretching and putting tension on it. But not too much." Sybella points at Hollis. "Make sure she doesn't try to fly quite yet."

Hollis agrees as Sybella gathers all the binding linens, removing them from the cage.

Hollis has been with Tristeh day and night for the last six weeks. Before the end of the first week, Hollis brought Ruby down—against Hellwig's wishes. I expected more violent thrashing and growling, but Tristeh stood in the corner like a wounded kitten. Though her hackles raised, she allowed the little red dragon in her cage without protest.

Over the past weeks, Ruby gradually made her way across the cage, closer and closer, as if taming her own mother. Now that Tristeh's wing is free, Ruby curls up near Tristeh and settles her head on her mother's front claw. Worries fill my mind as the two touch for the first time since their reunion.

Tristeh stands dead still. Her eye darts about, down at Ruby, over at Hollis. But she doesn't make a move.

Hollis leaves them to snuggle awkwardly and joins me outside the cage. "Let's fly Ruby to Balfour. That would be fun," she says, as though she's asking me to go sledding. The danger doesn't exactly match her tone.

"Is she ready?" Panic gurgles in my stomach. "Hellwig's only taken her out a couple of times." I'd rather ride a horned grizzlybull through a briar patch, but I wouldn't tell her that.

"She'll be fine," Hollis says with a wave of her hand.

I fear agreeing with her would make her more reckless. Instead, I say, "I have an idea about how to get all our men to the ground with Wilhelm's help."

"How?"

"Did you hear how the Lianminese got half their men onto Ellery? They used ropes on their dragon. I thought we could create a harness for Wilhelm, hanging two rope ladders on either side. We can stand on the rungs as he hauls us to Balfour. That way, the Ellerians won't have to carry us down one by one."

She smiles. "Good idea."

I appreciate her affirmation. "Want to help me build it?"

She loops her arm in mine. "Sure."

We miraculously find the rope ladder we used to exit the island in order to find Ciel's castle last year. Laying out the rope ladder in the courtyard of the castle, I check all the connections where the steps meet the rope and replace any rotting pieces.

"Let's cut them at about four risers." I pick up the blade.

"I think if you leave about six or eight, you can carry more people." She swishes her blonde hair out of her face.

"How many people do you think Wilhelm could carry?" I ask.

Her eyes gaze up the tower in thought. "Tristeh carried all five of us last year, no problem. Wilhelm is considerably bigger. I would say twenty men, but using your ladder idea, ten?"

I smile at her, thankful for her input, but she is a bit overoptimistic. She doesn't smile this time and sighs instead.

"Is everything okay?" I ask.

"Sure."

"Don't lie," I say. "You're terrible at it."

Hollis looks away. "I'm just sad. I can't stop being sad about Tristeh. My baby is wounded. And I hate being sad, so sometimes it makes me mad that I'm so sad. I want to be over it already, but then I feel guilty. If I get over it, then it's like I don't care enough about her. And I *do* care."

I stand and pull her up into my arms. "You can feel however you want, Hollis. But you and I know,—you care more about her than anyone else does. And Tristeh needs you."

She nods.

"Also," I continue. "There is a new baby down in that cave who needs you too."

"Grandbaby," Hollis corrects.

I roll my eyes and repeat, "Grandbaby."

The wind down the north hall carries with it the call of a shofar, filling the courtyard and my soul with excitement. Balfourians and Ellerians alike come dashing from wherever they were milling about. The shofar blasts again, alerting us that we are coming up on Balfour.

I catch sight of Belamy landing at the far opening of the north hall and dashing through, shofar in hand. He is about to blow it again when my father yells, "We heard the alarm. No need to blow it again."

"Yes, sir," Belamy says. "We are a couple hours from Balfour!"

I rush to get the two rope ladders cut to size and tie them together with several strips of rope that will fit around the saddle on the dragon. "Fetch Hellwig, in case he didn't hear the—"

"He's here." Hollis points across the courtyard.

As our people pour into the courtyard, I climb onto the basin of the empty fountain. "Can I get everyone's attention!" I say loud enough for only a few to hear. I clear my throat and yell, "May I have everyone's attention!" I raise both my hands and wave to those in the back.

Most of the Balfourians are present, and there are seven pairs of wings, including Hellwig's. They all fall silent. Their gaze makes my insides vibrate. I know what I want to say, but saying it in front of this many makes me strangely uncomfortable. I swallow my fear and it causes my hands to shake.

"I have an idea for offloading to Balfour." I turn to Belamy. "I'd like to know if the Ellerians would be okay offloading the stuff we've collected?"

Belamy nods, as well as Estefano, Zander, and Eljah. Swarley calls, "Of course. But who will offload the Balfourians?" He chuckles then stops short like he might have offended someone.

"I have an idea for that." I search the yard for Hellwig. He is standing beside Hollis. "Hellwig, I've fashioned a rope ladder to drape over Wilhelm to carry four or six men—"

"Yes, Hollis explained it. I think it will work perfectly. I'll need to create a perch for the dragon to sit on while each man climbs on board. Can someone help me build one?"

"Anyone want to lend a hand to build a perch?" Baer and Keseth volunteer as Luca and Berthold emerge from the royal hall.

"I'll help build." Berthold waves a fist in the air. His deep auburn hair hangs to his shoulders. His eyes remind me of Angus, and awave of grief hits me. I miss my cousin.

I refocus and say, "You three go with Hellwig, and let us know when you're ready."

It takes less time than I expect for them to build a strange, haphazard perch from three doors out on the surface of Ellery. Hellwig disappears into the castle to fetch the dragon. A line of Ellerians emerge carrying grain sacks filled with iron ore, gold, jewels, food, tools, weapons, and more. I march over to them to make sure they're okay with carrying so much weight.

"How far are we from Balfour?" I scan the horizon.

Estefano adjusts the satchel over his chest. "A twenty or thirty minute flight at the most."

"Are you sure you don't want to wait to offload tomorrow? It's a long way to carry stuff *that* heavy."

Belamy puts a hand on my shoulder, "This is way better than carrying *you* around. Plus, there is no sense making this first trip carrying nothing. We can always come back when the island is closer. But for now, we want to get back to our families."

I stand up straighter. "True." I hold out my hand, and he grasps my forearm in a friendly shake.

I release him, and he takes off eastward, toward Balfour. I put my hand out for Estefano, and he shakes it as well. I look each one in the eye and shake their forearm. Swarley and Zander. Terrowin and Char. I am so grateful for each one and couldn't have survived this year without them. When they take off, I watch their wings work the air as they disappear into the afternoon clouds that flood the eastern horizon.

Sybella and Alouette step out onto the rocky surface and walk slowly to me. Sybella gives me a hug and I say, "Thank you for keeping everyone alive."

Her eyebrows come together. "Not everyone."

Her sad voice drifts off into the wind, and I feel terrible for my thoughtless comment. "I'm sorry about Angus."

"Me too," she says. She walks out to the edge and leaps headfirst like she's diving into a sea of trees.

Alouette reaches for my hand and slides her grip around my forearm as warriors-in-arms would do. We stand together in silence. She doesn't say a word as all the memories of our life together flashes before my eyes. Our flights as children, the moment I saw her in Ciel's castle, when we were imprisoned in a cell together, the day Dayson carried her through the window after they attempted to execute her, her skillful negotiation with Wolfman, the joy on her face as we celebrated in Hartwynn, and the mending of her heart kneeling on her father's grave.

Emotion chokes me, and all I can muster is, "Thank you."

With a solemn nod, she doesn't say a word as her white wings unfurl, beat several times, and lift her into the air as she slips out of reach.

A loud sound of beating wings comes from behind me. Hellwig lands Wilhelm on the perch of repurposed doors. They were our dining tables for an entire year. It makes me a bit emotional now that our journey has come to an end.

As Wilhelm's four feet come to rest on the doors, they creak and crack but surprisingly hold the weight of the giant lizard. Hellwig flies off the dragon on his own wings and lands near me. I pick up the center of the rope ladders and hand it to him. "This long part goes over the saddle."

He flits into the air once more, letting the ladders drape from his arms. He hovers over the green dragon, slides the rope ladders on either side then lays the rope extensions across the back and front of the lip of the saddle. Exactly how I imagined. I smile, feeling like a champion.

The ladders hang over each side of the doors. The men of Balfour murmur about the rope ladders, and I reassure them, "As long as you hold on, you'll reach Balfour safely." I smile and wonder if it's the right thing to say. "Let us try three men on each side."

My father steps over to me and says, "Thank you, Ledger. You are a true leader."

I let him pull me into a powerful hug and resist the urge to cry as he releases me. He attempts to climb the nearest rope ladder, but it pulls down. Two men will have to climb up either side at the same time.

Brecken, Hollis's father, is about to climb on the other side.

"You and Fergus will need to climb at the same time." I put out my arm, and he shakes it. Brecken will return to his wife and two young sons. Hollis will join them later without Cullen, who died last harvest in the custody of those barbarians. I don't even want to think about how much he must have suffered.

As each man shakes my forearm and climbs the rope ladder, I think about who they are going home to. Grier and Keseth climb the creaky ladder. They are both going home to no one but a welcoming community.

I step back and signal Hellwig, who has strapped himself to the saddle. Five men, including Hellwig, is plenty for Wilhelm to carry.

"All set," I call. "Hold on tight, Father." My eyes connect with his. As the whole rope ladder of men lifts into the air, I catch a hint of fear in his eyes. Then he is whisked away toward the eastern horizon. Toward home.

***

After Hellwig flies off with his third and final load of Balfourians, I head to the dragon's cave below to meet up with Hollis. When I enter, Hollis is singing. I walk to the edge of the overlook and grasp the thick bars.

Below, Hollis is lying in the middle of the cave beside a resting red dragon. Her hair is long and sprawled out around her head. She is covered from head to toe in black leather clothes she pieced together from items we traded along the way. The light bounces off the smooth leather, showing her curves.

Her song is quiet and sweet as she lulls the baby dragon. Ruby is nearly full grown now, six months later, so calling her a baby seems ridiculous. But she still acts like a hatchling.

In the far corner, Tristeh lies facing the wall. It will take time for her wing to heal. We will let her rest for the week, while Ellery is near Balfour and devise a plan to get her off the island with her torn wing. Perhaps a sling of some sort.

"You ready to go, Hollis?" I keep my voice even, so I don't startle her.

"Oh!" She sits up with a jolt. "Yes, let's go home." She stands up, takes a deep breath, and walks to the gate. She whistles to Ruby. Her ears twitch and Hollis whistles again. Suddenly, the dragon leaps from a resting position, into the air, and flies to Hollis's side.

Hollis claps her hands. "Good girl!" She slips the dragon some sort of treat through the muzzle.

Hollis opens the gate slightly and pulls Tristeh's old saddle through.

I take a deep breath and try not to think about how terrified I am to ride on the back of an untamed hatchling. This could be quite dangerous. Hollis has taken her for only two rides so far. I walk all the way around the enclosure as Hollis expertly puts the saddle on Ruby, strapping it underneath and across her chest. She narrates what she is doing, as if Ruby understands words.

When I reach the enclosure gate, Ruby is ready. I have a weird sensation, like this has happened before, as Ruby dances on her toes like Tristeh used to do. The mother dragon doesn't stir.

"Are you sure she's safe to ride?" The bile churning in

my stomach makes me want to back out.

"It's perfectly safe." Hollis pulls open the gate, with the lead rope connected to the front flap of the saddle.

Luckily, Ruby is muzzled.

I hold the gate open as Hollis leads the dragon down the long corridor out the base of the island.

Hollis gives a double whistle at the edge of the opening. Ruby lowers her large scaly body to the ground and stretches out one wing to the side. Hollis climbs up and sits on the white saddle.

My whole body is shaking, not from the frigid air blowing in my face, but from sheer panic that I could die this close to getting home after all this time. *Why did I agree to this?*

"Come on, Ledger," Hollis says. "She is doing very well with her training. Hellwig has complete confidence she'll do fine."

I flash my teeth in a fake smile. My eyes are so wide they're drying out. I tell my feet to move forward and take the next few steps to the edge of the outstretched wing. I lean over and place both hands on the leathery wing's surface and climb on all fours to where it meets with the glossy red scales. I recall being braver on Tristeh.

"A little bit further." Hollis sounds like she is talking to a child. I want to stick my tongue out at her but realize I've been frozen in this spot for far too long. My body isn't obeying me. I pull my leg up to get myself to move forward again. Then I reach the saddle, sit behind Hollis, and with frantic fingers, strap myself to the saddle.

I can't quite catch my breath. Before I can ask Hollis to give me a moment, she leans forward. The dragon responds to her shift in weight and dives off the platform in one swift motion.

I flail backwards and almost lose my grip on the saddle. A squawk escapes my lips as I pull myself forward and wrap my arms around Hollis. I feel her laughing, stomach bobbing, before she giggles out loud.

Ruby spreads her wings out and soars across the treetops.

"Calm down, Ledger," Hollis shouts with her head turned. "You're not going to fall. Loosen your grip before I throw up!"

I release her and adjust myself, a bit embarrassed. *I guess if we die, we will die together.*

It doesn't take long to reach an area of familiar woods. I recognize the opening in the trees ahead: the Hundred Harvest clearing where our sacred tree used to be.

Hollis yells something into the wind, and as we reach the edge of the clearing, she leans forward. But Ruby holds to her course and doesn't descend to the ground. My heart is racing as I hold my breath. Ruby rebels by soaring across the village of Balfour and toward the river on the other side.

Hollis leans to the side, and Ruby finally obeys. I let the air out of my lungs as we round the village. Our men, women, and children point at us in the sky.

Hollis aligns Ruby with the clearing again, then signals her to land. The dragon gives a muffled screech and rejects Hollis's directions. Again. She flaps her wings harder and circles toward the north mountains.

"Come on, girl!" Hollis shouts and groans. She presses Ruby in another circle.

Thoughts of getting stuck in the air on a dragon for hours

and hours make my throat run dry. I imagine the worst and tilt my head skyward. *At least we aren't as high as those clouds.*

Another dragon's call comes from behind us. Hellwig and Wilhelm are gaining on us. He maneuvers his mighty dragon ahead of ours, taking the lead. Ruby follows close behind Wilhelm's left wing.

Wilhelm dips to the right. Ruby dips right.

Wilhelm slows. Ruby slows.

I take another deep breath, releasing the tension in my chest as Wilhelm descends toward the clearing and Ruby follows him all the way down. Wilhelm puts his feet out and his wings up, landing gracefully in the brown grass.

Ruby's wings go upward, and I feel the ground meet her feet. She comes to an abrupt halt and both of us on the saddle are thrown forward. We can only go so far before our saddle belts catch us. I shove myself back into my seat as Hollis laughs.

"Holy skies! I didn't think she'd ever land!" Hollis blurts then double whistles. She unlatches her belt and climbs down before I can get my shaky hands to obey.

The Shift 35

TOLLIVER

As soon as the third shofar blast echoes through our valley, I am out of the medical ward and running to find Ledger. Kava hollers something from inside, but I keep on running to find him. Grandmother has not improved. Her struggle to breathe has gone from her nose and throat, into her chest. This morning, I set pots of boiling water all around her cottage to release steam with eucalyptus, peppermint leaves, and lemon rind.

I've taken it as my mission to keep her alive. At least until Ledger arrives. But even that has been uncertain for the last few days. She's ashen like Clovis in his last days. My body surges with adrenaline as I remember his last breath. It haunts me and drives me to keep from losing another.

Red and green streaks across the sky as two dragons land on our sacred grounds. Picking up speed, I run full force through the short woods between Balfour and the Hundred Harvest area. My legs ache as I careen through the crowds gathered all around the space. Ellerians reuniting with Ellerians, Balfourians reuniting with Balfourians.

I spot my parents on the path between the sacred grounds and Balfour. I run to them. My father looks up in time to catch me in his arms. I hug him hard. "Father," I whisper into his neck. When I pull away, he holds my shoulders and looks me full in the face.

"Tolliver," he says, teary eyed. "My firstborn. Thank you for coming back to us. I'm sorry we did not tell you sooner about your birth family. I only found out after you and Ledger left last harvest. We have much to talk about."

"We do," I agree. "Right now, Grandmother wishes to meet with all of us at her cottage. She is not well, and she needs the family immediately."

He pulls me in for another embrace then releases me. "We will meet you there," he says.

When I reach the clearing, Hollis hands the reigns of a red dragon to Hellwig—a dragon I don't recognize. Ledger is lying in the dirt. At first, I'm worried he is not okay, and then he rolls over laughing. I come to a halt over him, and my shadow blocks the sun from blinding him. "Ledger, come quick! Grandmother needs you."

His eyes grow round, and he scrambles up from the ground. "What? What is it?"

"She asked me to bring you to her as soon as you arrived. It's urgent." I hear the panic in my own voice. I grab him in my arms in a big hug, thankful he made it back alive. "Welcome home, brother."

"Thanks," he says.

We separate and I wave for him to follow me. He keeps up with my swift pace. As we emerge through the woods, the bell at the village square rings over and over and over. I scowl. *What now?*

I redirect Ledger and Hollis toward the village square. The rest of our village emerges from their homes and join us on the path.

Our parents emerge from my childhood home with my three younger siblings. The little ones run to Ledger and hug him in a lump. He lifts little Hazel into his arms and tells her how big she's getting. When mother reaches him, she yanks him into a hug. She pulls away, kisses him on the cheek, and says, "Welcome home, Ledger. I've missed you."

We head for the village square as she takes my father's hand, pulling him through the crowd of wingless and winged people. The rest of us follow directly behind, like a family of little ducklings: Ledger holding Hazel, Hollis, Mila, Killian, and me.

"Welcome home, men of Balfour!" Elder Jubal shouts as the noise around the square dies down. "Welcome home, travelers! Thank you for your bravery in rescuing our men, and thank you for your endurance. I'm sure we will be hearing your heroic stories for many moons."

I gaze around; the entire village appears to be present.

"As you know, our way of life has drastically changed over the past year, with new friends moving into the village. We welcomed them with open arms, and now we wish to make them allies in the next phase of life in Balfour. We have merged our governments, elders and advisors."

When Jubal pauses, his mustache twitches in disgust. I move forward in the crowd, dragging my siblings with me, to get a better view. I lift Killian and put him on my shoulders.

"Our mutual queen has made a decree that we should

become a republic, all having equal say in how our village is run."

Murmurs skitter through the crowd in happy surprise. *I'm glad for that.*

Jubal continues, "Queen Huyana will join the council as an equal member. We will no longer be ruled by a king or a queen, but by our governing body. That body will be voted upon by everyone. It will not be filled with favored families. We have created the foundation of what we believe will be a good system of preserving the health and vitality of our combined people. We have all signed the documents and have handed them over to Queen Huyana to sign them now that our entire village is present."

Jubal's eyes make their way across the crowd and fall upon Ledger beside me. I turn to Ledger, and he tips his head in curiosity.

Jubal continues his explanation of how to nominate someone for the council. I consider nominating myself. I cross my arms over Killian's feet overhanging my shoulders and feel the satchel hanging at my side, full of medicines and oils. It reminds me of my current mission: *I need to deliver Ledger to Grandmother immediately.*

***

As soon as Jubal's announcement is complete, I set Killian on his feet, and Angus's voice calls from behind me. I whirl around in search of him.

Berthold, Angus's older brother, reaches for me and wraps me in a bear hug. "Hello cousin," he says, sounding more like himself now than Angus.

I clench my eyes until the tears subside. He releases me, and I say, "Welcome home, Bert." I shake my head and acknowledge Angus's absence. "I'm sorry about Angus."

"Me too," Berthold says as Ledger steps up beside us.

Ledger has grown while he's been gone. He towers over me by at least a full hand. Berthold and I look up at him. "I'm sorry I couldn't bring Angus back safely to you." He shakes his head. "He would have wanted you to have this." He holds out his hand, and I raise mine to meet his.

He sets a small, warm stone in my palm. I lift it to inspect it closely. *It's Angus's lucky stone.* A memory comes flooding back of the early days of learning how to hunt. Angus was getting more and more frustrated that he couldn't hit a moving target with an arrow. I knew all he needed to do was focus and hold fast. So I kicked through the dirt until I found this small stone. I laid it in his palm and said, "This will help you hit your target." The very next shot he took, he dropped an eight-point white tail. Ever since, he kept that stone in his pocket every time we hunted or went into battle.

Looking from Ledger to Berthold, I can't make out their expressions through the blurry tears. "Thanks, Ledger."

After saying goodbye to Berthold, we make our way toward Grandmother's cottage.

"Ledger!" Kava calls from Grandmother's porch. "Welcome home!" Baby Liam is strapped to the front of her, facing us. My son has round cheeks, dark eyes, and wisps of blonde hair framing his face. He gives us a toothless smile.

"Hi, Kava." Ledger scrambles quickly up the stairs. "Is this…?"

"This is your nephew, Liam." She rubs his fuzzy head.

Ledger puts his fingers in Liam's grip. "Hello, Liam." He tickles his belly, and a sweet little laugh bubbles out—and Liam's little feathery wings pop out from his sides.

"Oh my lands!" Ledger jerks back. "He has wings!" He flashes me a wide smile. "How did you do that?"

I laugh and shake my head. "It's not magic; we are all Ellerian, Ledger."

He strokes the tiny down feathers. "They're so soft." He chuckles and asks to hold him.

Kava pulls him from the pouch and hands him to Ledger. I ruffle the little hairs on Liam's head as I toddle up the stairs and into Grandmother's house.

"Grandmother," I call through the doorway as the strong smell of eucalyptus wafts in my face. "I've brought Ledger. But he's been detained by my handsome child."

My eyes adjust to the indoor lights, and my Balfourian parents are already there. Mother sits by her side. Father stands at the end of the bed. Mila, Killian, and Hazel are sitting on the bench at the table. Their silence worries me.

I walk to Grandmother's bedside. It appears she is waking from a nap. Her eyes are droopy as she tries to focus on my eyes. Her voice drifts from her still body. "Ledger?"

I put my hand on her forehead and find her temperature elevated again. I shake my head, knowing it's possible she won't recover from this. She's too elderly and weak.

"Ledger," I call out the door. "Grandmother needs you."

Ledger, Liam, and Kava join us in the cottage. I hand Mother a wet rag to help cool her dying mother.

Ledger hands the baby back to Kava, and he steps to

Grandmother's bedside. Mother lets him sit on the bed as she pulls up a chair.

"Ledger," Grandmother whispers with a weak smile.

"I made you something," Ledger puts his hand in his pocket and pulls out a silver ring. He pinches it between his thumb and finger, showing it to her. It bears the royal crest of a bird with a branch in its mouth. "Your own royal ring. Made for a lady."

He lifts her slender hand and slides it on her third finger.

A tear pools in her eye and trickles down the wrinkles in her cheeks. "Oh my boy," she says. "You are thoughtful and kind." She lifts her hand to see the ring, then lays both hands over her heart.

"I learned to smith silver on Ellery. We made a lot of good trades and ended up with some precious metals. You would not believe how hard it was to make that. But it had to be perfect. For you."

"Thank you." A tight cough escapes her lips, and she grips her chest as she hacks heavily. Mother reaches over with the cool cloth and wipes her face and neck as she lies back exhausted. She is still for a long moment, and I hold myself back from checking her pulse. *She can't give up now.*

Thrive 36

ALOUETTE

I pad quietly up the front steps of Queen Huyana's cottage. I need to see her. I want to tell her she was right. She knew I needed to let my father and, most importantly, myself off the hook

The front door is wide open, and voices drift through as I step to the doorway. I knock on the door jamb.

Many eyes meet mine: Ledger's entire family.

"Come in," a man's voice says from inside.

"Alouette," a woman calls behind me. "Is Ledger in there?" It's Hollis. She is jogging down the path, out of breath and quite disheveled.

I peer at every face in the cottage and find Ledger seated on the bed in front of his grandmother.

"Yes," I say to Hollis. I turn to the people in the cottage. "Should I come back another time?"

Queen Huyana whispers something and Ledger says, "You can come in. This is a family thing, so you should be here."

His words stop me in my tracks. *I am family?*

I gape at him and at the rest of his family. *My family?* Sadness and hope pull me in opposing directions. But hope thrusts me through the door, and I step to the foot of the bed next to Fergus. He smiles at me.

I don't know how to feel or what to say. I wanted to thank Queen Huyana and be gone. But this family won't let me go.

Ledger is the glue in this family I've gotten myself into. *How dare I think I could lose him, accidentally or intentionally.*

All my well-laid plans come rushing through my mind as Hollis stomps up the stairs and across the porch. "Ledger?" she calls.

"We're in here." Ledger waves her in. She flits across the room to his side and puts her hand on his shoulder.

I had plans of leaving this place. Leaving everyone I've ever known. Avoiding everyone that has ever caused me pain. But as I weed through it all, it doesn't seem that terrible: the pain of letting someone through my walls is outweighed by the happy tears of belonging.

I know I can't leave these people behind forever. This family. My family.

There is something I need to do, not only for myself, but for this family.

Hollis reaches forward and touches Queen Huyana's hand. "You're not well."

The queen peers up at Ledger. "They've made the announcement about the republic, and I need to tell you of our backup plan." She glances around the room at each one at her bedside. Something unspoken happens between each one.

When she meets my eyes, it takes all my effort to keep from bursting into tears. Her countenance radiates love, and it fills an emptiness that has pained me for far too long. As she looks at Fergus next to me, I inhale deeply.

The queen musters the strength to speak. "This is the rightful royal family of Ellery, here in this room. Look at each one of you. Strong, connected, loving, and compassionate. I could not have asked for a better family."

She closes her eyes for a moment. When they open again, Adaya sighs. Everyone braces for her end. I frown and ache inside. I don't want to lose her. I worry my toxicity has reached her too.

No. That's a lie. I let out the breath I've been holding.

This isn't because of me.

Queen Huyana takes a breath along with me and says, "Ledger, you are our backup plan." She takes his hands in hers. "Our family will always have a place on the council. It will pass from generation to generation as a royal right."

Ledger shakes his head. "That isn't fair to everyone else."

She smiles. "But this family is special. We are royal. I've hidden from it for far too long. I regret that. I've stood by and watched terrible things happen between our people. And the security I've built in this new government is the fact that our family will always be there to see it through. To ensure its success."

I am surprised by how similarly we feel, the guilt of being complacent. I wrap my arms around my stomach to hold myself together. I need to make sure this family survives.

I had planned to leave on Ellery once and for all.

Disappear into Hartwynn.

But now I know what I must do. Everything inside me shifts in an instant. *I must keep our trade agreements with all the peoples in Ellery's path and bring back what Balfour needs to thrive.* I smile at the thought.

Queen Huyana's voice pulls me back to the present. "If the transition into the republic doesn't work, Adaya will become queen. You, Ledger, will be king after her."

Ledger stands abruptly from the bed.

37

Kiss Goodbye

LEDGER

"King?" The word bursts from my lips. It's heavy and out of place as I stand gaping at my grandmother. Hollis takes my left hand.

My mother stands from her chair and takes my other hand. Her smile confuses me. "This is your birthright. Granted it's a birthright you never knew you had."

"What about Tolliver?" I ask. "He's—"

"He abdicated, to you."

I freeze. It's as though I've suddenly gone deaf. Confusing feelings work their way into words and out of my mouth. "I can't be a king." My throat is dry and my head is swirling. "I'm just a blacksmith's son. A nobody."

"It doesn't matter who you *think* you are. What matters is who *I* know you are," Grandmother says. "You are thoughtful and kind. And that is enough, right there, to make a great king."

"You are a true leader, Ledger," my father says. I meet his gaze. He uncrosses his arms and comes around the bed. He offers a hand. I release Hollis and mother's hands. He grips my forearm. “As I recall, that is the last thing I said to you before leaving Ellery. I knew you could do this.”

Everything inside me wants to fight against it. I don’t feel royal at all. I feel powerless and insignificant. I swallow, and the only thing I can say is, “What about Tolliver? He’s the oldest. He’s stronger, and smarter.”

Tolliver holds a sleeping winged child in his arms and gives a closed mouth smile as if he’s honored I would say it. “I am not blood kin,” he explains. “Though we are family by choice.”

My heart races, and I consider the magnitude of this responsibility. *The republic cannot fail. I can't be a king.*

I remember King Ciel with a regal countenance and intense eyes on his throne.

I think about Grandmother last harvest, descending from the sky on the back of a dragon and declaring herself queen.

I doubt my every thought, my every move. My cheeks grow hot, and I don’t know what to do with myself.

Then I mull over this past year on Ellery. It has been one challenge after the other, leading our men home. I look at my father. He followed my lead.

I look at Alouette, who joined my rescue mission. She didn’t have to, but I know without a doubt she did it because I asked her to.

I release my father’s grip and reach for Hollis. She would follow me anywhere. All the men of Balfour trusted me to care for them while they fought for their lives after being tortured by that barbaric tribe.

If they all believe I can do this, and I trust them deeply, then it must be true. This wasn’t what I was expecting when

I returned to Balfour. I thought everything would go back to the beginning, like nothing happened. But I see now how ridiculous that was.

I swallow and face Grandmother. She awaits my response. I sit and take her hand. It is small and frail. Her skin is pale and droops at her cheeks. I don't know how many harvests she's seen, but her eyes are full of wisdom and hope.

"Thank you, Grandmother, for the honor." I clear my throat to hold my voice steady. "I will do as you ask. I will do all I can to keep the republic alive, and if Balfour needs me to, I will accept the throne."

The words are a bridge spanning over a canyon of fears. Speaking it grants me safe passage.

Grandmother smiles at me and holds my gaze for the longest time.

I wait for her to release me. But I've blinked at least two or three times, and her eyes remain motionless.

My mother reaches over and brushes her eyes closed.

A shooting pain thrusts through my heart. *My grandmother is dead.* I struggle to breathe as my throat closes.

Tears well in my eyes and trickle down my face. People start moving around me. They walk away and murmur in hushed tones.

I'm not prepared for this. Any of this.

I can't look away from Grandmother Huyana. Her Ellerian name, her real name, was Paloma. She once told me it means dove, a symbol of peace.

She certainly brought peace.

Only two harvests ago, I wished for peace and friendship with the winged people of Ellery. It was something

Grandmother wanted too, for longer than I knew.

But I can't let her go. Not yet.

There is so much to tell her. I want to tell her about this year on Ellery. Our wins. Our losses. I want to see the proud look on her face with every story.

But she is gone.

Air finally reaches my lungs. I lean forward and cry silently over her. I pull her hand to my lips and give her a kiss goodbye.

"You were my best friend," I say. "You were the best listener. You had a way of pouring wisdom deep into my soul and a way of knocking me on the back of the head when I needed it."

Someone sighs beside me. I peer over at Hollis sitting in my mother's chair. She puts her hand out and I take it. She stands and pulls me from the bed. She hugs me hard and my tears fall into her hair. Her body convulses. She is crying too.

When she pulls away, she brushes her thumbs across my wet cheeks. "She's right, you know."

I tip my head in curiosity.

"You are thoughtful and kind," she says with a radiant smile and teary eyes.

"I wish I could have shown my grandmother how special she was to me," I whisper and lay my forehead on hers.

Hollis laughs and says, "You made her the most beautiful ring I've ever seen. You accomplished that."

I smile to myself. *I sure did do that.* I run my fingers through her hair and thank the skies for my Hollis.

Life is so fragile.

I wish I could show Hollis how special *she* is to me.

A thought strikes me, and I smile through the tears.

38
Like My Father

TOLLIVER

"And to this ground we commit Queen Huyana, Queen Paloma's body," Adaya says, tossing an olive branch on the top of her grave. The fresh dirt smell wafts in my face.

The sun breaks through the clouds and warms the crowd gathered in the field Ledger calls the baby graveyard. He demanded we bury her here among the children to whom she gave a resting place. It is the perfect place.

Several men helped haul three large flat shale stones from the river for us, laying them all out in a row. I take the first and largest, laying it at the head of her burial place.

Ledger walks over, lifts the medium rock, and lays it on top of mine. "Goodbye, Grandmother," he says.

Mila, with a bit of grunting, takes the smallest of the three and heaves it on the top of the stack.

Killian and Hazel place a few extra pebbles on top of the stack as their own commemoration, then walk back to mother, slipping their hands into hers.

Sadness touches every bit of my heart from the loss of Clovis, to the loss of Angus, and now the loss of my grandmother. I slip my hand inside my pocket and pull out Angus's stone.

Life and death are strange. It seems we must hold each other with an open hand. I lay the small round stone on Grandmother's memorial. *Goodbye, Angus.*

The others start walking away through the field, toward the village. Hollis and Ledger slip away. Mother gathers the children and follows them through the woods.

Father steps to my side. "Shall we walk together?"

We follow the rest of the family and friends, winged and wingless, who came to help commit her to the ground. I introduced him to my Ellerian father and sister yesterday. It was an awkward few moments, but they will be good friends in time. Tiberius has accepted that Adaya and Fergus are my parents. I will always love them and rely on their support. I'm glad Tiberius and Kailani have grown closer to my family since being in Balfour.

My father and I walk in silence through the crunchy grass until we reach the shadows of the wood. He stares straight ahead and says, "Did you hear they announced the nominations for the council?"

"No, I didn't. I was helping with Grandmother."

He walks with his hands behind his back like he's holding a secret.

"Were you nominated?" I ask.

"I was not. It is in the signed documents that two people from the same house are not permitted. And luckily for me, the royal line gets one seat on the council." He smiles and it confuses me.

"Luckily for you?" I peer at him, confused. "You don't

want to be on the council?"

"Oh, Tolliver, don't you know me? I am a battalion leader, a teacher of hand to hand combat. I never enjoyed sitting in a room arguing over the greater good. Meeting with the elders exhausted me. Oh, and smithing? I was filling my father's shoes. Now we have old Deveraux smithing for the whole village." He snickers and pats me on the back. "I am finally free to do what I desire."

I guess I never took the time to understand what truly drives him. "You are the best battalion leader, speaking as one of your previous students and warriors."

"You've always had a lot of skill with the sword, Tolliver."

The river of words I haven't shared with him starts backing up. I wonder if the dam will break before I am solid enough in my decision to let some of it flow. *Will he judge me?*

"Baer and I will start training and getting our men back into shape, so if the savages ever return, we are better protected," he says.

"Now that all our efforts aren't wasted protecting ourselves from people on that island?"

"Yes," he says. "We will also train the guardians on ground warfare and defensive strategies."

I nod in agreement. "So, who was nominated for the council?"

"All the current elders except Chasen. A few Ellerians, Advisor Tiberius and Advisor Gabriel. Oh and, Advisor Samhul. Also, Laurid, Espen's wife. And a handful of Ellerians I haven't met yet. I guess voting will happen at the

Harvest Festival. Each one nominated will have a chance to introduce themselves and invite people to vote for them."

We walk in silence long enough for me to open the floodgates and just tell him. "Well, Father, you raised me well. I learned many skills in your care. In this past year, I learned even more about myself. I started apprenticing as a healer alongside Kava, and I must tell you, it is fulfilling work."

"Really? A healer?" He purses his lips and tips his head.

What could that mean? I brace myself for judgment.

"I helped deliver my own son into this world," I say.

"Oh?" His eyes widen.

"It was beautifully terrifying. More challenging than any battle, more fulfilling than any elders' meeting."

"So you've found something you can be passionate about?"

"Yes, and quite by accident. It wasn't what I would have originally chosen. But now that I'm in it, I could never walk away from it. I am a husband, a father, and a healer," I say, walking confidently to the edge of the river. The rest of our people have already crossed ahead of us.

Father smiles wide through his graying beard and puts his hand on my shoulder, stopping me before I cross. "There are only two things that carried me through my early years: be true to yourself and commit to a good woman. You've done both quite magnificently."

I put my chin up and say, "Thank you, father."

We both forge the flowing river, and I notice halfway across that I walk like my father, hands behind my back, leaning slightly forward, and a smile on my face.

39 The Honor

ALOUETTE

"Can I talk to you?" I approach Ledger inside the workshop as he looks up from the anvil.

"Sure, Alouette."

I walk outside, hoping he will follow. When he steps to the door, I break the news quickly. "I'm going to stay on Ellery."

His smile slides into a frown.

"Hi, Alouette," Hollis calls from down the path and waves to me. "I'm looking for Ledger."

He steps outside into the evening sun. "I'm here."

Hollis touches his arm and slides her hands into his. "Did you get a chance to make my new buckle?"

"Yes." He ducks back into the workshop and returns with a strip of leather and a mended buckle on the end.

"Thank you!" Hollis smiles. Her blue eyes shine at him. "I can't wait to marry you!"

"Yes, I'm looking forward to the spring and getting married on Delineation Day," Ledger says awkwardly. I wonder why he is being so formal.

"You're my favorite," she says.

"Alouette, we want you to be there, at our wedding." Ledger's eyes are scrunched with pleading. "Please say you'll be there."

"Why wouldn't she be there?" Hollis scowls in confusion. "Everyone's going to be there."

I wring my hands. "I've decided to stay on Ellery."

"What? No!" Hollis crosses her arms in protest.

"When are you going to stop running away?" Ledger asks. "Your life is here. Your family is here."

I'm not looking for an argument. I resist the urge to cross my arms.

Belamy walks around the corner and knocks into Ledger. Belamy reaches out and catches him before he slams into the workshop wall. "Sorry, little buddy." He stands Ledger on his feet and says to me, "There you are."

"Do you know about this?" Ledger asks Belamy. "She wants to leave on Ellery again."

Belamy smiles and flaps his black wings one time. "Of course."

Ledger is taken aback with his mouth open and his eyes wide. He looks at Belamy, then me, then back at Belamy.

I cut in. "I'm not running away, Ledger. I think it would be best if someone stayed on the island and upheld the trade agreements we made this year."

"But you'll miss our wedding." Hollis reaches out and takes my hand. "I consider you my sister. I've never had a sister. You're the only one I've got. And I need you there."

"I know. But Balfour needs the supplies Ellery can provide. Belamy has agreed to go with me."

Belamy interjects, "And Estefano, Swarley, Zander, Hellwig, and a handful of others."

"I thought you hated that island," Ledger says. He eyes Belamy like there's something he's hiding.

"I don't like someone telling me where I can and cannot go. We were trapped on Ellery before." Belamy loosens his stance. "Now, I can go where I please, when I please, with whomever I pretty please."

Hollis giggles at his remark.

I make eye contact with Ledger. "Who do I talk to about getting a large supply of grain to initiate the trades?"

Ledger blinks several times, then says. "My mother, I guess."

"Will you ask her?"

He looks down with sadness in his eyes. I know he wants to argue more, but something about the way he stands up straighter tells me he understands.

"Excuse me, Hollis. I need to find my mother."

"Okay," she says with a sigh. "Goodbye, future mate."

"Goodbye, future mate," he repeats, watching her jog up the path.

Belamy laughs at their cuteness.

Ledger sighs deeply, and when Hollis is out of sight, he turns to me. "I have to tell you a secret!"

My head jerks back. "What?"

Belamy steps closer to hear. He puts his hand on the small of my back.

The evening sun shines on Ledger's face. "I hate keeping secrets, and I hate surprises, but Hollis loves surprises and springing them on me. I thought it was time to give her what she loves. To show her how much I—" He looks up at Belamy. "You know what I mean."

He leans in. "We aren't getting married in the spring."

I raise my eyebrows and lean in too, concerned there is a rift between them.

"I've arranged with Jubal to wed us tomorrow at the Harvest Festival." He clamps his teeth together in an intense smile. "She has no idea."

"That is so sweet, Ledger. She will love it." I'm happy they have each other. I think about my own wedding and wonder if that day will ever come. I've only ever dismissed the thought, feeling unworthy of happiness.

Belamy cackles a little too loud. "It's about time you caught up with her, Ledger."

I scrutinize him. He is muscular and handsome. Would he make me happy? I'm pretty sure I'm the only one in charge of my happiness, but he would make a nice addition to that. After all, he is going with me on Ellery.

Ledger explains, "All she ever does is surprise me, so I figured she needs a really big surprise!"

"You two could not be more opposite," I say. We laugh together about his spontaneous bride.

"Right you are," he says with a loud sigh. He snaps back to the present. "Please tell me you won't be leaving until after the Harvest Festival."

"I wouldn't miss it," I say with a smile.

Ledger flicks at one of my feathers. "Let's go find my mother."

***

After loading more grain than I ever dreamed they would agree to provide, Belamy and I descend toward the village with a basket of items Ledger needed me to fetch. I scan the people below, looking for Ledger. His parents and sister are there, but he is nowhere to be found.

"I'm going to find Ledger," I say to Belamy as my wings carry me downward.

He slips his bronze hand in mine. We stop our descent for a moment as he kisses my hand. His raven-black wings work the air. I meet his eyes as we are suspended in the cool autumn wind. His eyes are full of hope. He smiles and says, "I'll meet you at the feast."

I can't hide my smile and the way he makes me feel.

"Thank you for coming with me," I say.

"I love a good feast," he says, still holding my hand.

"No, I mean, back to Ellery."

He tilts his head and gazes at my lips. My heart flutters in my chest, and I can barely breathe when I say, "You can kiss me now."

"You sure?" He glances below. "The whole world can see."

"I think the whole world saw this coming."

He grins, sliding a hand around my waist and the other against my jaw.

I lay my cold hand on his shoulder and hold the basket off to the side. His body heat radiates through his tunic and longcoat. He leans into me and stops before our lips touch. I press in and kiss him first. Something inside me bubbles to the surface. I can't hold it back, and it sneaks out in a giggle as I pull away first.

"What is so funny?" he asks. I don't open my eyes, because I don't want to see him feeling as insecure as he sounds.

"I'm happy," I whisper, pressing my forehead to his.

"Whew, I'm so relieved. I thought you hated my kiss."

I snort, and he joins my laughter. I open my eyes to his joyous face, wide smile, and big brown eyes.

I release him and fly toward the sacred grounds with my basket. He lets me go without another word, and I don't turn back to make sure he watches me go. I know he does.

As I touch down in the clearing around the old tree stump, I gasp at the sight.

There is a metal tree standing on the knee-high platform over the stump. Ledger lights the lanterns hanging from its metal boughs.

"What is this?" I motion to the tree.

Startled, he whirls around.

"Oh! Alouette, you scared me." He rubs his head with his free hand and waves a lighted stick in the other. His brown curly hair is trimmed tightly to the sides of his head with fluffy curls on the top. "I made Hollis a Hundred Harvest Tree to get married under."

The sun is setting behind the tree and the orange light casts a lovely glow all around him and his creation.

"It's beautiful!" I say.

"Thank you. Did you find what I needed?"

I nod and hold up the basket. A bell tolls in the village and a drum beats in the distance.

He announces, "Here they come!"

He lights the last lantern in the large metal tree which

reaches wider than my wingspan. I can't believe he made this in a matter of days.

The drums grow louder with the strum of a lute and several trilling piccolos as the hum of joyful voices draws near.

Ledger stomps out the lighted twig and steps to the edge of the platform. He nervously straightens the collar of his crisp white tunic and pale blue longcoat. It fits him perfectly, as if it were tailored for this day. His eyes light up as he watches the path, waiting for Hollis.

The path strewn with bright yellow, orange, and red leaves stretches from the village, through the woods, straight to the platform on which Ledger stands. The sun hits each face and lights up every eye as they emerge from the dark of the woods. More and more of our people pour into the clearing. It becomes increasingly difficult for me to see who has arrived, but Ledger gasps. *Hollis must be here.*

As soon as each person sees Ledger, they seem to know why he is standing there. They part the way and exit the path of leaves, standing on either side, opening the way for Hollis.

Her eyes light up as she catches sight of him. Her mouth hangs agape, and her hands press to her heart. Her pale cheeks blush as though the sight of it all has taken her breath away. Her golden dress sparkles in the evening light. It hugs her tightly around the waist and drapes to her toes. Her hair is pulled up halfway and the rest cascades down to the middle of her back.

I can't hear what she says to her parents, but her father nods, and Hollis bounces on the balls of her feet. She kisses his cheek and dances up the path toward Ledger.

I've never seen a Balfourian wedding and wonder what it entails, especially with all the odd things Ledger asked me to collect. I hold the basket tight as Hollis comes to rest at the foot of the lighted metal tree. Her face and hair glow in the warm sunlight.

Ledger pulls her up onto the platform and whispers, "Surprise."

Adaya climbs the left side stairs. As the queen, she will lead the ceremony. Her long, silver-gray dress swishes softly on the wood platform. Overlooking the crowd, she raises her hands and all the voices hush.

"We bless this union of Ledger and Hollis and speak life to their future offspring," she declares.

Beside me, Tolliver and Kava hand Ledger and Hollis a bundle of leaves. With bubbling excitement, they accept, kiss the leaves, and toss them over their heads. They fall gently all around, raining down a sense of joy and anticipation. Murmurs go through the crowd all around. The word *bless* drifts through their soft words.

Ledger whispers to me, "Alouette, the white cloth."

I jolt to attention and open the woven lid of the basket. I pull out the beautiful cloth Adaya made. It is a crisp white fabric with lace all along the edges. Ledger gently takes it from my hands. He unrolls it, and the light glints off certain parts. There is silver thread throughout the lace. It is truly a beautiful piece, fit for royalty. But I have a feeling Adaya would have made it the same even if there weren't royalty.

Adaya addresses the crowd. "This covering represents their mutual agreement to provide safety, security, comfort, and intimacy to one another."

Ledger lays the most ornate part over the top of Hollis's head, and the rest flows down her back, the way of a bride's veil. Adaya tucks a hair pin on either side to hold it in place.

Hollis's eyes well with tears, which she dabs away, as she says thank you to Ledger and Adaya.

As soon as Adaya steps away, drums pound a loud rhythm as all the wingless people stomp their feet and dance. The Ellerian people follow their lead and dance as long as the music lasts. Joy abounds as if we are agreeing to their long happy union. I dance and move my body to the music with the basket in hand.

The drums stop abruptly. Silence falls on all our people. Ledger and Hollis lean into one another and kiss for the first time as husband and wife. As soon as they separate, the people cheer and clap. My heart bursts with love for this new world I'm a part of. I almost wish I were staying longer to enjoy it. But I have work to do.

Ledger turns to the crowd and raises his hand. "It is not our tradition to trade trinkets, but I wanted to give my bride a gift." He pulls a small item from his trouser pocket and holds it into the light. The sun glints off its surface, and my breath catches in my throat. "I want to give you my grandmother's ring with the royal crest. I love you."

Hollis's eyes well with tears as Ledger slides it on her finger. She wraps her arms around him in gratitude. Behind me, there is a commotion as three men with torches make their way through the crowd.

Elder Jubal, Advisor Tiberius, and another Balfourian I don't know approach the neatly stacked pyramid of wood beyond the metal Hundred Harvest Tree. They toss their torches, and the pyre begins to burn. Ledger and Hollis descend the stairs behind Adaya.

I thought the ceremony was complete. I'm confused as the crowd moves beyond the tree and platform.

"Alouette, come on," Ledger calls. He waves me toward the fire. I have no idea what is going on.

When I reach Ledger and Hollis, she asks, "You knew about this surprise?"

I nod. She hugs me as I say, "Sisters, remember?"

Ledger opens my basket and pulls out the iron ore he needed. "Hollis gets the holly branches."

I carefully reach in and pull out the spiky bunch. I tip it so Hollis can take it without getting sliced as many times as I did while picking the hideous plant. She pulls off a short branch and gives it to her mother, another to her father, and one each to her two younger brothers.

Ledger takes his handful of iron ore and hands the gray rocks to Adaya and Fergus. He hands one to Tolliver, Mila, Killian, and Hazel. Then he holds out the last piece to me. I take it, nervous about what I'm supposed to do with it.

Hollis's family steps toward the fire alongside Ledger's family—my family. They all speak at once, "Through life into death, we combine into dust, never to be separated." I repeat it, whispering under my breath having not known the words. Then her family tosses the holly branches and we toss our stones into the flames.

The words make tears come to my eyes. I've never been in such a large family. I've never felt like this before: connected and unconditionally accepted.

Hollis smiles at me. "Definitely sisters now."

I hug her and say, "Congratulations on your union."

She lets me go, and both families exchange hugs. The rest of the village fades to the southern side of the tree where the feast is being served. Mila hugs me, and as I turn around, there stands Belamy with two golden rings. One large, one small.

My heart races.

This is one tradition I am familiar with, and I can hardly breathe as I hope he's doing what I think he's doing.

"Fergus, sir," Belamy says.

All of Ledger and Hollis's family stop and gather around. Fergus raises his eyebrows at Belamy, which feels strangely rehearsed.

"May I have the honor of marrying Alouette?"

My breath catches.

Fergus clears his throat and looks me deeply in the eyes. "Alouette, do you wish to marry this guardian?"

I blink at his formality. These are the words I thought I'd never hear after my father left this world.

I don't even need to think about it. "Yes. Yes, I do."

Fergus says to Belamy, "I give you my blessing to marry Alouette."

Fergus takes my hand and sets it on top of the rings in Belamy's hand. We grip them together as tears stream down my cheeks.

Ten Years Later

Epilogue

LEDGER

"They're going to be here today; I can smell it!" Hollis calls from the front porch.

I pull on my worn, brown leather coat and join her out front. Hollis is wrapped in a floor-length black cloak with speckled fur cascading over her shoulders. An autumnal wind blows back her cape, revealing her favorite black leather trousers and pale pink tunic. Her mother constantly tries to guilt her into wearing dresses again. I smile at my little rebel with weightless blonde hair dancing in the chilly morning breeze.

As soon as my feet hit the dusty path beside her, the shofar blasts three times in the distance.

"I knew it!" Hollis says then calls for our children. They all come running from around the cottage. In the chaos, I drift off in thought about when this cottage was my grandmother's. I smile at her memory and miss her with my whole being. The outside is exactly the same, but the inside is full of the signs of messy children and a carefree mother who finds cleaning to be secondary to fun.

"Ellery is here! Who wants to fly today?" Hollis asks all five of them.

"I'm riding Ruby!" my oldest son, Baofire, declares. He

is nine years old and as pale as his mother with golden hair and blue eyes. He isn't quite as tall as my shoulder yet, but his personality is as big and fierce as Angus once was.

"We are riding in Papa's flying contraption," Hollis says with excitement. She enjoys getting them all worked up. They cheer in unison except Baofire, who puts his hands on his hips in protest.

My youngest, Della, is carried around the corner by my father. She might be his favorite. He really enjoys being a grandfather. He says it's even better than being a parent. He lets Della down, and she runs to me. I scoop her into my arms, swish her mousy brown hair aside, and kiss her squishy round cheek. She will be two harvests old at the next full moon.

My father waves to us and continues on his way to the training grounds. I catch sight of my mother skirting between the cottages to catch up with him. She kisses him through his silvery beard, and they go their separate ways.

Dove, Jasper, and Opal, my three middle children, rattle off too many questions. Thankfully, Hollis fields them all, even though she encourages the chaos.

"Remember, Liam and Rosie wanted to come with us this time, so let's fetch them." I herd my wildcats toward my brother's house. I'm pleased that I told Deveraux to ready the flying contraption this morning. We've tested it several days in a row now.

As we reach the front porch of the medical ward, Sybella is ascending the steps. "Good morning," she calls, ducking her wings to fit under the low hanging porch ceiling.

"Good morning, Sybella." Hollis climbs the stairs behind

her.

The front door opens, and Liam flies out, nearly knocking the two women over. He suspends in midair above us on white wings that have grown longer than he is tall. "I heard the alarm! Come on, Rosie," Liam calls to his little sister.

Rosie comes clomping out. The little thing has her auburn, curly mop tied in ribbons on the top of her head. "Let's go, let's go, let's go," she shouts as she runs down the steps past her aunt. She shouts to her winged brother in the sky, "I bet I can beat you there!" It is a strange thing, who gets wings and who doesn't. I guess I'll never understand why.

"No way," Liam shouts and shoots through the sky toward the village square. My children follow Rosie's lead and chase after their cousins.

Tolliver and Kava appear on the porch as Sybella goes in.

"Will you be joining us?" Hollis follows them down the steps, joining me on the path.

"Wouldn't miss it," Tolliver says. "Besides, Sybella has the medical ward covered. Right, Kava?"

She gives an irritated look, as though she's uncomfortable leaving the place in Sybella's hands. Sybella is quite capable and a great addition to their team, serving all of Balfour.

The four of us pick up the pace as our children disappear around the bend ahead. Kava says hello to Rylan and his daughter sitting on their front steps. Tolliver waves to Kailani, who was the first Ellerian to marry a Balfourian, Bernhard. Many other folks emerge from their homes because of the shofar announcing the homecoming of our merchant ship:

the island of Ellery. This is the most happy, exciting time of year in Balfour. It is a stark difference from how I grew up, hiding in the cellar, fearing the annual battle with the winged people who lived on the island. Who knew that one choice by a young blacksmith's son could change the course of our history? I sigh at the memory and all the years of peace since.

The children eventually tire out, and the four of us parents walk up on them before entering the village square. Suddenly, a red dragon soars over the tips of the trees and along the thatched rooftops. She lights up the sky with her beaming scales. Someone rides her, but I can't see who. The children gasp and scramble around.

"Ruby's gotten bigger," Hollis says.

Sometimes, I can't tell the two red dragons apart from far off.

When Ruby returns, she dives into the square and glides along the ground. She stirs up the dust in her wake, nearly touching the cottage porches with the tip of one wing.

All the children squeal with joy at her arrival. She lands before us on her back feet, then her front, and claps her wings closed. Zander unlatches himself from the saddle and climbs down. He greets me with a handshake then walks off toward his family's cottage.

My children rush to Ruby's side, petting and hugging her bright cherry scales.

I wrap an arm around Hollis and kiss her head. "Your grandbaby is home."

She sighs in my embrace.

Alouette and Belamy took all the dragons to Ellery this last year to help load more and more goods onto the island, bringing them back to Balfour.

When the sky fills with voices, Hollis and I gaze into the blue to see who has arrived.

Over the tree line, Belamy's black wings appear, then Alouette's white ones. They descend into view and drop gently to the ground. Hollis breaks free from my arms and scuttles to Alouette, greeting her with a hug.

"Welcome home," I say to our world-traveling friends.

"Thanks, Little Buddy," Belamy says with a well-meaning smile, but the nickname doesn't bother me much anymore.

He greets Tolliver and Kava with a hug. "Wait until you see what I've brought you. It will transform this village!" His eyes grow large as he describes some sort of metal sheeting to replace our thatched roofs.

"That could seal up the leaks and keep the animals out," Tolliver says, nodding with approval.

When Hollis starts a high-pitched squeal standing with Alouette, I wonder what all the excitement about. "Holy skies! Ledger, guess what?" She leans into Alouette. "Can I tell him?"

Alouette must have said yes, because Hollis whirls around. "Alouette is with child!" She rubs Alouette's noticeably rounded belly.

How did I not see it when she arrived? I gape at her, looking from Alouette to Belamy.

"Congratulations!" I refrain from adding the word *finally* to the end of my sentiments. They've been unsuccessful in having children for these ten years traveling as merchants on Ellery.

"Thank you," Alouette says.

Kava hugs her, and Tolliver claps Belamy on the back.

"When are you expected to deliver?" Hollis asks.

"We calculate sometime in the next moon."

Hollis clasps her fingers together. "Does that mean you're staying in Balfour?"

Alouette looks at Belamy, who tips his head and shrugs. "You knew she was going to ask. I'll do whatever you want," he says.

After a sigh and a long moment of suspense, Alouette says, "We *will* be staying."

In the distance, a dragon caws. Hollis turns her attention to the sky with an anticipatory grin.

Tristeh soars high above, circling round and round, descending with every rotation. Eventually, she dips into the square, landing gracefully across the wide space without a rider, but her white saddle is securely in place. She pulls in her wings and settles onto the solid ground of home. She hasn't been able to close her right wing all the way since the Lianminese dragon tore it from joint to tip. It was stitched and healed, but the long, gnarled scar keeps her from holding herself the same ever since. She is tamer, and after Ruby rescued her, she somehow overcame her instincts, allowing Ruby to be a part of her world. Seems family is stronger than instinct, even for dragons.

My children take off running, except for little Della. She wanders around picking weeds she thinks are flowers.

Tristeh flaps her wings at the children as they dance around, making them topple over in the wind. Now I can tell the difference between them; Tristeh's scales are a deeper crimson than Ruby's.

Baofire is back on his feet in an instant and directing his siblings. "Jasper, you ride Tristeh. I'll ride Ruby, and we'll race!"

When Ruby stretches out her wing, Baofire climbs up and sits on her saddle.

"Baofire, get down from there!" I yell. My son is too at ease on a dragon. It shouldn't bother me, being that I'm married to the *queen dragon mother*. I call her that sometimes when she gets overly angry at the children. The thought makes me smile.

"I've got this," Hollis says, stalking toward the green-eyed dragon. I can't hear her words, but something she says causes Ruby to tip to the side and make Baofire fall off into the grass. The kids laugh. Hollis puts out a hand, and Baofire allows her to pull him up. She leans in and says something to him. His face brightens. They both look at me. I know what they are asking. I nod and my son scrambles up Ruby's outstretched wing. I watch him carefully as he secures himself to the saddle, pulling the adjustable strap tight. I let out the breath I'm holding. His face is full of wild-eyed pleasure, ready for the signal to go.

Hollis pets Ruby on the shoulder and heads toward her first baby. Tristeh bows her head. Hollis takes the giant scaly jaws in her small hands and presses her forehead to Tristeh's. She coos at her. I'm too far away to hear, but the scene brings tears to my eyes. Her love for that dragon abounds.

The children chant, "Fly-ing, fly-ing, fly-ing!" I roll my eyes at their impatience, even though I would have joined their excitement about flying when I was a boy. My face would have shined like Baofire's as Alouette took me into the world above.

Alouette laughs. "Take them flying, Ledger."

"Are you coming with us? My contraption should be all ready to go. I've got Deveraux heating it up near the Hundred Harvest Tree as we speak."

"Yes," she says. "Let me deliver my news to the rest of the council, and I'll meet you there." She takes Belamy by the hand, and they saunter toward Balfour. Something inside me feels settled anytime she is home, as though I spend the year worrying and now I can rest.

"All right, little flying beasts. To the sky!" I shout.

Hollis kisses Tristeh on the nose, whirls around, and flashes a beautiful, mischievous smile. "I'll meet you in the sky, Love."

She ascends Tristeh's left wing, straps herself in, and they dart into the blue together.

***

We step into the clearing of our sacred grounds where my flying contraption fills the air. The billowing float, made of the thinnest silky fabric crafted by Ellerian weavers, drifts above it. It is rounded at the top, ballooning into a big ball of vibrant red. Hollis requested it match her dragons.

On the ground beneath is a large woven basket, big enough to hold ten men. The furnace is mounted on four angled posts at the corners of the basket. It feeds hot air into the massive float. I smile at *my* baby. My wings. My way into the sky.

Deveraux stands beside our creation with his hands on his hips, belly hanging over his belt and wings hanging limply behind him. He gives me a wave then helps my middle children climb into the basket with Rosie.

I carry Della as I walk alongside Tolliver and Kava.

"Thanks for taking them up again, Ledger," Tolliver says. He pats my back, and Kava nods in agreement.

"Rosie would die if she couldn't fly with her brother," Kava says.

"No problem. Now that it is functioning properly, I'll be taking them up more often," I say, unable to stop smiling. The excitement builds in my belly. "Are you coming up this time?"

Tolliver shakes his head. "Maybe next time."

Kava agrees, "Next time."

Standing beneath my floating contraption, I gaze over at my other creation. The metal Hundred Harvest Tree I built for my wedding to Hollis stands nearly double its height and width now. Over the years, I've added more branches in an attempt to recreate the enormous living tree that used to stand in this spot.

"Come on, Papa," Jasper calls. "Baofire is winning." He reaches for me over the basket's side.

"Get your belts on. I'm coming." I hand Della to Kava.

While I climb over the side, Dove and Rosie help each other latch themselves in. The pair of eight-year-old cousins are best friends.

"Papa, I'm afraid," Dove says, holding the leash connected to her belt with white knuckles.

"We are perfectly safe in this basket, Little Dove." I

gently cup her chin and whisper, “Don’t think, just fly.”

She smiles up at me, and I kiss her on the head.

Then I check Jasper’s belt. The proud six-year-old already has it wrapped around himself and hooked over the safety bar on the basket’s interior. It allows the children to freely walk around without the risk of falling out or giving me heart palpitations—which almost killed me on our first flight. Opal is only four and is almost as tall as Jasper. They look like they could be twins with their unruly, brown hair. I belt Opal in tightly and turn to Della.

“Do you want to go up?” I ask my little one, pointing to the sky.

She bounces in Kava’s arms. “Uppie! Uppie! Uppie!” Della has not been flying yet. So far, every last one of my children love to fly. Kava carries her to me.

I wrap a belt around Della’s waist and cinch it tight, then hook the end over the bar. Taking her in my arms, I give Deveraux the signal to untie us from the stakes securing us to the ground. He walks from corner to corner, bends over, and unties the ropes. The basket jerks beneath us, and the children squeal with delight.

The ground drifts away as the clouds beckon us higher, like an old friend calling me home. I watch the faces of my children and niece. Their eyes are wide with wonder looking upward. Once we reach the treetops, Jasper happily points to the North Mountain. “There’s Baofire!”

He and Hollis are taking off again from the dragons’ cave Hellwig built in his few years living in Balfour. He had a series of caves dug from a naturally forming one on our side of the mountain. Hellwig died on Ellery several years ago, and Wilhelm didn't do well without him for a while after that. Wilhelm emerges from the cave sans rider, spreading his wings and joining Tristeh and Ruby in the sky. He must have been dropping off supplies.

Dove and Rosie gawk and point at the village as it gets smaller and smaller. I soak in the serene view of our village. The four concentric circles of cottages and workshops have grown to six, expanding to the woods on either side. The southern fields lay in a haphazard quilt pattern, not quite square, stretching into the distance beyond the brier.

The river to the east twinkles in the morning sun. There are a handful of cottages dotting the eastern ridge. Our village has expanded its borders beyond the bustling village below. Beside the mill, to the northeast, the market is filling with the winged and wingless, bringing their wares to sell and trade.

I think about all the effort we've put in over the years. My time on the council has been hard work and an honoring experience as they accepted me as a peer and leader. The republic has held nicely, and though some wish to get their own way, what Grandmother set up and Mother has upheld has worked wonders. *Thank the skies!*

Baofire and Hollis dart to our spectacle in the sky and circle us. Baofire stays far off, unable to ride with precision quite yet. Hollis brings Tristeh in close, wings outstretched, leaning Hollis toward us. We watch her go round and round. My heart overflows with love for her, watching her pale hair ripple and cape flutter behind her in the wind. She smiles and leans forward, directing Tristeh in a nose-dive. Baofire follows her lead, and my heart leaps into my throat.

Before too long, they pull up on their dragons and zoom

past us, over our heads, followed by Wilhelm.

Out of nowhere, Alouette and Belamy are hot on their tail. The children cheer for all of them.

Alouette flutters over to us and does a somersault in midair.

"Maybe you should take it easy," Belamy says, touching her rounded belly.

Her eyes smile as she laughs. "Good point."

Belamy performs aerial stunts with his jet-black wings for the children, over and under, round and round. Alouette hovers beside our basket, clapping for Belamy as he takes a midair bow. The children applaud with her.

A deep relief fills my soul. *My whole family is together now.*

The morning rolls swiftly by as we enjoy the smooth eastward flight. The furnace above us begins to cool, and we drift lower and lower in the air. I don't attempt to stoke it because I know it's time to go.

Before we touch down, Dove turns to me with hope in her eyes. "Papa, can we do it again tomorrow?"

"Yes, Little Dove."

THANK YOU

Thank you for reading *Wingspan* by Heather Trim. Independent authors rely heavily upon reviews and word-of-mouth to reach new readers. If you have a moment to spare, please leave a review on your preferred site. Honest reviews, short or long, are greatly appreciated.

Leave a review on Amazon:

Leave a review on Goodreads:

ACKNOWLEDGEMENTS

Thank you, Reader, for joining me in the world of *Wingbound*. Thank you for getting wrapped up in the lives of the people who live there. Thank you for letting them surprise you, irritate you, make you laugh, and make you cry.

Thank you to each and every person who encouraged me on this journey of writing.

To my husband, who watches me with grand curiosity to see what I'll do next, it's been a joy to surprise you and entertain you. Thank you for always believing in me and helping me see there is value in this weird thing of writing words, creating stories out of nowhere.

To my babies: Daisy, Daphne, Gabriel, Amaryllis, and Violet. Thank you for always being available to hash through what the characters would and would not do. Thank you for your strong and sometimes harsh opinions. Your vibrance helps me write better characters!

Mom and Dad, thank you for your support and encouragement. You make it easy to take flight and live my dreams.

Hey Big Fam! I love all of you. Erin, Jason, Natalie, Sam, and Julia. Lucas, Pam, Alex, Isabelle, Zane, and Lucas. Amber, Justin, Eli, Jackson, Tobias, and Abby. Thank you all for being such weirdos so I have a source of strangeness to draw from. I think we have the best family on the planet, and even if we weren't blood, I'd have chosen you anyway!

Thank you to my amazing team of Beta Readers: Laurel Pinson, Will Pinson, Shannon Johnson, Jessica Domelle, Robin Willson, Eileen Dudley, Rebecca Czerwonka, Melinda McCuan, Bill Gilmore, Rebecca Marsh, Pam Mather, and Lisa Coetzee. You continue to prove to be the best team of manuscript evaluators ever. Long live Tristeh!

To my Critique Group: Linda, Scott, and Ted. I appreciate how you sharpen me and make me a better writer. (I said, pushing my cheeks back. Haha!)

Thank you Jessica Nelson, my fantabulous editor, for fixing my dangling modifiers and hedge words. You turn my art from rough to right.

To my handy dandy proofreaders, Timmy and Comma Queen Lydia Clothey. Thank you for being such skilled gatekeepers of my words and punctuation!

Thank you, my invisible King, for the gift of imagination. Your imagination is mind-blowing! Thank you for infusing me with the courage to step into the realm of writing. I am nothing without you. You make me fly.

ABOUT THE AUTHOR

Heather Trim, an award-winning author, the executive director of Bear Creek Ranch, and a professional daydreamer inspires with her unique perspective of spirituality and the world. She lives in Georgia with her husband, Kevin, and five lively children. Heather enjoys bullet journaling, graphic designing, and reading too many young adult novels. She can be found on Facebook, Instagram, and her website: www.heatheraine.com.

Sign up for Heather's newsletter:
http://eepurl.com/cLd0D1

Connect with Heather:
Facebook: facebook.com/heatherainetrim
Instagram: instagram.com/heatheraine5
Goodreads: goodreads.com/heatheraine
Amazon: amazon.com/author/heathertrim

www.ingramcontent.com/pod-product-compliance
Lightning Source LLC
Chambersburg PA
CBHW060537310726
48982CB00009B/1289/J